PRAISE FOR CHRIS MULLEN

"Things are heating up down on the border..."

— CRAIG JOHNSON, *NEW YORK TIMES* BESTSELLING AUTHOR OF THE WALT LONGMIRE MYSTERIES

"Chris Mullen crafts a twisty tale of Texas-sized intrigue and larger-than-life characters..."

— BRUCE BORGOS, AUTHOR OF *THE BITTER PAST*

"Cass Callahan is a can't-miss character."

— JAMES WADE, TWO-TIME SPUR AWARD-WINNING AUTHOR OF *BEASTS OF THE EARTH*

"Chris Mullen's writing is sharp and action packed. His talent and enthusiasm are enviable."

— CHRIS ENSS, *NEW YORK TIMES* BESTSELLING AUTHOR

"Chris Mullen crafts a gripping tale of suspense, resilience, and an unbreakable spirit set deep in the heart of Texas."

— JACK STEWART, BESTSELLING AUTHOR OF *UNKNOWN RIDER*

TEXAS TERROR

ALSO BY CHRIS MULLEN

Rowdy Series

Rowdy: Wild and Mean, Sharp and Keen

Rowdy: Redemption

Rowdy: Dead or Alive

Rowdy: Rescue

Rowdy: To Catch a Killer

Rowdy: Return

Cass Callahan Series

Dead Land

Kill Order

Hunting El Despiadado

Darkness Rising

TEXAS TERROR

CASS CALLAHAN
BOOK FIVE

CHRIS MULLEN

WOLFPACK
PUBLISHING
— EST 2013 —

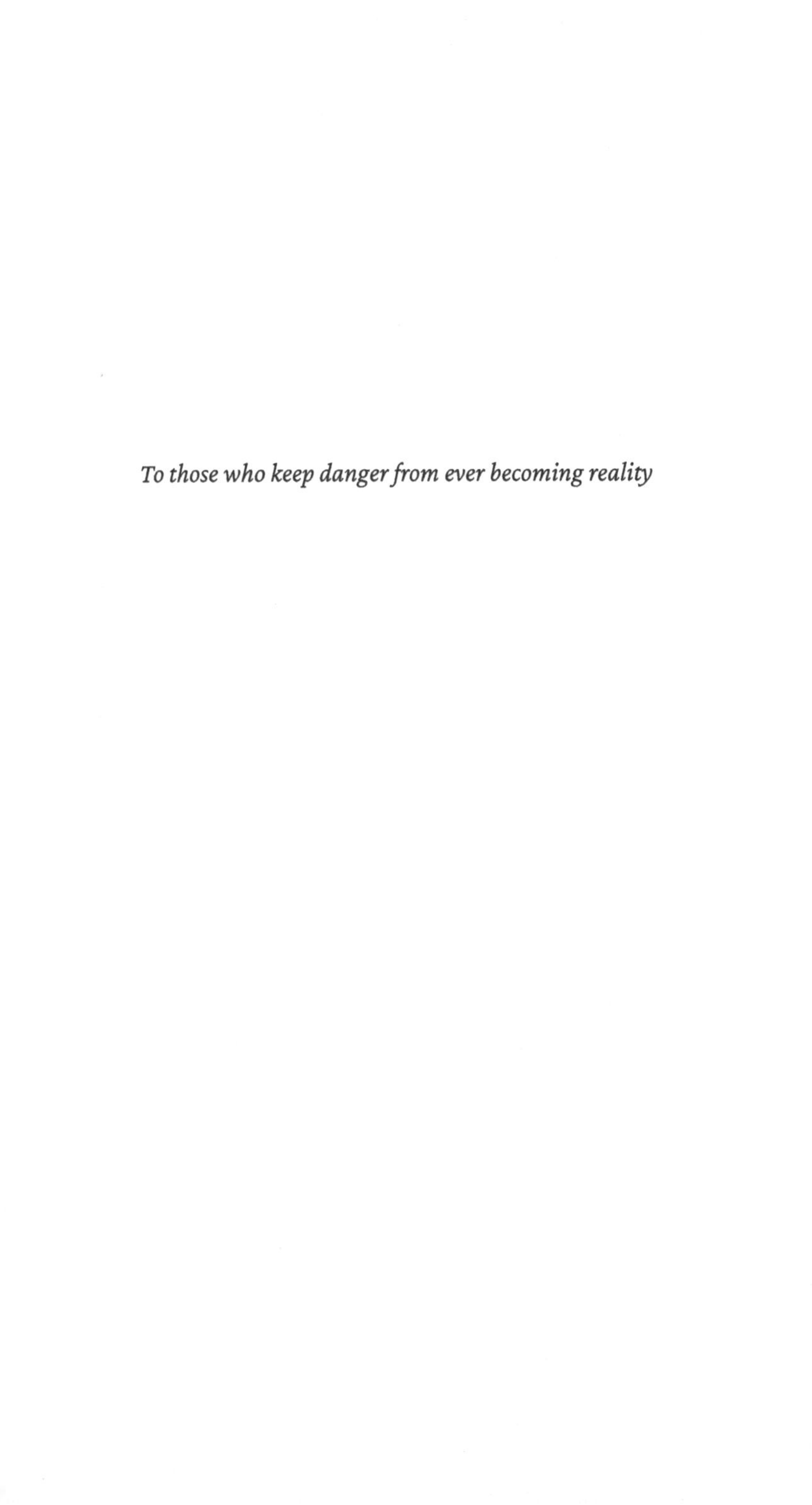

To those who keep danger from ever becoming reality

TEXAS TERROR

PROLOGUE

29.26550° N, 95.9000° W

3:03 a.m.

A low hum hung in the air like distant bees swarming toward their hive as the padded clicks of keys on a laptop enter the final lines of code needed to upload *Zhou Xin* via a patch terminal RTU at the base of Transformer Six at the Newgulf power substation. The computer virus had one very important protocol—to infiltrate and override SCADA, the *Supervisory Control and Data Acquisition System*, and send twenty-five thousand square miles of Southeast Texas back to the Dark Ages. Newgulf was the first of thirteen critical targets located across the state. This substation, the most vulnerable of the ERCOT network, was an easy first assignment for *Sūn Tiān*. With eyes glued to his screen, he entered the final lines of code.

```
# Final trigger command to initiate
blackout
```

```
print("Final command: Activate blackout
protocol across target grid…")
time.sleep(1)
```

The air felt still, the humidity thick like wet cotton. Sweat clung to Sūn Tiān's clothing beneath his denim uniform jumpsuit. The hard hat covering his head completed the façade but added to the stifling heat. Beads of sweat dripped from his brow, free falling before splashing onto the keyboard and then trailing into the creases beneath the keys. He used his bare hand to wipe the sweat away but the moisture on his skin only aided the damp keyboard causing a smearing effect across the keys.

"*Ai-Ya!*" Sūn Tiān whispered, then, again in practiced English, "Damn!"

A thrum from the transformers overhead surged louder, then fell quiet again like thunder rumbling off in the distance. He looked up. The night sky was overcast. The substation's security lighting caused the low-hung clouds to glow. Sūn Tiān glanced back at the screen, then at his wristwatch.

Too easy, he thought. *And in record time. I should be commended by my superiors.*

A smile creased his face as he closed the laptop.

The skin on his hand tingled and the hairs on his arm began to stand at attention as he reached out to disconnect the laptop from the RTU. Pinching the cord, he flinched, pulling away when a sharp sting of static shocked him. His heart thumped harder as his body felt a jolt of adrenaline surge through him. Using his pant leg as a wiping surface, he rubbed his hand over the denim before reaching for the cord again.

His eyes followed his fingers, shaking this time as he stretched his hand out to the RTU a second time.

"San...er...yi..." he counted backward, then with a sudden pinch, grabbed the cord, depressed the safety lever, and slid the housing out of the control box.

The hum above Transformer Six grew louder as he coiled the patch cord and slid it into his bag.

"*Wán le.*" Sūn Tiān paused. "No, no. English only," he said to himself. "All finished."

A *crackle* and *zap* broke the hum, followed by a resounding chorus of *sizzles*. White light *popped* just above his head causing him to jump. He turned to run, but instead, threw his body back against the base of Transformer Six when he saw the security office door on the opposite side of the substation swing open.

Two figures appeared in the doorway, their heads twisting one way, then another as they scanned the compound.

Sūn Tiān froze. His pulse quickened. Had they seen him? His sweat-soaked clothes felt like lead. The weight of the shoulder bag and tool belt added to the mounting pressure he was feeling now that there were guards inspecting the grounds.

Without warning, a second, more brilliant flash of white light exploded overhead, causing Sūn Tiān to cover his eyes and brush his body back against the metal bushings of Transformer Six.

The men across the yard saw the flash, one yelling at the other and pointing. Sūn Tiān watched the men, and thinking they had spotted him, grabbed his shoulder bag with one hand and looked in the direction of his planned escape route. When he repositioned, the closed, steel jaws of the pliers sticking out from his tool belt knocked into the metal bushing.

As Sūn Tiān began his sprint, a long arc of searing heat and light exploded from the transformer, crackling like fireworks. Deadly strands of electricity danced toward him. The flash was brilliant. The surge hit him in an instant. His muscles clenched. The whole world turned white. His body convulsed, caught in the fatal current as fire consumed his clothes and hair. The laptop in his shoulder bag melted in the flames like chocolate under the scorching sun but the virus was in place, waiting to bring Southeast Texas to its knees.

CHAPTER ONE

HOUSTON, TEXAS

7:32 a.m.

Coffee steamed under my nose as I sipped a fresh brew at Mugz Coffee and sat with Ray Tucker, my former partner, longtime friend, and royal pain in the ass.

"You're a freakin' mess, Cass. Last time I saw you this way, you had just come off an all-nighter in Mid-town waiting for," Ray began to pick his teeth with a business card from his pocket. His speech became muffled as he continued to speak. "You know what I'm talking about. The double homicide guy. Used the pointy end of a paint-brush to kill his girlfriend and her sister."

The smell of dark roast fuming into my nose was glorious and almost carried my thoughts away with it, but Ray pressed on.

"Anyway, after hearing about all the crap you've been dealing with back home, what with those Ching Chong SOBs, ain't a wonder why you're so fucked up."

I stopped mid-sip and looked over the rim of my

coffee mug. Ray caught my glare, added a smirk to his questioning face, and reached under the table for something in his back pocket.

"Here." He slid a small, silver-plated flask across the table. "Might as well make it Irish."

I looked at the flask, then back at Ray.

"I'm good."

Ray leaned forward, placed his elbows on the table, and laced his fingers.

"Look." Ray's tone softened, which was unusual for a tough jackhole like him, but it held my full attention. "No bullshit, Cass. From what you've already told me, it seems like you're on a never-ending mission. Just as you think you're wrapping things up, you're pulled in a different direction. Isn't it too much for one man?"

I set my mug on the table and took a deep breath before answering. In some ways he was right.

"Listen, Ray. I appreciate your concern. Hell, that's all I have been showered with these past few weeks. Concern."

Ray leaned back and draped an elbow on the back of his chair.

"I'm not overdoing it. I'm not overstepping my boundaries."

"What about that night with Flint on the ranch you told me about? How's that for boundaries?"

"Fine. I admit that was not a good decision, but still, I wasn't wrong."

A barista with a blue durag and wearing a retro *Smells Like Teen Spirit* Nirvana t-shirt approached our table. Her arms were inked with intricate tattoos of anime characters, and a silver hoop ring pierced her nose.

"You two need a refill?"

The innocence of her voice and the natural beauty in her face made me question why she had styled the rest of herself the way she did, but who was I to question what others did when I, myself acted in a similar, self-scarring way.

"Thanks," I said, sliding my mug over to her.

Ray removed the flask from the table and shook his head as he answered a buzzing on his phone with an irritated glance.

"Better make that to go, Cass."

I looked to tell the barista, but she was two steps ahead of me, already pulling a Styrofoam cup and lid from a stack behind the counter for my morning roadie. She flashed a wink at me, in which I saw both her quick-witted initiative and raw, beautiful human nature.

Ray huffed as he slid his phone into his pocket.

"Trouble?"

"It's Houston, Cass. What do you think?"

CHAPTER TWO

CALLAHAN RANCH, "THE CR," WEST TEXAS

aster! Raven urged, kicking Tucker's flank. His nostrils flared, eyes wide and focused, as horse and rider charged across the barren terrain toward the grove. *Gotta move faster!* With the wind in her face and stomach muscles clenched, Raven held tight to the reins, riding the gallop.

The first line of cottonwood trees loomed ahead, whizzing by at breakneck speed as Tucker raced around the outer rim of the grove. Branches swayed in the breeze like arms cheering for her, encouraging her to ride on. A burden of canyon wrens took flight, escaping the chaos. Making the final turn, Raven's smile widened at the sight of riders on the horizon, their distant whoops and hollers ringing in her ears.

Almost there!

Her pulse quickened.

Come on, Tucker. Don't let me down!

Out of the corner of her eye, she caught a flash of brown and blue and heard a high-pitched *yip* sound out above the thunder of hooves. Risking a quick glance over her shoulder, Raven saw Gilly right on Tucker's haunches. Strands of her blue hair whipped across her face as her horse gained ground.

Raven had grown up as a daddy's girl, where princesses, tea parties, and cheerleading ruled her world. The thought of getting dirty or playing with the boys was out of the question. But since arriving at the CR just months ago, she discovered a passion for riding that ignited her spirit. The thrill of galloping, the bond with Tucker. It was intoxicating. There was no turning back, and she had the bruises to prove it. If only her daddy could see her now.

Gilly had challenged her to race from the herd, around the grove, and back again. With the eyes of the other ranch hands falling on her, Raven stood her ground. She had become proficient in the saddle but racing posed a different set of skills she had yet to conquer. But to back down would have shown weakness, though everyone already knew the depths of her resolve.

"Let's do it," she had said with a competitive tone.

Ranch hands had a tradition to uphold, one of which was competition among each other. There was no fame or fortune on the line, but to be king of the hill, or in this case, queen of the ranch, plenty was at stake for both women riders.

The horizon and the cheering riders grew larger before the racers. The thunder of hooves quickened with each pounding step. Raven's legs were tight, the insides of her thighs rubbing raw, her knuckles white from her fierce grip on the reins.

Closer. Faster. The riders pressed on, each movement in perfect sync with the fluid motion of their mounts.

Sudden cracks erupted to the south drawing the immediate gaze of the ranch hands waiting at the finish line. Raven's heart dropped when she realized the sounds were rapid gunfire. Immediate visions of her recent kidnapping and Cass's fight to save her jammed the forefront of her mind. The atmosphere shifted, and the excitement of the race faded into an unsettling tension. She pulled back on the reins, bringing Tucker to an abrupt stop. Gilly sped past but slowed her pace to circle back to Raven.

"That comin' from the Flying H?" Gilly asked, pulling up next to her.

"Think so."

The breeze came to a standstill as Raven squinted, scanning the horizon for signs of trouble. She wiped her brow and cleaned the sweat from her hand on her jeans. She had heard plenty of gunshots while on the range before, but not like this. What she, and everyone else was hearing, sounded like someone on a rampage.

"Let's head over to the rest," Gilly said. "We'll call this race a draw."

Suppressing her rising anxiety, Raven smirked at Gilly.

"That'll be the second one between us," she said, recalling their first clash—a knock-down, drag-out brawl in the corral. It had been a necessary scuffle that ultimately brought them closer together.

Gilly balled her hand into a fist, showing it to Raven. "Yeah, but they were both fun as hell. C'mon."

With Gilly in the lead, the two galloped the final distance and met up with the others. Cody, Jesse, and Pedro had reined their horses around to watch the horizon and point out where they thought each shot had originated. When the girls arrived, Jesse was the first to notice them.

"That's some shit goin' on over there," he said.

Another volley of gunfire cracked and echoed over the open terrain.

"Think it's Huckabee's crew?" Raven asked.

"Could be. Sounds like the shots 'er all comin' from the same spot. Don't sound like a fight ta me," Pedro said.

Cody, the Six M's lead hand, walked his horse forward, then reined it around to face everyone.

"We need ta check this out. Follow in line. I'll lead us south of the shots. If I say git down, get the fuck down. Hear me?" Everyone nodded. Cody focused on Raven. "No hero shit. This may be your ranch, but out here, I'm in charge of everybody's safety when Flint ain't around."

Raven nodded. "Got it, Cody."

"All right. Let's ride."

Raven's stomach twisted with nervousness as they rode toward the gunfire. It had been only a little over a week since the dangerous events at the Bar S, but Raven had insisted on getting back in the saddle at once. And, with Cass gone to Houston, she needed to have some kind of normalcy in her life. The problem was gunfire had become all too normal for her liking.

CHAPTER THREE

EDITH L. MOORE NATURE SANCTUARY, WEST HOUSTON, TEXAS

Twigs crackled under my feet along the Creekside Trail. A plague of grackles sat perched on limbs high above us as Ray and I walked along the edge of Rummel Creek. As if in perfect sync, their heads cocked, tilting further as we passed beneath their canopy of judgment. The drumming of a woodpecker foraging in the brush added a calming undertone to the morning, but the day was just beginning.

On any other day, a walk through this nature sanctuary would have been rejuvenating. The sounds of animals scurrying in the underbrush, the wisps of wind that always seem to sail through at just the right moment, the sway of the trees as they danced in that breeze, and the bird songs that ring out in melodious calls, echoing through the reserve would bring anyone a taste of peace.

But add in a corpse stuffed beneath a fallen Live Oak tree, the very one we were walking toward, and the entire preserve loses its appeal. It transforms into something more akin to Fangorn Forest, where nature itself becomes a killer.

"You believe this place?" Ray said, swiping a hand in front of his face. "All this nature crap right in the middle of the city."

"I like it. It's peaceful. Where else in town you can simply disappear, close your eyes, and enjoy the sounds around you?"

"Who are you, David Attenborough?"

"I'm just saying, it's great for communities to have places like this."

Ray snorted, then covered one nostril with a finger, and blew a thick glob of mucus, sending it sailing into the brush. He wiped his hand inside of his pocket and sniffed.

"It jacks up my allergies. And another thing," he said, pointing out a patch of decaying leaves soaking in a muddy pool of runoff. "Goddamn mosquito nests. Look, they're all around us. We're at ground zero, looking like the main course at an Zika Virus convention."

Damn it, Ray.

We continued down the trail to the head of Oxbow Loop, where the forked path was blocked by a taut line of yellow police crime scene tape. A young-looking uniformed officer stood guard, watching our approach. His freshly pressed Houston Police Department uniform looked brand new. His badge glimmered. Raising a hand, he commanded our attention.

"That's far enough."

We stopped. I could hear the steam hissing from Ray's short-fused ears.

"You believe this prick? HPD has got to be scraping the bottom of the barrel these days."

Ray stepped forward, his sudden movement startling the officer, and flashed his badge.

"Detective Ray Tucker."

Ray took a moment to size up the patrolman, his eyes falling upon his nameplate. "Brantly? That's your name?" Ray's voice squeaked with sarcasm. "Step aside, Officer Brantly, or would you like to haul our deado back there to the morgue in your patrol car?"

I watched the color on Officer Brantly's face turn from pink to white, then red, but he held his tongue and lifted the police tape so Ray and I could pass underneath. Ray barreled ahead. I paused to stand next to Officer Brantly.

"Ignore him. It's what I do on a daily basis."

Brantly nodded.

"Keep up the good work, kid," I said before catching up to Ray.

"Fucking rookie."

"Ease up, Ray. Everyone has a job to do. We were both him once."

Ray gave me a side-eye glare. "Speak for yourself, Cass."

Twenty paces farther, the path dipped, then curved around a bend in the creek. At the base of the path were two more officers, one plain-clothed man wearing brown suit slacks and a matching jacket that looked like something straight from the rack at Dillard's, and our victim of the hour. I vaguely recognized the man in the suit, sifting through my HPD memories to recall his name.

"That's what I call a deadfall," Ray said, pointing to the body.

Shrugging off his inappropriateness, I offered a hand to the man in the suit.

"Cass Callahan," I said, introducing myself, omitting my FBI team TITON title.

As we shook, the man's eyes dilated just enough for me to know that he recognized me as well.

"I know you, Callahan. I was working the CRU when your house bur..."

Ray stepped between us, cutting off the handshake.

"Put a sock in it, Reese. He doesn't need you dredging that shit up."

I laid a hand on Ray's shoulder.

"Simmer down, old timer."

Ray huffed, then walked past us, heading to chat with the officers on scene. Reese watched him go, his eyes simmering with contempt.

"Reese," I said, pointing at him. "Charlie Reese, right?"

"The one and only."

"Thank God for that," Ray sputtered over his shoulder.

Reese lowered his voice.

"You were Tucker's partner for so many years. How did you survive?" he said with a hint of sarcasm.

"Keep him fed and full of coffee," I said. I turned and walked to the edge of the path where the tree and the victim lay. "Guess there's a gang element in all this. That why you're here?"

Reese joined me overlooking the body.

"Yeah. It's too early to tell for sure, but I am pretty sure this guy was running with the West Side Primera Flats gang."

"Shit." My mouth was too slow to withhold my thoughts.

"You know the bunch?"

I knew them all right. Too well, in fact. One in particular, Guillermo Morales, a.k.a. Gordo, had deep ties to the Tiny Flips, a clique within the West Side Primera Flats gang. He was the one that broke into our house and assaulted Raven—the one she shot and killed. It was that home invasion that marked the beginning of Raven's downward spiral, the catalyst that ultimately drove us to move to the CR.

"Yeah, I know 'em."

Rot in hell, Gordo!

I leaned closer, careful not to disturb anything near the investigation site or the body.

"Looks like a clean kill," I said. "GSW to the chest. Another to the shoulder."

"And one to the head," Ray added, breaking away from the officers on the opposite side of the crime scene. "Come around here and take a look."

Reese and I walked over to get a look from his vantage point.

"Lower caliber than the others," Ray said, pointing to the distinct entry wound near the temple. "No exit wound. Probably why you missed it from your angle."

"Not so clean then," Reese said. "The shot to the chest looks like it would have been enough to kill him, but it appears whoever did this wanted to make sure the job was done."

I looked at Reese, wondering what, if anything, he might be withholding.

"Who found the body?" I asked.

"Older couple. Bird watchers out for a morning stroll. I took their statement. They were pretty shaken up, so I let them head out before you arrived."

"Then why the hell did I get the call to respond if you were already here?" Ray said, nostrils beginning to flare.

I knew the look. It was one of those, *everybody better duck and cover* moments that Ray let trickle over from our days in the Army.

"Look, Tucker. I got a call. You got a call. Maybe we work this together? Same team and all, right?"

Behind us, new sounds invaded the sanctuary. Footsteps, clanking metal, squeaking hinges, all recognizable but not native to the calm preserve. I turned to see a CSI team accompanying two women in lightweight jackets, the letters HCIFS—*Harris County Institute of Forensic*

Sciences—emblazoned across their lapels, as they hauled a gurney along the trail.

"The cavalry has arrived," Ray said, his arms outstretched before him and clapping slow, sardonic claps.

"Good morning to you, too, Detective Tucker," one of the women from HCIFS replied.

Ray lowered his hands, his face blossoming into a smile.

"Maureen Prescott, what are you doing out here this morning?"

"Heard there was a body in the woods stinking up the place. Was told to remove it."

Ray stepped aside and waved his arms like a welcoming maître d'. Without hesitation, Maureen walked right up to Ray, grabbed him by the collar, and pulled.

"Let's go, Ray."

Caught off guard, Ray stumbled forward a step.

"Hey!"

"Ease up, Ray," I said. "Let the lady do her job."

The other woman from HCIFS snickered, as did members of the CSI team and Charlie Reese. Ray raised his hands in surrender, then looked around at the bunch laughing at him. Maureen gave Ray a final tug before letting go. He cut a smile himself, then returned to good ol' Ray Tucker form.

"All right, assholes. Get back to work."

CHAPTER FOUR

THE CR, WEST TEXAS

Raven and the Six M crew remained on horseback at the fence line separating the south rim of the CR from the Flying H, unaware that a rider raced toward them from behind. The sun hung high, burning bright yellow, heating the air and killing the breeze. A hint of burned gunpowder drifted past on the last breaths of wind, thickening the stale, questionable atmosphere.

"We just gonna sit here?" Pedro asked.

Cody shifted his gaze from the direction of the gunfire to Pedro, then back again.

"We're wastin' time," Gilly added. "All that blastin', someone's up ta sumthin'."

Cody flexed his legs, the leather of his saddle groaning as his boots pressed into the stirrups. At first, he said nothing. The tension in the hot, stagnant air and the crackle of distant gunfire weighed on him, as did his concern for his crew. He knew they all shared a similar urge to engage in the action.

Behind them, the oncoming rider's gallop quickened,

the steady drumbeat of hooves creeping closer with each passing second, yet it remained overlooked, lost in the gunfire and growing mystery beyond the fence.

With his eyes fixed ahead, Cody gave the order. "Pedro. Jesse. Make a hole in the fence so we can pass through."

The two hands dismounted and walked the few paces from their mounts to the fence when a single gun blast from behind them halted them in their tracks.

"Touch one board on that fence and I'll save Huckabee the trouble of shootin' ya fer trespassing."

Flint glared at Jesse and Pedro as he pulled his horse to an abrupt stop between them and the others. His angered gaze quickly shifted to Cody.

"What the hell are ya thinkin'?"

Cody's jaw tightened. When he did not answer right away, Flint nodded and passed his glare around for the others to have a taste.

"Sounds about right," he said, his gaze stopping on Raven.

She stared back at him, her gut tightening. Flint squinted. He had seen that look in her eyes before—the one that always meant she knew something was wrong.

The silence between them all shattered when more shots rang out from the Flying H. Cody looked downrange and shook his head. Flint noticed and nudged his horse over to Cody's side.

"Listen up, young buck." Flint leaned in closer, his words low but sharp enough for the others to catch through the gunfire. "Yer doin' good work out here. Don't fuck it up."

Flint's head snapped back toward Pedro and Jesse

"Since you two seem ta have a hankerin' at fence work, ride the north line from the river to the road. You see somethin' needs fixin'. Fix it." He turned back to Cody. "You an' Gilly see to the herd."

All eyes fell on Raven. She felt the weight of their looks, a flicker of worry rising within her. Were they wondering if this was one time she got off easier than the rest? She had always worked as an equal among the ranch hands. Why should now be any different? Straightening herself in the saddle, Raven masked her thoughts with a calm expression.

"What about me, Flint?"

Her tone was deliberate, nearing subordinate.

The air around her seemed to thicken. Tension swirled between them as Flint's gaze hardened and the Six M crew exchanged uncertain glances.

"Ya carryin'?"

Raven slid her right hand to her waist, fingers brushing the grip of her Purple Demon, a Ruger EC9S 9mm. A sharp flicker of anger coursed through her at being singled out, mixing with the familiar thrum of anticipation. She swallowed it back, forcing a calm nod at Flint.

"Good. Yer comin' with me."

Two more shots echoed from the Flying H, drawing everyone's attention but Flint's.

"Ya waitin' fer an invitation? We got shit ta do!"

Pedro and Jesse reined their horses away at a trot. Cody and Gilly paused a moment to share a glance with Raven.

Cody's face hardened like stone, but he did what any cowboy would do—he followed orders.

"C'mon, Gilly."

"Y'all be careful," Raven said.

"Same," Gilly replied as she reined her horse away to follow Cody back to the herd.

Flint moved next to Raven.

"No bullshit, Flint. What the hell is going on?"

Flint glanced back over his shoulder, his gaze sweeping the open land south of the CR. The gunfire rattled in the distance, but it wasn't the bullets that concerned him, it was the silence between the blasts that held more weight.

"You gonna keep me in the dark, or what?"

Flint leaned over and spat, rubbing his horse's neck before finally speaking.

"Raven..." He paused, his voice dropping. "Ain't never kept anything from ya, but this is one of those times I'm gonna have ta ask ya to just trust me."

"You know I've always trusted you, Flint. What is going on?"

Flint huffed, hands resting on his hips.

"Got a call from Huckabee. Ya remember Curly Yates?"

Raven tilted her head, considering the name. "He's the one you got into it with a while back. Broke his finger as I recall."

"A-yuh. Curly's been with the Flying H as long as I can remember. We've all had our run-ins with illegals tres-passin', leavin' trash, sometimes killin' cattle, or worse—each other on our land. Seems like Curly's done fed up. The son of a bitch is out there right now takin' shots at a group of Mexicans workin' their way along the far side of the river."

"Huckabee's not stopping him?"

"Huckabee's back at the Flying H headquarters. Curly radioed in, said he saw 'em and he's fixin' to handle it. Huckabee tried hailin' him back but Curly ain't respondin' anymore. That's why he called us. With the sheriff laid up...hell, I don't have to tell you how thin things are. It's the Wild West out here today, Raven. Huckabee's headin' out, but he cain't ride fer shit. We're closer."

"Why send the others away?" Raven asked, glancing at the dwindling dust trails made by Gilly and the rest.

"This is yer ranch, Raven. Ya want ta risk the lives of those hands? Get Gilly shot? I know any one of 'em would go with us, but they don't know Curly like I do. One wrong word an' he may take aim at us. You an' me are the only ones who might have a chance at stoppin' him before it's too late."

Two more blasts rang out. Raven flinched, her grip tightening on the reins. She exchanged a grim glance with Flint.

"Sounds like we're already too late."

CHAPTER FIVE

HOUSTON, TEXAS

Construction was a perpetual asphalt plague, causing a sea of brake lights to litter the south-bound lanes from San Felipe to Richmond Avenue. There was never a good time during the day to drive on Loop 610 near the Galleria. Traffic was crawling. Ray and I drifted with the blacktop current, creeping ahead with what seemed like the rest of Houston. But there was always at least one impatient driver whose sense of urgency on the road was never quenched.

"Get a load of that," Ray said, pointing at a blue Nissan Quest minivan. "Another freakin' Karen behind the wheel."

We watched the minivan pull in one lane, get trapped by a slower flow of traffic, then cut another driver off only to find itself back where it started. Horns honked and sign language was exchanged, but the anxious driver pressed on, forcing its way through the mucked up, midday traffic.

"You'd think with the soccer mom stickers and the

yellow 'baby on board' sign in the rear window she'd take a little more care," I said.

"Cass. You know as well as I do, these drivers think the world revolves around them. It's fucked up, but that's life."

Karma has a way of righting wrongs, or at least provides an opportunity for those in need of reflection with a little extra, unscheduled time. In this instance, in the minivan's quest for expediency, it happened to cut off an unmarked patrol car. When our slow, but steady pace caught up, I could see the driver—oversized sunglasses, baseball hat with hair pulled through the back, dangling earrings, a pure product of uptown entitlement—but most satisfying was how she strangled the steering wheel as the ticketing officer walked back to his patrol car after securing our speed racer soccer mom's driver's license.

"Check it out, Ray," I said as we rolled past.

Ray tapped the horn and waved. Her response was immediate, and predictable.

"Fuck you, too, lady." Ray backhanded my bicep. "Look who I'm callin' lady."

As we passed by the exit for the Southwest Freeway, the construction zone ended, and traffic picked up. Ray breathed an exasperated sigh of relief as we accelerated to posted speeds.

Eventually, Loop 610 curved east and NRG Stadium came into view. I used to love this part of town, especially back in the '90s when all you could see was AstroWorld on one side and the Astrodome on the other. Now, where AstroWorld had been, was nothing but an open lot. I closed my eyes, remembering all the time I spent riding the Texas Cyclone as a kid. The *click, click, click* beneath the roller coaster as it slowly climbed to stomach-lurching heights, the inevitable plunge over the harrowing summit with hands thrown above my head, and the thrill of hurling through the tight curves at what felt like break-neck speeds bore a feeling I would never forget.

AstroWorld had so many exciting attractions that cemented their way into my memories, but it was Dungeon Drop that always took my breath away. On a clear day the views of downtown looked like a picture-perfect postcard from atop the ride. My feet would dangle, and for a moment, I was lost in the Houston cityscape as the colors of the buildings seemed to shimmer in the distance. It took only a moment, and then blood-curdling screams rang out when a sudden euphoric sense of weightlessness escalated into a heart-stopping, one hundred and thirty-foot drop at over fifty miles per hour. With my hands gripping the shoulder harness and the wind whipping by, I always managed to keep my eyes open to watch the skyline disappear as I plummeted toward the ground.

Ray eased onto the exit ramp at Fondren, our slowing speed grounding me in the reality of the day and reminding me of where we were going. We had one very important stop to make before heading to the Houston Contract Detention Facility, the ICE detention center where a group of three Chinese and two North African illegals were being held following their arrest at the Port of Houston last week.

We navigated the curves and obnoxious traffic lights until we found ourselves in the middle of the Houston Medical Center. Ray rolled his window down and stuck his hand out, swimming it up and down as if he was a kid on the way to somewhere special. He had been quiet since exiting 610, but I did not push for conversation. Over the years, we had shared many details about our lives with one another, but it was the most recent news he dropped that helped me understand why he seemed to hate the world now, more than ever.

The whir of sirens echoed among the tall buildings. Ray barely noticed. People littered the sidewalks, some strolling, lost in thought or engaged in conversation with those beside them, while others looked determined to reach their destination. It was a somber place where hopes and dreams were realized or lost. It was the one part of Houston that found a way to dig inside of me, regardless of why I was passing through.

The brakes squeaked and the car's blinker clicked. Before us, in large black letters, was the name *M.D. Anderson Cancer Center*, a long red strike through sliced the word cancer as a stark reminder of their ultimate mission—eliminate the disease. We pulled into an adjacent parking garage and found a lucky spot near the entrance.

"Want me to wait in the car?" I said.

Ray drew in a long breath, then turned to look at me.

"No."I could see in his eyes, how the brown of his irises swirled with tiny black flecks, and the red webbing streaks of emotional irritation spread out in all directions, that Ray needed someone right now more than ever.

"I'm not sure how many more trips we'll make down here, but Ruth Ann will want to see you, Cass."

Ruth Ann, Ray's wife of nearly twenty-seven years, was his rock. She could handle Ray like no one else and loved him more deeply than any woman could love a man. Though smaller in frame compared to Ray, she had a commanding presence that could captivate a crowd with just the sound of her voice. One glance from Ruth Ann could either melt your heart or strike fear to your core. Without fail, every time I visited, she had something simmering on the stove or baking in the oven and would not let me leave without sharing a meal. Toughest of all, she was the one who waited and worried at home over the years, praying for his safe return when we were deployed overseas or back on the job in Houston.

Now, it was Ray's job to wait and worry. And pray. Ruth Ann had been diagnosed with late-stage pancreatic cancer just before Ray and I made our deep dive into Mexico to confront the Camargo cartel, but she insisted that he be by my side instead of hers. "Cass needs you," she had told him. "I just need you to come back." Ray never said a word about her condition until this morning. The news hit me like a hot branding iron, but I could not let Ray see it. This was not about me. It was not my place to show weakness, not with Ruth Ann fighting a battle that doctors said only a miracle would help her win.

Ray cut the engine and gripped the steering wheel. He let a long, slow breath of air escape his lips as his fist tightened to show the whites in his knuckles.

"Goddamn cancer."

CHAPTER SIX

29.71168° N, -95.64324° W

A blue Chevrolet Malibu with Pennsylvania plates and a Budget Rent a Car sticker on the rear bumper flashed its hazards and eased to the shoulder of northbound Highway 6 just past the Westpark Tollway. The car idled but no one got out. Sounds of urgency filled the roadway as cars sped by. Most moved over a lane out of courtesy, but some disregarded the Malibu's flashing lights with thoughts of *sucks to be them* as they careened past.

Minutes ticked by. Still, no one got out of the car. Tinted windows concealed subtle movements within the vehicle. Curious rubberneckers only gained a glimpse within the car. A tilting head, a sweep of the hands and arms, a definitive lean toward the center of the vehicle, all masked behind the darkened glass.

A motorized hum accompanied the passenger side window as it opened a third of the way. Shadows moved again, leaning toward the passenger side of the car, and then after a moment, the window closed. The momentary gap was enough for the cool of the vehicle's interior to mix with the thick Texas air, leaving beads of condensation on the lower windshield. The would-be stranded vehicle was absorbed in the monotony of carpools and commuter traffic. No one pulled over to help. That was the way of things in the big city and was what the driver had counted on. No one had time for more than a glance, too consumed by their own hurried lives. Hide in plain sight —a key strategy to implement by any seasoned foreign operator.

The flashing hazards ceased as a deep red filled the taillights and the Malibu's left turn signal was activated. Checking the side-mirrors, the driver eased back into the right-hand lane, blending into traffic as if never having stopped at all. The driver glanced in the rearview mirror, mind swirling with thoughts of what came next as the West Park overpass and Barker Substation faded into the background.

CHAPTER SEVEN

THE CR, WEST TEXAS

The West Texas sun was relentless, high in the sky, and beaming with an unseasonable heat for early spring. Flint and Raven rode close together, their horses making good time as they crossed an open stretch of the Flying H terrain. A small coppice similar to the grove on the CR jutted from the ground a mere two hundred yards from the Rio Grande, making it the perfect spot to hide with a clear line of sight across the border. The two looped their way around to approach the cluster of trees from the east, careful not to draw fire from Curly.

As they drew near, Flint waved a hand, signaling for them to slow their pace, then stop altogether prior to reaching the border of the trees. Raven followed his lead, dismounting, then ground tying their horses before continuing.

Flint left his Winchester .308 in its sheath on his horse but double-checked the cylinder on his revolver. When on the range, he holstered a Smith and Wesson model 25. Raven rubbed her Purple Demon, hoping she would not need to pull her weapon. She knew what that meant. Both Cass and Flint had told her on separate occasions, never draw your weapon unless you intend on pulling the trigger.

The trees stood still under the harsh sun, casting shadows that offered little cover. Flint paused, scanning the small grove one last time.

BANG!

Another shot rang out. Raven and Flint flinched, then shared a look of silent urgency. Not wasting more time, Flint nodded to the grove, then double-timed his pace, advancing in a low, crouched position. Raven mimicked his posture, following right on his heels.

They reached the tree line, taking cover behind opposing cottonwood trunks.

BANG!

The hardened rapport of another blast stung Raven's ears. A sharp smell of burned gunpowder assaulted her nose. Peering around the trunks, they saw Curly in a prone position just below a felled cottonwood fifty feet from them. Flint pointed at Raven, motioned to stay put, then tapped his chest and pointed into the heart of the small grove.

Raven's heart thumped.

BANG!

The shot seemed louder than the last.

BANG!

She felt herself jump, her temples pounding as intensity coursed through her.

BANG!

Raven's teeth clattered. She tried to swallow, but her mouth had gone dry. She pressed her back against the trunk, forcing herself to remain hidden, but felt compelled to keep Flint in her sight. With wide, concerned eyes, she watched him step from his covered position and creep ahead to a younger tree halfway between her and the volatile Curly Yates.

Kneeling behind the smaller trunk, Flint glanced back at Raven. Realizing she had been holding her breath, she gulped fresh air and nodded. Flint pressed a finger to his lips, then motioned to Curly.

BANG!

"Curly Yates," Flint called out following the blast.

Curly whirled around, gun at the ready.

"Who in the Sam-Hell?"

"It's Levi Flint, Curly. Got a call from Huckabee sayin' that ya might be needin' a hand?"

Curly's eyes scanned the grove. He slid the action of his rifle back and ejected a spent cartridge.

"Damn tired of these Mexicans, Flint. It's time someone did somethin'. Somethin' they'd 'member an' pass along if they're lucky. Ain't no slap on the wrist gonna keep 'em from comin', but a blast to the head'll teach 'em. Teach 'em real good, too."

"We got that in common, Curly. Ain't much a nothin' else, but that." Flint paused, locking eyes with Raven. He squinted, then turned to peer around the tree at Curly. "I'll tell ya this...killin' them folks ain't the way. Why don't ya put the gun down an' let's come up with a differn't plan?"

A steely scrape and distinctive click broke the silence between the men as Curly chambered another round.

"Not this time, Levi. Not today."

Flint watched him resume a prone position and aim his rifle at a point beyond the Rio Grande. Gritting his teeth, and having failed to get through to Curly, Flint's mind raced with thoughts both good, and bad.

"Fuck 'im," one voice whispered. "This shit is his problem, and his problem alone."

Flint stood with his back against the tree. Taking a deep breath, a new voice filled his head.

"Nah. As much as ya don't like 'im, or them people he's shootin' at, ya know it ain't right. Quit stallin' and stop the son of a bitch."

Flint began to motion to Raven but stopped and stared at the empty space near the tree where she had been. He scanned the tree line, twisting his body around in time to see her move past to his position to approach Curly from his flank.

"Shit!" Flint said with bated breath.

If he called out, he would alert Curly that more than just he was there in the grove. On the other hand, Raven might find herself in his crosshairs.

Flint lunged out from behind the tree and raced toward Curly. His legs pumped faster with each step. Adrenaline pulsed through him.

BANG!

Curly's rifle screamed. Scorching smoke and fire erupted from the barrel as another bullet zinged across international borders at another probable live target.

The blast echoed, but Curly heard movement behind him. Rolling to his right, he dropped the rifle and pulled a pistol from his belt. The whites of Flint's eyes seemed to flow blood red as he charged. Caught by surprise, Curly took aim.

BANG!

CHAPTER EIGHT

MD ANDERSON CANCER CENTER, HOUSTON, TEXAS

"Looks like you could use something to eat, Cass," Ruth Ann said, her voice shallow and weak.

"Now that you mention it, I could eat. You wanna get outta here?"

"Sure thing. Tell this big lump to pick me up and let's blow this joint."

Her words rose, soft and delicate, like the fluttering wings of a butterfly caught in a breeze. I felt the warm glow of her strong persona in her reply, but it was only a feeling. The person lying in bed before me was but a fraction of who I remembered. She was thin, frail, the illness aging her far beyond her forty-eight years, as if it had stolen decades from her in a matter of weeks. Her jaundice gave her skin a sallow, yellowed appearance.

I leaned over and kissed her forehead, my lips absorbing her clammy coolness. The disease had a firm grip on Ruth Ann. It was squeezing the life out of her and there was nothing neither Ray nor I could do but keep a stiff upper lip and be by her side. God, how I wished what she was going through was not real. Our light-hearted banter was genuine and would be forever cherished.

Ruth Ann shifted her gaze at Ray, her eyes telling a longing story of want and need, a plea beyond what words could ever express. She mustered a smile and closed her eyes. I imagined she had transported herself to a time when she and Ray were younger, exploring love and life, with the future wide open before them, believing with all their heart that they had all the time in the world.

Time. A killer of us all, yet it never runs out for itself. Calling it unfair feels like a hollow excuse, but time still holds us in its ever-loosening grip.

"What can I do for you, dear?" Ray said, cupping her hand between his palms. His voice deep, tender, the sound of true love mixed with a breaking heart.

Ruth Ann opened her eyes again. Fixed on Ray, her smile returned, and for a moment, she seemed to glow with a revival of energy. But, as moments do, it passed all too quickly. The patient monitors next to her bed characterized her life with simple lines that jogged up and down across the screen. Numbers displaying her blood pressure, oxygen level, and heart rate ticked up and down, recording her progress or decline, whichever the case was at the time. There it is again. Time for Ruth Ann was slipping away.

"How about you just sit for a while? Until I fall asleep." Her words crackled through exhausted lips. "You and Cass have things to do. People to save."

"The only one I want to save is you," Ray whispered.

A massive lump in my throat made it difficult to swallow my emotions, but it was the single tear running down Ray's cheek that broke the dam.

Ray eased into a chair next to her bed, never once taking his eyes off her, never once letting go of her hand. I worked my way into a corner of the room near the door and leaned against the wall, making sure to wipe my face clean. My eyes burned as did a fire scorching the backside of my throat and chest.

The intercom speakers in the hall announced a code that was immediately followed by a rush of footsteps and the squeaky wheels of a cart being pushed past Ruth Ann's room. I could hear growing sobs that seemed to stop just outside the door. A man, possibly a teenage boy, their grief blending in muffled bursts of pain and loss.

I could not help but think of my son Spencer, safe at college, a mere ninety-minute drive from where I was, and Raven, who I left back at the CR. We had all experienced traumatic events but had pulled through. I folded my hands, thinking of them. I squeezed my palms together, grinding skin and bones, hoping the pinch and pain would help the anger and fear and hopelessness of this hospital room subside. What if that was Raven stuck in that bed. What if it was Spencer sobbing into my shoulder just outside the room. What if...what if...

I pulled my cell phone from my pocket and typed a message to Spencer.

10:53 A.M.

Callahan: Hey, son. I hope you are having a good day. I love you.

I pressed send and began typing a similar message to Raven, but nothing I wrote seemed to say exactly what I wanted her to read. I deleted everything, then simply typed the letters:

ILU

I did not know what she was up to, but whatever it was, I was sure she was in a much better place than me.

CHAPTER NINE

THE FLYING H RANCH, WEST TEXAS

An agonizing scream replaced the echoing blast of a single bullet as Curly grabbed his wrist, supporting his injured hand. His weapon lay in the dirt, its polymer grip shattered, rendering it useless. Raven stood in the open, Purple Demon drawn and smoking. Flint had tucked and rolled to the side, dodging Curly's line of fire but quickly jumped to his feet. With three swift steps, he kicked Curly's gun away and towered over him.

Curly rocked back and forth, veins bulging in his neck and face, his skin darkening to a purple shade as he groaned through gritted teeth. Blood streamed from both sides of his hand where the bullet had torn clean through.

"Sum bitch," he cried, glaring at Flint. "What the hell did you do?"

Flint glanced away from Curly, and grimaced. Curly followed his gaze until his eyes landed on Raven.

"You? You shot me?"

Raven held her Purple Demon with two steady hands

as she stepped closer. She had fired weapons many times since moving to the CR, once to save her life, but this time felt *different*. Since deciding to act, her heart rate normalized, and her breathing calmed. She was laser focused. It was as if the gun had become an extension of her, and the world around had become but a blur except for Curly Yates in her sights.

Flint cocked his head as he looked at Raven, unable to decide if he was pissed or damn impressed by her taking action.

"Go on, Raven. Put that away. Curly ain't gonna do nuthin' now."

Raven sidestepped three more paces, then returned the Purple Demon to its holster. She felt a warmth radiate on her hip. Her fingers buzzed, as did the crick of her neck, one from the vibration of the blast, the other from the rush of adrenaline coursing through her.

Flint walked around Curly and picked up his rifle.

"Remington 700, huh. Leupold scope? Damn, Curly. Ya screwed the steer this time. What in the hell were ya thinkin'."

Curly sneered, his coloring fading from purple to a clammy sheen of white.

"Ya know damn well, Levi."

Flint leaned close to Raven. "Run an' grab my saddlebag. Got a first aid kit and a radio in there."

Raven looked at Curly, then to the rising cliffs beyond the Rio Grande. Flint sighed.

"Ain't nuthin' we can do fer anyone over there." Raven continued to stare into the distance. Into Mexico. "Go on, Raven."

"But?"

Flint turned and placed his hands on her shoulders. "We take care of what we can, when we can. Help me get Curly patched up 'fore he passes out an' we have ta drag 'im home. Then, you an' me 'ill ride to the river fer a look-see."

With guarded reluctance, Raven walked to the horses, all the while wondering how many people Curly might have injured or even killed. Her compassion for humanity took charge, causing her to pause and succumb to emotions she had previously subdued. She leaned against her horse, her eyes streaming tears.

Tucker snorted, then twisted his neck to its fullest, and nuzzled Raven's shoulder. Still leaning against him, she turned and looked into his large brown eyes. Tucker bumped his nose against her chest, coaxing her to smile between the tears.

"Oh, god, Tucker. You are the bright spot in my day."

She wrapped her arms around his neck, stroking his coat. The horse's warmth and regard for Raven grounded her emotions, but it was his snort and wriggling lips that made her laugh.

"Always hungry, huh?"

She let go of him and wiped her cheeks, her face smeared with dirt and grime. She rubbed damp, soiled fingers against her leg as she stepped away from Tucker and retrieved Flint's saddlebag. Before returning to the grove, she reached into her own bag and found a small pouch holding three sugar cubes. She removed two cubes, popped one into her own mouth, then offered the other to Tucker. His lips flared and his eyes dilated with delight. With an open palm, she fed him the treat before returning to the grove. As she walked, she glanced over her shoulder at her mighty companion. He bobbed his head, padding his front hoof, watching her as she went.

"There's more of that when the day is done, fella," she said, before disappearing into the trees.

The aftertaste of sweetness in her mouth helped remove the sour taste on her tongue that had formed following the shooting. She did not notice the change until she reached the horses and fell into a brief rift of emotion. Transitioning to ranch life and working alongside Flint had hardened her in ways she never expected, so her fleeting moment of vulnerability reminded her of who she was on the inside. Yet, there was one change she felt above all else, and it concerned her. Drawing her gun, taking aim, pulling the trigger—the flow of attack from beginning to end felt *satisfying*. The feeling was separate from her concerns about Curly's potential victims, which was what bothered her most of all.

"Here," Raven said, tossing the pack to Flint.

Flint opened the flap and rummaged through the contents. Curly had calmed down but looked like he was in extreme pain.

Good, she thought.

Shaking her head, Raven marched to the western tree line and looked toward the Rio Grande. Nothing looked out of place. The only sounds were the sharp screech of a red-tailed hawk soaring on the upper-level winds and the distant rumble of building storm clouds just beginning to poke above the Mexican cliffs.

Flint powered on the small two-way radio.

"Floyd Huckabee, this Levi Flint. Ya copy?"

Raven turned and sat on the felled trunk where Curly had positioned himself. Ten feet away, he sat on the ground, wrapping gauze around his hand, making it look as though he were affixing a baseball to the end of his arm. Flint stood close by holding the radio in one hand and Curly's rifle in the other. He lifted the mic to his mouth again.

"Come on, goddammit. Ya there er not?"

Flint released the transmitter and listened for a reply. The speaker chirped once, followed by a line of static, then Huckabee's raspy voice.

"I read ya loud and clear. We're headin' your way as we speak. Tell me ya stopped that son of a bitch."

Raven cocked her head and considered who "we" might be. Flint must have been thinking the same thing.

"Oh, he's stopped all right." Flint glanced at Raven. "Who is *we?*"

"Tell me ya didn't kill 'im." Huckabee's voice crackled over a bad connection.

"He ain't dead. Prob'ly outta be. He damn near fired over a dozen shots." Flint lowered the receiver. When Huckabee did not speak, Flint spoke into the mic again. "Who ya got taggin' along, Floyd?"

"Levi?" A new, familiar voice came over the box. "It's Deputy Marie Bostwick."

"Boss?" Flint replied, a surprised hitch in his voice.

Raven hopped down from her spot on the truck and joined Flint.

"Roger that. You still at the horse junction?"

Raven nudged Flint, "Horse junction?"

Flint lowered the mic.

"It's what Huckabee's been callin' this place fer years. This been a spot fer many a cowboy an'..." Flint made a quirk of the lips, then spouted out the rest. "Their buckle chasers to meet up after sunset for a roll in the hay, so ta speak."

Raven looked around the small group of trees and cringed. "Here? Not what I'd call a cozy spot."

"Flint?" Boss's voice was sharp.

"A-yuh, same spot."

"Roger that. See you in twenty. Out."

Flint lowered the mic.

"I hate talkin' on that thing." Looking at Curly, Flint decided to get a few things off his chest before Huckabee and Deputy Bostwick arrived. He placed the radio back in his saddlebag and walked over to him. "Yer a son of a bitch, all right. Just like Huckabee said. First time I think I've ever agreed with the ol' cuss. I been out here all long time. Dealt with many a brown-skinned, wet-haired, greasy river swimmer, but I ain't never killed one just because. So, ya got an itch in yer pants. Figured if ya pick a few off, might slow 'em down er kept 'em form crossin' over. Never did consider that maybe, just maybe, ya dumb fuck, that them people might be getting' handled by a cartel. Now ya done shot at people ya don't know, maybe hit some, maybe kilt a few, but what ya mighta just done could cause the rest of us a pain we ain't even know, Curly."

Flint paced back and forth, his mouth churning, his thoughts reeling.

"What ya gonna do if some cartel jackass decides ta shoot back? Maybe gather a small crew an' make a run on the house? Ya gonna kill 'em all? Ya know that's Mexico right there???" Flint pointed toward the river with a furious finger. "RIGHT THERE. They ain't got no law way out here. Not on that side. Only thing they know is what the cartels on that side of the river tell 'em. Ain't nobody gonna cross the cartel. There's too much at stake."

"You don't know shit, Flint."

Curly started to get up, but Flint put a boot heel on Curly's thigh as he tried to stand and kicked him back to the ground. Raven looked on. There had been a time when she would have asserted herself and jumped in with a diplomatic suggestion, break up the argument or fight and try to calm the waters, but not today. She was having none of Curly. As far as she was concerned, Flint had about sixteen minutes left to get across whatever point he was trying to make.

"Stay down, Curly."

"I ain't no dog, Flint."

"Yeah? Right now, ain't a dog on this earth than yer better than."

Flint flashed a look at Raven. Curly caught the glance and looked at her as well.

"I see," he said, eyes flicking between Raven and Flint. "You two out here, alone, an' yer playin' hero." Curly smirked. "Maybe when this is all over, the two of ya can keep the tradition of this place alive. Bet she'd love ta loosen yer buckle. Give ya a taste of what a city woman is like."

Flint growled, but Raven was fiercer. She charged Curly, landing one solid, Tecovas kick, square on his damaged, bandaged hand. He doubled over, his scream tearing through the grove as he crumpled in fresh agony. The bandage began to stain red, fresh blood seeping through the gauze. He retched, spat, tried to curse, then retched again. Raven's lip curled into a snarl as she caught her balance and turned for a second run at Curly.

Her initial attack had moved quicker than Flint could react, catching him completely off guard. He had seen Raven handle herself before, but not like this—not with such raw, unchecked fury. But it was not just the speed of her assault that surprised him, it was the way she squared up for a second round, her eyes blazing with a fierce determination, as if one strike was not enough to satisfy the rage boiling inside her. Flint's stomach tightened. This was a side of Raven he had never seen before.

Bending at the knee, Raven exploded toward Curly once again. This time, Flint moved faster, stepping between them and catching her before she could land another kick. As much as he would have enjoyed letting her have another run at Curly, he knew Raven would punish herself later for what she had done. She struggled with him, fury raging in her eyes.

"Let me go!" Raven screamed. "No one disrespects me like that. You hear me, Curly Yates? No one!"

Flint lifted Raven, carrying her out of reach of Curly. He forced his face in front of hers. When she moved to look past him, Flint moved in her way.

"Raven," he said. Flint's tone was calm, grounded. "You've made yer point. Let it go."

Raven's face was red, complimenting all that she saw at the moment, but the sound of Flint's voice, the oddly soothing reverberations of his simple message connected with her. The fire within her settled, and the realization that she had lost control began to set in.

With eyes bloodshot and filling, Raven lifted her head to look at Flint.

"I...I..."

"Don't you say a word, Raven. You've every right, ya hear me. Every right."

Flint guided her past Curly to the edge of the trees. Shade began to stretch beneath the limbs, waving back and forth in dark ripples across the floor of the tiny grove. The cliffs across the border now stood beneath a darkening sky. It was too early to tell if the brewing storm would head their way, but it did not matter. Raven had a storm of her own to weather, and with Cass away, she would have to ride it out alone.

"I think we'll just set a spell an' wait fer the cavalry ta arrive. Ain't no more ta do right now, Raven. Ain't no more ta do."

CHAPTER TEN

NEAR CLEAR LAKE HIGH SCHOOL, CLEAR
LAKE, TEXAS

Excitement buzzed among the students and faculty gathered around the perimeter of a closed off section in Clear Lake High School's senior parking lot, eagerly awaiting the First Annual Soaring Falcon AeroShow. Cosponsored by the Robotics Club and the Future Falcon Flyers Club, the event promised a thrilling demonstration of coordinated flights, filling the sky with student-created projects showcasing technical skill and creativity. Drones of various sizes sat inside mini hula hoops landing pads, each featuring designs that included original modifications for speed, maneuverability, operational range, ceiling capacity, as well as innovative craftsmanship. Anticipation swelled among the student teams as they prepared to showcase their aerial creations. The school mascot, an oversized Falcon head bobbing on the shoulders of a student wearing feathered sleeves and pants, spread its arms and zigzagged across the makeshift tarmac, as if soaring through the clouds, further ampli-fying the crowd's energy.

The rising murmur of excited students and teachers filtered into the nearby neighborhood. Thelma Snippet, a seventy-five-year-old retired high school English teacher, heard the noise while sitting in a wicker chair on her front porch. She closed her eyes, reminiscing about her time in the classroom, but there were too many memories to recall from forty-nine years of teaching. Most were worth remembering, though some were better left to linger in the dark.

A yard crew rumbled past her house, heading to their next job. The sharp rattle and clank of tools in their trailer and the blare of Tejano music through open windows made her open her eyes and squint, just as she often had at students who would not stop talking during her lessons. "*Noise pollution*," she had called it. "There is no place for that here."

Students had called her "Snippet the Sniper," for all the extra-curricular conversations she had shot down during class. When she first overheard the nickname, it caught her by surprise and stung, but once she realized how sharp her aim truly was, she embraced it, becoming an expert marksman for classroom chatter.

She glared at the truck and trailer as it drove away, then shifted her eyes to a white van parked along the street next door. Service vehicles were common in the area, especially with her neighbors always knee-deep in some renovation project, but the plain, unmarked van triggered her *Snippet the Sniper* instincts, prompting her to stand and walk to the edge of the porch.

What are they fixing now?

Thelma crossed her arms and watched.

Sharp feedback from a loudspeaker, followed by a man clearing his throat, reverberated over the airways.

"Students. Settle down. Settle down. The air show will begin momentarily."

The voice drew a mix of low-toned groans and mocking retorts.

"Principal Whitfield," she muttered. "You never could manage a crowd."

A high-pitched screech erupted from the speakers, followed by a woman's voice on the microphone.

"Falcons...are you ready to fly?"

The crowd responded, this time with cheers and admiration.

"That's more like it, Ms. Macias."

Thelma smiled, recalling her former, younger, and more formidable vice principal, but the sudden slide of the van's side door wiped it from her face.

Cocking her head, she stepped off the porch and strolled down her driveway, her eyes peeled and watching for any movement from the van. She went to her mailbox, peaked inside, and removed a stack of envelopes she had placed there earlier for her mailman to collect. Standing next to the curb, she shuffled the letters, pretending to examine each one while she spied on the van.

Back at the school, the announcements continued.

"First up, we have Stella Rufio and Hanna Ortega with their 'bird' as they like to call it, and Milo Stavinoha and Frankie Appleton with their drone, 'Soarin' Screecher.' Let's give these two groups a hand as they demonstrate their signature Falcon looptie-loops!"

Thelma glanced at the sky over the school and saw two drones rise into view over the neighborhood rooftops. Wobbling at first, the two drones circled once, then rose and rolled over in the air, earning a thunderous roar from the crowd of high school students and teachers watching. The hum from the student's drones was faint, but the sound grew louder as a similar noise began much closer.

She turned to see two black drones now sitting on top of the van. Thelma had seen similar machines before, but only on television. Squinting her eyes again, she saw alternating lights blinking in a red, orange, red pattern on the bellies of both units, and the spinning propellors, but the drones stayed put.

Replacing her mail in her mailbox, she closed the door and lifted the flag.

The hum quickened.

Thelma looked on as both drones lifted off the roof of the van and raced away in different directions—one toward the school, the other into the distance beyond her rooftop.

"What are they doing?"

Thelma heard the van's engine rumble to life. Determined to find out who had just launched the drones, she marched down the sidewalk.

"You," she called out, using a well-honed accusatory teacher's voice.

The van door began to slide closed. Thelma's face crinkled, the wrinkles on her cheeks and forehead deepening into familiar furrows.

"Oh, no you don't!" she said, quickening her pace before stopping next to the van. "What do you think you're doing?"

The sliding door had yet to close. Thelma heard a distinct rumble from inside the van, followed by what she thought was a voice.

"I can hear you in there. If you don't come out. I'm going to call the police."

The movement in the van stopped. The door creaked open, this time with a slow, cautious slide.

"I wrote down your license plate," Thelma lied. "Don't think they won't..."

With a swift jerk, the van's door flew open. A man

wearing blue jeans and a black turtleneck lunged out, grabbing Thelma by the collar. With a violent tug, he pulled her into the van and slammed the door closed.

Thelma's shrieks were drowned out by the van's engine, the roar of her former students' excitement, and the gloved hand clamped over her mouth, pressing hard enough to break her two front teeth.

CHAPTER ELEVEN

HOUSTON, TEXAS

The police radio in Ray's car crackled as we pulled out of the Medical Center and headed northeast on MacGregor Way past Herman Park, but neither he nor I made any mention of it. The silence between us carried the weight of our visit with Ruth Ann. Our emotions were spent, our interest in the world around us at that moment, nonexistent. We moved along with traffic as if on autopilot. Our first step was simply to make it through the rest of the day.

Houston, on the other hand, had other plans in store. The high-pitched beep of an impatient horn blaring behind us following a stop at a red light, now turned green, jolted us back to reality. A friendly tap would have sufficed, but the obnoxious, continuous wail from the car behind us stirred more than it intended.

Ray slammed the gear into park.

Shit, Ray. That was all my brain could manage at that moment. Before I had time to react, he was already out the door, storming toward the vehicle behind us. Cars passed in the other direction, avoiding the escalating incident. I jumped out in time to see the driver's eyes behind us fill the windshield like the cartoon wolf gawking at Red Hot Riding Hood in Tex Avery's 1940s cartoons. Asshole drivers are a dime a dozen, but most shrink like testicles in winter when confronted. This driver was no different.

Ray approached the front of the vehicle, a compact white Chevrolet Spark, and the horn stopped. The driver, a middle-aged man with a dark mustache and medium-brown skin, suggesting Indian or Pakistani descent, was caught by Ray's fiery glare and tilted his head in clear surprise at his reaction. His little man syndrome bluff had been called, and now he had a choice: get out of the car and meet Ray head-on, or back up and drive away.

As most telephone tough guys do, the man broke free of the trance, threw his car in reverse, and backed off. Luck was on all our sides as the lane behind us had emptied during the green light. Ray raised his hands in the air.

"Where ya goin', jerkoff?"

Gaining some distance and, with a bit of misplaced confidence, the driver stuck his middle finger out the window before yanking the wheel hard, sending the car into a wobbly, one-hundred-eighty-degree skid. The Spark's engine buzzed like a neurotic bumblebee and the tires squealed over the pavement as the driver attempted a fast getaway. Ray took three quick steps and kicked the bumper, denting the plastic just below a sticker that read, *Zero Gucks Fiven*.

"Ray!"

My shout was reactive and made little difference. The confrontation was over the moment Ray stepped out of the car. Everything else was an unfortunate blend of pent-up rage and bad timing.

The driver zoomed off, peeling his tires around the

first corner he came to, and was out of sight in a matter of seconds. Ray stood with hands on hips. His breathing was heavy.

"You, okay?" I asked.

Ray dropped his arms to his side and turned around.

"I'm tired, Cass. Freaking, goddamn tired."

His face sagged, aging him in an instant, burdened with regret. The root of it all was painfully obvious, and without the miracle we both prayed for, things were bound to get worse.

We walked back to the car, got in, and resumed our auto pilot status as we navigated the streets and highways north to the ICE detention center.

My mind drifted, revisiting Ruth Ann's hospital room, then replaying Raven's rescue from the Bar S, and further back to the assault on the Camargo cartel compound in which Ray was shot and nearly killed. There had been so much gross negativity in my life, I was ready for a win without the collateral damage. As I sank further into the past, my cell phone buzzed, yanking me out of my trance. I glanced at the caller ID before answering. The number read, PRIVATE.

I let it vibrate two more times before it drew a response from Ray.

"You gonna answer that?"

If I had to guess, I had a fifty/fifty shot at knowing who was on the line. The phone buzzed a fourth time before I pressed the *ACCEPT* icon.

"Callahan," I said, answering the call.

A familiar voice came through the line, the kind that irritates the senses like nails on a chalkboard or the sudden pain of brain freeze from a frozen margarita.

"So, as I expected," the voice replied, sounding as if he had smallish bees up his nose. "Enjoying your little soirée in Houston, I gather?"

Ray side-eyed me. "Jesus, what now?"

Special Agent Dylan Sharp was a prick if I ever knew one but had gained my respect during my operation in Mexico. His actions saved Ray's life and helped me track down and eliminate El Despiadado, my number one, most wanted killer. Following our incursion, and to my surprise, he was promoted to Special Agent in Charge of the FBI field office in El Paso, thus becoming Liaison to the Governor of Texas' newest task force, TITON—the Texas Intelligence and Tactical Operations Network. As much as I hated working with the man, he had recruited me to join this elite covert team, now making him my superior. Fuck me sideways, but it gave me life when I needed it most.

Our mission was to be the first line of defense against threats targeting civilians or law enforcement, with statewide jurisdiction and significant latitude. TITON's primary focus was to combat the influx of South American gangs illegally migrating and regrouping in major Texas cities. However, terrorism knows no boundaries. Becoming a TITON agent gave me carte blanche to pursue my investigation into potential threats involving an illegal Chinese presence that seemed to be spreading across the state.

"What's on your mind, Sharp?"

"There was an explosion southwest of Houston I think would be worth your time."

"Don't have much of it to spare, Sharp. I'm heading to depose a few..."

"I hear what you are saying," Sharp said, his interruption dripped of condescension. "But in truth, you are the closest asset I have and I need a report filed expeditiously."

"Expeditiously," Ray mocked, having overheard most of the conversation. "Sounds like he's enjoying the new title they crammed up his ass. Expeditiously."

Sharp did not miss a beat.

"I'll text you the location. Make this happen, Agent Callahan."

Agent Callahan. It was the first time anyone had called me that, and I decided right then I hated it. But, like Uncle Stewart used to say, "Sometimes you gotta stomp through shit ta reach the meadow." It was an old hunting metaphor, but I thought it fit this scenario to a T.

"Roger that," I said.

"Oh, Cass, one more thing."

I took a deep breath. "And, what's that?"

"Tell Ray he can kiss my ass. Expeditiously."

The line went dead. Even from over eight hundred miles away, SAC Dylan Sharp had a way of getting under my skin. Ray's too. Prick, indeed.

"That slack-jawed, *maricon*."

We shot ahead as Ray's foot rammed the accelerator.

"Let it go, Ray. We both know Sharp is an acquired taste."

"More like the backwash from Nana's left tit."

"There's a visual I could have done without," I said. "How about we slow down, and I'll remind you how Sharp got us both out of Mexico. Alive."

Ray let up on the gas and gave me a wicked grin.

"Well, at least the son of bitch got something right."

My cell phone chimed with an announcement of an incoming text.

"That your new detail?" Ray asked.

The car slowed to a stop at a red light two blocks from the detention facility.

"Yeah. If you want, drop me at the house after we're done here and I'll head out alone."

The light turned green, but Ray did not go. Instead, he turned and placed his hand on the headrest behind me, his eyes narrowing with a sharp resolve.

"Like hell."

CHAPTER TWELVE

THE FLYING H RANCH, WEST TEXAS

Raven stood near the horses, now tied to a deadfall on the western face of the small grove, rubbing Tucker's neck and watching the sky over Mexico grow angrier as the once bulging white clouds had turned dark gray and jagged. Gusts of cooler air blowing across the border made the branches bend and sway until the sudden, random bursts subsided. Flint leaned against a cottonwood trunk near Curly. The radio was on, but no further communication had been transmitted. Aside from the leaves shrieking with the bend of their branches, nobody talked.

Her eyes scanned the horizon, looking for movement. Was what Flint said about cartel retaliation possible? She was all too familiar with their brutality having survived what can only be characterized as a manhunt by *La Sombra Negra*, a female sicario sent by the Camargo cartel whose sole mission was to seek and destroy. Raven's friend, Cruzita Vasquez, owner of the local *botánica La Mariposa Mística*, The Mystical Butterfly, had been with her and suffered severe trauma. She also survived and has since returned to as normal a life as one could expect, but her former bubbly personality was now guarded, as if caught in a riptide and had yet to reach the safety of shore. The memories still clung to her like a bad tattoo, regretful while impossible to erase. The thought of crossing paths with the cartel again churned in her gut.

A clap of thunder rumbled beyond the cliffs causing Tucker's ears to prick and twist. Raven took his muzzle in her hands and kissed it.

"Don't worry, fella."

Don't worry, Raven.

Tucker snorted and bobbed his head out of her grasp to stare in the direction of the coming storm. Flint's horse was no different. Raven offered it a consoling rub of the neck as well.

Behind her, she heard the crunch of dead grass and fallen twigs beneath the hardened soles. Raven spoke without looking back.

"You think he hit anyone?"

Flint joined Raven at the tree line and looked out across the land, following the dirt to a point where rocky crags and muddy banks disappeared behind the swaying patches of switchgrass and cattails along the river.

"Dunno. It's possible. Curly's rifle and scope er made fer distance, but he ain't the best at aimin'."

"Should we..."

"I knew ya were gonna bring this up sooner er later," Flint interrupted. He walked around to block her view of the distant border. "If, an' I do mean *if*, Curly hit anyone over there, ain't a damn thing we kin do about it."

"But," Raven started to say, leaning to the side to look around Flint.

"Let's say fer a minute we do ride up ta the river an' see some unlucky bastard..."

Raven cocked her head, glaring as she jammed her fists on her hips.

"...fine," Flint continued. "Poor soul lyin' on the ground. What are ya prepared ta do? Cross illegally inta Mexico? Put yerself in harm's way, 'cause ya know they ain't really alone over there."

Raven's cheeks drooped, her stern expression giving way to worry. Flint read her change. It was something he had learned to do, which surprised him more than he would ever admit. He turned around and looked to Mexico, a place he hated, not for its culture or history, but for all the bad things he had endured during a lifetime of living on the border. The crime, the sorrow, the under addressed and unrelenting struggle of people: some wanting a better life, others wanting to destroy what life others had made.

"Before we leave, I'm riding over for a look. Come with me. Don't come with me. Your choice, but I'm going."

Raven's tone was firm, her message unmistakable. It was in her nature to be a humanitarian, though Curly might have had something to say about that.

Flint flashed her a hard look, but even his best glare was unable to break her intent.

The low rumble of a motor grew from the east, catching both their attention. Raven turned, ducking and adjusting her head to see through the trees.

"Think that's Boss and Floyd?"

"A-yuh." Flint glanced at Curly sitting on the ground and supporting his injured hand. "This should be good."

Together, they walked to the opposite side of the grove, where their view opened to the expanse of West Texas. In the middle of it all, a lone Brewster County Sheriff's Bronco edged closer. They stood and watched as the vehicle approached, the occupants of the inside coming into focus.

"Couple things before they get here, Raven. Boss is going to ask you to hand over yer gun, may even need ya to ride along back ta town with 'er. We'll cross that creek if we have ta."

"Yeah, I've already considered that," she replied, looking over her shoulder, though the trees blocked her view of the border and beyond.

"An' Huckabee's gonna be fiery. I'd say let's see how things play out. Now that Boss is here, it's her show. We'll just see if he sees it that way."

Flint gestured to Floyd Huckabee in the passenger seat. His scowl was noticeable through the windshield.

Deputy Bostwick circled around and parked with the driver's side door parallel to the tree line. She stepped out of the Bronco and straightened her utility belt. Huckabee got out and slammed the door behind him. As he rounded the front of the Bronco, only his hat was visible above the hood, bobbing up and down like a lop-eared bunny crossing the road. When he came into view, Raven had to hold back a smirk, remembering Cass having referred to Huckabee as an angry Oompa Loompa in a Stetson—though, to his credit, he was a tad taller. His voice sounded gruff as he grumbled and walked.

"He kill anyone? The dumb SOB. Where's Curly Yates!" Huckabee stormed over to Flint, his head level with Flint's chest as he looked up at him. "Ya tell me where he is so's I can put a bullet in 'im myself."

"Slow down there, Mr. Huckabee," Deputy Bostwick said. "I agreed to let you ride along, but that's all. Please stand aside and let me do my job."

Flint looked down at Huckabee. "Well, that's already been done, Floyd. Ya know, maybe if'n ya kept yer people in line, we wouldn't have ta be over here doin' it for ya."

The veins in Huckabee's neck pulsed.

"I regretted callin' ya in the first place. I ain't had no choice in the matter."

The argument might have continued, but Deputy Bostwick pinched her lips together and made a sharp, high-pitched whistle that pierced their ears, breaking the unwarranted standoff.

"Say that again, Levi. Curly's been shot?"

Flint shifted his gaze to Raven.

"That's right, Boss," Raven said. "It was the only way to stop him from shooting Flint."

"He ain't dead," Flint added. "Shot clean through the hand is all. We gave 'im first aid, wrapped a bandage ta stop the bleedin', but he's been wailin' on crazy like up until you pulled up. Must be hurtin' somethin' fierce."

Boss looked at Raven, more professional than normal. "Where is he?"

Raven pointed to the trees near the spot he had laid out on the ground.

"There. I'll bring you over."

"No. You stay here with the guys. I'll handle Curly." Deputy Bostwick walked a few steps, then turned around. "Raven, where is your weapon now?"

Raven glanced at her holster. Boss instinctively moved her hand to the grip of her service weapon, a gesture that startled Raven. Realizing what she had done, Boss shifted her hand to her hip, then pointed at Raven with the other.

"Remove the weapon, release the magazine, lock the slide back, and place both pieces on the hood of the Bronco before I get back."

Deputy Bostwick's voice was firm. Raven nodded.

"I know you, Raven, so I won't cuff you as long as you cooperate." She looked next at Flint. "Levi, you, too."

"If it'll make ya feel better," he said, shaking his head.

Deputy Bostwick marched into the trees to collect

Curly. Huckabee sized Raven up, a noticeable impression dawning over him.

"You shot Curly?" Each word dripped from his mouth.

Raven looked Huckabee in the eye. "Damn right I did. He was firing shot after shot like a lunatic. When we got here, Flint went in to talk to him. When he wouldn't stop shooting, Flint moved closer. That's when Curly whirled around and pulled a pistol from his belt. That's when I shot him."

"Crack shot, too," Flint boasted. "Took Curly in the hand and popped his gun outta reach in one shot. Saved me fer sure."

Something Raven had seldom seen on Huckabee began to form at the corner of his mouth, but she did not like it. Not now.

"How can you smile at a time like this?"

"Hell, Mrs. Callahan. I never thought ya had it in ya."

Flint became defensive.

"Ain't none of this have ta happen, Floyd. Ya know Curly's better than the rest of us. Ain't a stretch ta say he's been off his rocker fer a long time. It's no wonder we're standin' here right now." Flint's nostrils flared. "Ya said ya didn't want ta call fer help? Weren't no pleasure a mine to give it to ya. Like it er not, ranchers look out fer their own. But now Raven's caught up in this an' you think it's funny."

"Hold on ta yer britches, Flint. Ain't no one said a thing about this bein' funny. I was only admirin' her wherewithal." Huckabee turned back to Raven. "A city woman such as yerself ought not have stayed around after what y'all been through these past months, but now that I git a good look, I see there's somethin' different about ya. Ya seem tough as me."

"I'm different, all right, but I'm not anything like you.

Just because I acted, don't think for a second, I forgot who I am."

A rustling in the trees reminded Raven and Flint to secure their weapons for Boss. Brushing past Huckabee, they stepped over to the Bronco, disassembled and placed them on the hood as instructed. Raven looked at her Purple Demon. It was a fashionable piece, bought as a training tool, but had turned into so much more. Now, catching the dimming light, it looked *wrong*, like the toys she used to buy for Spencer as a child. Looking at the miniature Ruger, a wave of embarrassment came over her.

"Flint." Raven's voice sounded low. "I don't think I want this anymore."

Flint turned around and leaned against the front fender.

"Ain't nuthin' ya did was wrong, Raven. Ain't no reason ta give up the gun. I'm sure Boss er the sheriff'll give er back when they can."

"It ain't the gun, Flint," her words blending for the first time with his. "It's just that..." She turned around and leaned back next to him. "...I don't want to carry a Barbie gun anymore."

She looked ahead, not bending to Flint's curious gaze.

"Tomorrow, drive me into town. It's time to ditch this toy."

Flint and Raven stepped away from the hood as Deputy Bostwick came into view, leading Curly, his wrists cuffed in front of him. He supported his injured hand with the other, his face cringing with each step. The bandage looked soiled. Huckabee took one glimpse at Curly and marched right up to him, blocking his path.

"I've had you on fer god knows how long, Curly," he said, jabbing the air with his finger. "Trail drive's over. Damn sure it is."

Curly glared down at Huckabee, but did not say a word.

"Let us pass, Mr. Huckabee," Deputy Bostwick commanded. "Or would you like to join us for processing?"

Snarling, he stepped aside. "Get 'im off my property."

Deputy Bostwick led Curly to the Bronco and opened the rear driver's side door. Curly looked back before getting in the vehicle.

"Ain't never gonna be over. Not fer you. Not fer me."

Deputy Bostwick placed a hefty hand on his shoulder, coaxing him to turn around, but he resisted.

"What's a few dead Mexicans, anyway? They'll keep comin'."

Curly's face twisted into a malevolent grin, as if he had predicted a future more grim than the present. It made Raven shudder. The sight of Curly made her sick to her stomach—for what he had done, and for what she had done to him—but she kept her glare fixed on him until all she could see was her own reflection in the window as Deputy Bostwick got him into the seat and shut the door.

Walking to the hood, Deputy Bostwick inspected Flint and Raven's weapons. Satisfied, she walked back to the rear of the Bronco, opened the glass hatch, and retrieved a box before returning to the front of the vehicle. She set the box on the hood next to the guns and took out two clear plastic bags along with evidence tags. She recorded the details on each tag—make, model, and location. When she finished, she looped the tags through the trigger guards. The crinkle of the bags broke the silence as she slid each weapon inside, sealing them before placing the collected evidence in the box. After securing the box in the rear of the vehicle, she turned to Raven and gestured toward the grove.

"Walk with me back to the scene."

Raven nodded, hearing a deputy's voice rather than her friend's. They had shared many conversations in the past, but this felt different. It *was* different.

"Remember," Flint whispered as she stepped away from him. "Ya ain't done nuthin' wrong."

Raven agreed, yet a part of her still felt she might have crossed a line when she attacked Curly after the shooting. Words were just words and should not mean anything, but when tempers flared, and insults stung, right and wrong blurred into shades of red.

At first, they walked in silence, just as Raven had once led her share of misbehaving students to the principal's office when she was a teacher, but now it felt like the shoe was on the other foot. The rumble of thunder grew louder, sounding nearer with each resonating boom. Overhead, branches swayed in the breeze as if warning Raven that there was more at stake than just a simple explanation.

They stopped at the tree line where Curly had taken roost. The remnants of his damaged pistol lay scattered where they had fallen, and blood spatter stained the brown earth near their feet—dry reminders of what had happened. His rifle still leaned against the tree where Flint had placed it following the confrontation, its slide open and barrel empty.

"So," Deputy Bostwick said, turning to Raven. "Tell me what happened."

CHAPTER THIRTEEN

29.6073° N, 95.1588° W

A swift, high-pitched buzz soared over Bay Knoll, a residential community near Clear Lake High School, catching the attention of a man walking his dog and triggering the early detection warning system for unauthorized aircraft in Ellington Field's main tower. Though a general aviation airport, Ellington Field is more critically a NASA operations facility for the Johnson Space Center and strategic base for the Texas Air National Guard, U.S. Coast Guard, and Army National Guard.

Inside the air traffic control tower, Senior Airman Jacobs squinted at the monitor, where a flashing red indicator showed an unauthorized UAV entering restricted airspace. His headset crackled as he called out to his NCOIC, or *Non-Commissioned Officer in Charge.*

"Unidentified UAV entering southeast perimeter airspace. Altitude holding at approximately fifty feet, moving toward Runway One Seven Right. Activating early warning system."

The tower's alarm sounded, a shrill tone echoing across the airfield. Jacobs grabbed the radio.

"Attention all personnel, we have a UAV perimeter breach. All aircraft hold positions."

Behind him, Technical Sergeant Miller, the NCOIC for the shift, leaned over the radar console, eyes fixed on the UAV's flight path.

"SITREP," she said, her voice calm but urgent.

"UAV inbound at seventy miles per hour. Heading Three One Five," Jacobs answered, locked in.

"Maintain radar contact," Miller said. "Alert base security and get electronic countermeasures online."

Jacobs keyed the mic again.

"Base security, this is ATC Tower. We have an unauthorized UAV breach, confirmed near Runway One Seven Right, bearing Three One Five. Requesting electronic countermeasures. Scramble ERT (Emergency Response Team) for ground intercept."

As Jacobs relayed the information, Miller moved to the communications panel and punched in the line for NASA's operations center.

"This is Ellington Tower. Be advised, we're initiating an immediate ground stop pending interception of a UAV over the airfield. Move to FPCON (Force Protection Condition) Bravo protocols. Recommend you secure your assets."

Down on the tarmac, aircraft engines whined to a halt. Security vehicles, blue lights flashing, roared across the airfield in pursuit of the intruding UAV. Senior Airman Daryl Savage and John Vesey were the first to respond on the ground.

"ATC Tower," Savage called on the radio. "We've got eyes on your UAV. Looks like a kid's drone. Not much bigger than a pizza box, but it is traveling at significant speed."

A light on the console illuminated signaling that Ellington's jamming system was online.

"Roger that. Remain in pursuit. Be advised, we're activating countermeasures," Miller announced over comms, then keyed the final code for initiation.

Multiple signals aimed at disrupting the drone's controls swept across the airways. The RF jammers engaged first, broadcasting a high-powered signal attempting to sever the UAV's communication link, while the GPS spoofing system projected a false location aimed at tricking its navigation system into believing it was miles away from its current location. It would take only moments for a commercial drone to lose signal, causing it to cease functionality and crash.

Despite the RF jamming and GPS spoofing systems working in tandem, the drone maintained its course, as if unaffected by the barrage of electronic interference. Instead, as it passed over the center of Ellington Field, it increased its speed.

"Damn, look at the thing go," Vesey said, then into his radio. "Tower, be advised, we're seeing no change in course from our position, but it seems to be increasing its speed."

"Roger that. Initiating level two protocol," Miller replied.

Should initial measures fail, a high-powered microwave emitter is brought online that could fry the UAV's circuits, but first it had to lock onto the drone's dynamic position.

Airman Savage and Airman Vesey shared a look.

"That thing is flying so low and so fast, it'll be over south Houston before that emitter can track it," Vesey said.

The drone zinged closer to the northwest border of

Ellington Field. Lights on the control panel in the tower turned from amber to dark green. The radio crackled.

"Initiating targeting sequence. On my mark. Three... two...one."

The microwave emitter activated, sending a directed pulse aimed at disabling the drone's electronics. At first, the drone shimmied, its flight path beginning to falter. As it crossed the outer boundary of the base, the shimmy intensified into a pronounced wobble, causing the drone to dip lower with each erratic motion. Its descent grew steeper by the second, struggling to stay aloft as the effects of the pulse seemed to tighten their grip.

"Looks like you got it, Tower. It's headed straight for Clear Creek Golf Course," Savage said over the radio. Releasing the mic, he looked at Vesey. "Some kid just lost an expensive toy."

"Yeah, and as soon as we recover it, they'll be getting an unwelcome visit from the authorities as well."

The two airmen sat in their Air National Guard response vehicle and took a moment to revel in the trouble some kid had caused the base and the consequences they would soon face. Their relief was overshadowed by a sudden thunderous explosion that rattled the vehicle's windows, followed by a swirling plume of black smoke rising in the direction the drone had gone down.

"That wasn't a clean splash on the golf course," Vesey muttered, eyes widening as the smoke thickened. The airmen exchanged a glance as the black cloud rose and sirens began wailing in the distance.

"Shit." Savage's disbelief caused him to pause. Vesey grabbed the mic.

"Tower, this is Vesey. The drone is down, but..." He took a breath to steady himself. "There's been a major explosion west of our location. I think it just hit E.P.P."

Radio silence followed for what felt like minutes before a response came over the air.

"Roger that. Tower can confirm an explosion at Enterprise Products Partners. Alerting emergency services."

Airmen Savage and Vesey sat a moment longer and watched the billowing black cloud grow larger.

"What the hell just happened?" Vesey said.

Savage shifted to reverse, taking one last look. "Maybe that wasn't a kid's toy after all."

CHAPTER FOURTEEN

HOUSTON CONTRACT DETENTION FACILITY

The room was cool, dark. A rattle from deep within the airducts festered as if dried leaves had been caught in the aluminum folds and flapped against the metal siding, trapped until the air conditioning had run its course, or they became too brittle and cracked under the constant pressure. A large, one-way mirror separated the room Ray and I were in from another, larger room where the three Chinese illegals sat on one side of a long, industrial-sized table. Each was handcuffed and secured through restraint rings bolted on the table's surface.

"Rough looking bunch," Ray said. "Let's get this over with."

"Keep your head on straight when we're in there, Ray. My gut has been twisting around this for days. If there is a connection between them, the guy that was killed in Big Bend, and the Chinese son of a bitch, Li, back in Brewster, I'll need them, any of them, to cooperate."

"Good luck with that." A man wearing khakis, a pink

Ralph Lauren polo beneath a tweed Herringbone blazer, walked into the room and joined us at the observation window. "I'm Agent Thomas Somel, U.S. Immigration and Customs Enforcement."

"I can read your nametag, Agent Somel. Clearly," Ray said.

Agent Somel pursed his lips as he glanced down at his ID badge. He left Ray's comment hanging and turned to look at me.

"I'm Agent Cass Callahan, TITON group, FBI." *I hated the sound of that.* "What makes you say that?"

"Cass. Can I call you Cass, or do you prefer Agent Callahan?" Thomas said, offering a hand. I answered as we shook.

"Cass is fine."

"Good," he said, letting go. "We'll get through this faster if we drop the formalities. All on the same team, right?"

"Kumbaya," Ray turned away from us to glare through the window.

"Sure," I said. "Have they been a problem for you?"

"No problem, really, other than they tried sneaking through a U.S. Custom's warehouse with fake creds."

Ray huffed, amused.

"What is it then?" I asked. "Do they speak English?"

"That's the thing. We don't know."

Thomas pressed his palm against the one-way mirror and leaned toward the window squinting his eyes.

"They haven't said a word since they were detained. No facial expressions, no visible cues, nothing. They act hardcore but look as timid as an eighth-grade badminton team."

I looked at the men sitting at the table.

"Maybe they need a little American persuasion," Ray said, still focused on the detainees.

"Let's go with procedure first, Ray. If the sight of you alone sitting next to me in there doesn't break them, I doubt anything will," I said. I turned and headed to the door. "You leading us in, Thomas?"

"Help yourself," he said. "Word came down the chain to give you full cooperation. As long as you don't go full-on Batman versus Joker in there, I'll just sit here with my popcorn and watch the show."

"Fair enough." I reached for the door handle. "You comin', Ray?"

"Oh, yeah," he said, turning around. "I haven't had sit-down Chinese for ages." He ignored Thomas's disapproving head shake. "Let's go see what's on the menu, Cass."

We stepped into the hall and walked down a short corridor to another door marked, *Interrogation Room C*. I pulled the handle, but it did not budge. To the right of the door was a small security box with a slot to insert an ID card. There was also a small camera embedded in the frame of the box with a red bulb glowing beneath and a small speaker with a call button on the side. I pressed the call button and looked into the camera. Agent Somel's voice rattled through the speaker, followed by the sharp mechanical click of the security lock.

"You're all clear."

The red bulb turned green, and the door nudged open on its own.

Ray and I stepped into the room, approaching the three detainees from behind. I walked to the left of the table, Ray circled right, his hip bumping the man on the edge making his chair squeak across the polished tile floor.

"Pardon me," Ray said, turning around and putting his hands on the table in front of the man he had just bumped. "You all right, fella?"

I took a seat on the opposite side of the table from the men, placing a folder on the surface in front of me. Ray was still focused on the detainee, now to my left, eyes locked on the man as he slowly made his way around the table and sat down next to me.

The room felt meat-locker cold.

Now I understand why Agent Somel wore a blazer.

I pulled my cell phone from my pocket and set it on top of the folder.

"I'm Agent Callahan. This is Detective Tucker. Seems the three of you were in the wrong place at the wrong time."

Each man stared straight ahead, their gazes the product of a perfect poker face. No eye twitches, no subtle jaw movements, no clicking of their teeth; each seemed a master at hiding his thoughts or emotions, but I held what I felt was an ace in the hole that might get their attention.

Not yet. Wait for the river, then push.

I looked at the man in the middle. His face was smooth, as though his chin and cheeks were untouched by the signs of puberty. Stringy, black hair fell across his forehead in a straight line from temple to temple, reminding me of the home haircuts Raven used to give Spencer during those long elementary school summers to save money. His fingers were laced together beneath raw, red marks around his wrists.

"Tell me your name, and I'll see what I can do about those restraints."

Still, the man stared ahead, seeming to look past me as if I were not there.

"No name?" I glanced at Ray. He looked ready to toss the room. "Let me help you out. If they don't want to tell us their names, I'll give you names of my own."

Ray pointed to the man on my left. "You're Hong."

He pointed to the man on my right. "You're Ding."

He pointed at the man in the middle. "And you're Dong. There. Now we can tell you apart."

Ray smirked.

"As you were, Agent Callahan."

I reached for the folder beneath my phone and pulled a paper with printouts of the photos Ray had sent me after the Chinese men were captured.

"Now..." I paused, holding up the paper. "These aren't the best shots. Mug shots would have been better, but for our purposes today, these will do fine."

I set the paper down on the table and rotated it so they could see. None of them moved, their gazes locked, their demeanors conditioned to be unresponsive.

"You see? This is you," I said, pointing to one of the pictures, then pointing at the man Ray had dubbed Dong. "And these are your buddies."

I slid the paper closer, the edges crinkling against the man's knuckles.

With a sudden shove of his chair, Ray stood up and pounded both fists on the table. The metallic thud echoed in the tiny room. The detainees flinched, as anyone's instincts would cause them to do when startled, but their facial expressions never wavered.

"One of you yellow-faced bastards are going to answer his questions, or I'll Bruce Lee your asses into next week. *Comprende?*"

Ray's slur made my stomach turn, but I let him run his bad cop routine. He moved around the table, squeezing between the detainees, and leaned in close enough to Dong that the straight hair on his forehead puffed aside beneath Ray's breath. Ray stayed put while I continued.

"As you can tell, Detective Tucker is passionate about his work. Here's the thing, fellas, these are pictures of you. You've seen yourself before, no big deal. I get it."

I reached for my phone and unlocked the home screen, then pressed the text icon, displaying recent texts first. I scrolled through the list as Ray scooted further between the men and rested a hip on the table. When I found the text I was looking for, I tapped the message to expand the pictures within the thread.

"Now." I paused, looking at the image I selected, pressing my lips together as if seeing it for the first time and was impressed by what I saw. "This looks a little different, but I'd bet you'd recognize this man."

Time to go all in.

I turned the phone around so all three detainees could see the image. Ray stood up.

"That's nasty, Callahan. Why would you carry that on your phone?"

Hong did not budge. Ding looked on without regard for the image, but the Dong showed me his hand. His eyes widened and his lips parted. It was slight, but enough.

"I'm guessing you recognize the man, or what is left of him, in this picture? A *Mr. Li*, but you already knew that." I studied the Dong's face. "Never did catch his first name. I'd also bet that if I asked Detective Tucker to remove your shirt that we would see a tattoo on you like the one on what's left of Li's torso?"

I noticed tension in the Dong's throat as I watched him try to swallow.

"What do you think, Detective Tucker?"

Ray walked back to his chair and sat down next to me.

"What I think is these guys are hiding something big, and you just cracked their fortune cookie."

"Let's make this easier on everyone." I looked at the mirrored glass. "Agent Somel, can you please have two of these men removed. I'd like to speak with one of them alone."

A moment later, the door buzzed and Agent Somel walked in with two detention officers.

"Who would you like to speak with first?"

I pointed at Dong, his cheeks growing pink with what I felt were signs of concern.

The first detention officer unlocked Hong's table restraints. At the same time, the other detention officer did the same for Ding. Dong seemed to grow more nervous as the seconds ticked closer to our being alone. His eyes became shifty. Though still laced together, he flexed his fingers.

As the officers turned to lead the two men out of the room, Hong yelled.

"*Měiguó qù sǐ!*"

He threw his arms in the air, repeating the phrase over and over. The detention officer who was leading him out struggled to control his thrashing, which drew the attention of the second officer, as well as Ray and Agent Somel. They converged on Hong, attempting to regain control of him. I watched as the situation exploded before my eyes, then shifted my gaze to the other detainee who had been released from the table.

When our eyes met, his mouth cracked open, showing his crooked teeth beneath a growing, sinister glare. With a flash of movement, Ding looped his shackles around Dong's neck and twisted his wrists with one violent, sudden jolt. I had no time to react except to yell.

"NO!"

My single word was met with a heart-stopping *SNAP*.

Ray whirled around, as did Somel and the officer responsible for releasing Ding. Ray slid behind him, wrapped his right forearm around Ding's throat. The left locked vertically around his head, clenching the detainee in a powerful headlock while Somel pulled his strangling handcuffs away from Dong's neck. Ding's crazed look and crooked teeth burned into my memory, something I would have to file away as a living nightmare.

As Ray and the detention officers cleared the room, I was left to look across the table at what was supposed to be the next step of gaining information for my investigation into an illegal Chinese presence in Texas. All that was left was the chill of the room, the rattle in the air ducts, and the blank stare of a man whose head hung to one side of his body and whose fractured vertebrae jutted out unnaturally from under the skin of his throat.

CHAPTER FIFTEEN

29.55617° N, -95.07505° W

An unmarked, white van pulled into the guest lot of the Clear Lake Hilton and parked in the shade of the high-rise hotel. Nassau Bay's waters looked like glass, its smooth sheen reflecting the sun as if it were trapped just below the surface. Three gulls tussled over a dead crab on the warm asphalt, their high-pitched cackles and wing flapping bird hops reminiscent of The Three Stooges squabbling over a dame.

The van idled, its engine purring with menial vibrations. Eyes flashed to the driver's side mirror, then a hand toggled the controls, angling the reflection to grab images from the sky behind the van. On the distant horizon, a plume of black smoke billowed higher and higher into the air, trailing to the west with the gentle, onshore breeze. Masked by the smoke, yet coming into view, was a tiny black speck shooting across the sky, growing larger by the second.

Tapping the steering wheel, the man fixed his gaze on the mirror until the distant speck transformed into an approaching drone. With the press of a button, the van's side window opened wide enough for the driver to reach an arm out and place a flat magnetic device on the roof, then closed again. The drone shifted, recalibrating its course as it soared closer, locked onto the van's position. Unhurried, the man moved to the cargo area of the van, careful to avoid the body lying in the back. With arms raised over her head and legs crossed at the ankles, the corpse looked relaxed, as if asleep. If not for the strangulation marks around her neck and bloodied, swollen lips revealing the jagged remains of broken teeth, she might have looked peaceful.

Three spaces behind the van, a Lexus SUV pulled in and parked. Two children hopped out of the rear doors, followed by a young mother from behind the wheel. The kids ran around the vehicle holding their arms out and whirring like airplanes.

The woman waited patiently for them to complete their circle, then, on final approach, snagged them both like arresting grips on a naval aircraft carrier. With one child holding each of her hands, the three walked toward the entrance of the hotel as a buzzing sound grew overhead.

"What's that noise?" one child asked.

"Sounds like bees," said the other.

The mother ignored their observation, leading them along, while both children watched a small drone zip over the parking lot behind them and land on the roof of a white van.

"Wow," they said in unison, but their wonder was cut off as they were pulled through the revolving door to the hotel lobby.

The side door of the van slid open. A man in blue jeans and a black turtleneck appeared in the doorway and removed the drone as its propellers came to an abrupt halt while in his hands. Vanishing into the van as fast as he appeared, the man got behind the wheel and drove toward the parking lot exit. His movements were a blur but the curious eyes of two children still buzzing from NASA's Martian Matrix—a hands-on experience at the Johnson Space Center—saw everything from inside the lobby. Faces pressed against the window, wide-eyed, they watched the strange man with the drone drive away as their mother spoke to the concierge.

CHAPTER SIXTEEN

"Twice in one day? What are the odds? Seems like you're piling up the dead bodies around town, Detective Tucker."

"Maureen, you are as grim as the reaper himself," Ray said.

"Oh, if you put it that way, I'm still better off than you."

They have no idea what you're going through, I thought.

I stood next to Ray and watched Maureen Prescott, his *ball buster* from earlier today, and another HCIFS technician tag, bag, and remove our dead detainee.

"This keeps getting better by the minute," I said, my voice swimming with frustrated sarcasm.

Agent Somel reentered the room after escorting his detention officers and the two other detainees back to their holding cells.

"I'll need confirmation that they're being sent for processing downtown, Thomas," I said.

"As soon as our investigation is complete," he replied.

"What investigation?" Ray shot back. "Watch the fucking security footage. It's all there in high def. One guy kills the other. You do have cameras rolling, right?"

"We do, Detective Tucker." A degree of formality settled between us.

"So, what's the holdup?" I asked, my patience thinning as much as Ray's.

"Agent Callahan, we—"

"It's *Agent*, now?" I interrupted. "What happened to 'We're all on the same team?'"

"Oh, I'd like to assume we are. But seeing as how the two of you managed to get one of our detainees killed while under your supervision..."

"Our supervision?" Ray was pissed. His fingers flexed at his side. I could feel the heat radiating from him with each steamed word. "Your guys failed to follow REP—*Risk Evaluation Protocol!* This isn't the first day of kindergarten, for Christ's sake. High-risk prisoners are to be individually escorted and or removed from detention one at a time!"

Agent Somel faced Ray, locking eyes with him and speaking with an enhanced, more combative tone.

Big mistake.

"Detective Tucker, these men were not deemed high risk. Their silence may have been questionable, but their profile suggested they were seeking asylum."

"Oh, their profiles suggested they were asylum seekers. Why didn't you say that in the first place. That makes everything better." Ray turned, ran his hand over his head, then stepped into Somel's personal space. "You didn't know dick about these guys. Probably felt another couple chinks wouldn't buck the system. Maybe slip them into a program in some damned sanctuary city when they should be back on a plane, or better yet, a slow boat to China or wherever the hell they came from. Typical bureaucratic bullshit. Admit it, Somel. ICE just crapped the bed."

Ray stood a good four inches taller than the younger ICE agent. His barreled belly surged in and out with each heated breath. Somel, looking more like the quarterback about to get sacked in the end zone, stood his ground. He leaned forward, tilting his chin and cocking his head. His eyes firm and focused on Ray's.

"Perception, Detective Tucker. The only thing that changed since detaining those men was *your* visit. Following their arrest and arrival here, their interactions, while limited, showed zero signs of hostility. Not toward us, and especially not toward one another. Then you guys show up." Somel turned to look at me. "You're not getting a thing out of a dead Chinese detainee."

The hair on the back of my neck prickled as the pressure in the room thickened, and I was drawn into the line of fire. It was time to put the full weight of my new role with TITON into play.

"Thomas," I said, "I'm assuming control of the body and the two surviving Chinese detainees. Separate them and keep them here until I arrange their transfer." Agent Somel opened his mouth to protest, but I turned away, cutting him off. "Detective Tucker, catch up with Maureen. I need the body redirected from HCIFS custody. Make sure they don't leave the premises before I speak with them."

Ray sneered at Agent Somel, bumping his shoulder as he left the room. Thomas straightened his jacket, shook his head, and smiled.

"Agent Callahan, you're overstepping..."

I shot him a glare, talking over him with finality. "Not a goddamn thing. Take it up with Special Agent in Charge Dylan Sharp, FBI Field Office, El Paso." I produced a business card from my wallet and handed it to him. "Or better yet, see if you get any pushback superseding my authority from this guy."

Somel glanced at the card.

"Office of the Governor of Texas, Greg Abbott," he read aloud, his voice teetering between frustration and subjugation.

"TITON has authority," I said, my voice steady and unyielding. "As an agent on the governor's special task force, I have the power to do whatever's necessary to protect the people of Texas—by any means." I stepped past Agent Somel, pausing at the doorway to Interrogation Room C. "You mentioned earlier that we're on the same team," I continued, my tone hardening. "You're right. But I'm in the game, and you're just holding the towels."

CHAPTER SEVENTEEN

Heat waves rippled across the horizon beyond the Rio Grande, blurring the cliff tops and creating the illusion of distant spirits dancing along the ridgeline. A cascade of bright yellow rays made Raven squint as she gazed ahead. Perspiration dripped down her neck, soaking into her loose-fitting wild rag. The rumble of Deputy Bostwick's Bronco faded as it carried Huckabee to his ranch house, then Curly to Brewster General, and finally, the county lockup. Raven's stomach knotted as she slid her hand to her side, feeling the empty space where her sidearm should have rested in its holster. Her fingers traced the leather lining, its smooth sheath sending a chill up her arm.

"It's gettin' late. Best we start headin' back."

She heard Flint but continued to scan the land beyond the river.

Did Curly hurt anyone? Kill anyone?

"Raven." Flint placed a hand on her shoulder. It was a gesture he would never have offered another in the past, but his affection for her changed him in more ways than one. It felt natural, the way a brother might seek to console his younger sister. "Hear me?"

Raven took a long breath, letting air slowly escape through her nose. Her shoulders rose and fell with unspoken turmoil as Flint withdrew his hand.

"Yeah, but I have something I want to do first." Before Flint could object, she walked over to the tree where Tucker was tied, loosed the reins from the low-hanging branch, and mounted up. "I'll meet you."

With a nudge of her boot heels and a click of her tongue, Tucker carried her into the yellow haze beneath the sun's steady descent.

CHAPTER EIGHTEEN

HOUSTON CONTRACT DETENTION FACILITY

Stepping out of the ICE detention facility in North Houston felt like walking away from a blind date gone bad. Horribly bad. Ray stood with Maureen next to a dark blue HCIFS van, engaged in what looked like a deep conversation. As I approached, Maureen leaned into Ray and wrapped her arms around him. Ray's arms dangled at first. Our eyes met and his hands rose to Maureen's elbows, coaxing her back to let go. His face looked disconcerted. Maureen glanced at me, then wiped her cheek.

"I feel like such a shit," she said as I joined them. "I had no idea about Ruth Ann."

I pursed my lips, knowing nothing I could say would make a difference.

"It'll be fine," Ray said, breaking the awkward silence. "She's a tough cookie."

Maureen grabbed his bicep.

"Please let me know if there is anything she needs." She paused and squeezed her fingers. "Or that you need."

"That's very kind, Maureen." Ray flashed me a look. "Right now, what I need is for you to listen to Cass."

Maureen released Ray's arm and shifted her gaze to me.

"I need the body transported out of Houston, tonight, and can have a plane at Sugarland Regional Airport in a few hours to pick it up."

I watched curiosity shift Maureen's demeanor, but she kept her thoughts to herself. Ray noticed as well.

"Can you handle the transfer, Maureen?" I said.

She looked at Ray, her face brimming with questions.

"It's important," Ray said.

Her fingers twitched and her jaw tightened. I could tell by her mannerisms that she was not comfortable with the request, caught between wanting to help and being unsure if she should.

I tried to ease her concerns.

"I'll make sure all the appropriate paperwork is filed with the county, but this needs to happen before all that is processed. I know we're working the system backward, but this cannot wait."

Maureen crossed her arms, then looked at the van. I read her eyes as they scanned the lettering on the side, *Harris County Institute of Forensic Science.*

"I can assure you that you will not get any flack from the Chief ME." I turned to Ray. "Sabrina Bridger still heads up the examiner's office, right?"

Ray nodded.

"Sabrina and I go way back, Maureen. I'll give her a call and fill her in as soon as we leave."

Maureen looked at Ray, then at me, and dropped her arms. "What time?"

I pulled my phone out of my pocket to check the time, but my eyes fell upon the notification banner across the top of the screen, widening as I read the message:

*Drone crash sparks explosion in Southeast Houston rocking
pipeline near Ellington Field*

"There a problem?" Ray asked when I failed to answer
Maureen.

"Yeah. Another local disaster about to get national
attention." I glanced at the time.

5:18 p.m.

"I'll have a plane waiting for you in two hours and will
text you the details of the transfer as soon as I have confirmation of its arrival."

"All right," she said. "I'll do it. Just make sure I don't
get shafted if your plan goes sideways."

"He means what he says, Maureen. Cass'll have your
back." Ray shot me a glance, then turned back to her.
"He's had mine for more years than I'd like to count."

I offered Maureen my hand. Her smaller, bony fingers
wrapped around mine with a firm grip and solid shake.

"I better get rolling, then. May take me that much time
just to navigate rush hour traffic."

"What about your partner?" Ray asked, motioning to a
pair of eyes popping in and out of view in the passenger
side mirror.

"Who? Casey? He's a teddy bear and will do whatever
I ask. The kid's raw and needs experience. Nearly puked
this morning at the sanctuary when we were bagging
your first stiff of the day."

"The gangbanger. Right." Ray's reply was course, but
accurate. "You drive careful now."

Maureen lifted on her tiptoes and grabbed Ray around
the neck, giving him a final squeeze before loading up and
driving off.

"Now that she's gone, you wanna tell me where you're
sending our dead buddy, Dong?"

We walked to Ray's car and talked over the roof.

"I've got a friend out West who can give me a detailed analysis of the body. Mostly, I want her to take a close look at his tattoo. In the pictures you sent me, it looks exactly like the ones on the other two Chinese corpses. If there are any connections or subtleties we can decipher as clues, she's the one who'll find them."

CHAPTER NINETEEN

THE FLYING H RANCH, WEST TEXAS

"Raven!" Flint yelled as he watched her lead Tucker into the heart of Curly's kill zone. "May not like what ya see."

His voice carried but did not dissuade Raven from continuing ahead. Knowing there was only one thing to do, Flint walked to his horse and mounted up, grumbling.

"Woman gets somethin' in her mind...ah, shit! Ya think she'd seen enough?" He kicked heel, and his horse bolted ahead.

The cliffs loomed larger as the staggered riders drew nearer, the sky above the jagged rim darkening from light gray to ominous charcoal. The clouds bulged as if fighting to contain something unnatural within. Thunder rumbled behind a kettle of turkey vultures soaring higher and higher on the raging thermals from the approaching storm. Amid the chaos, the large birds remained graceful in flight. The wind whipped over the edge of the cliffs on a suicide dive, crashing down on a patch of creosote shrubs and tarbush—now barren of their seasonal yellow blooms

—and causing their branches to lash in a frenzied dance within the blustery gusts.

Flint ran his horse to catch up with Raven. A distinct chill, carrying the sweet scent of impending rain, brushed past his face. A dull throb pulsed in his right leg, a lingering ache from an angry gunshot and a hardened reminder of a fight he would rather forget. Pulling alongside her, he considered his words.

"Ain't no tellin' what's ahead. Why don't we turn back. See if'n we can beat the storm. Looks like a real gully washer."

A flash lit the sky, casting the brooding clouds in an eerie, washed-out brilliance before the turbulent gray overtook the sky once more. Thunder rolled, its warning lost on Raven.

The soil softened beneath heavy hooves, and Raven found herself twenty yards from the banks of the Rio Grande. Pulling up, she slid out of the saddle and led Tucker by the reins, walking closer to the water. She eyed the ground where the river met the land, then across its ripple to the soggy foreign shore.

Flint remained on his horse and pulled his rifle from its saddle sheath. With squinted eyes and his head on a swivel, he scanned the brush and felled rocks beyond the water. He knew, more than he felt, that they were being watched.

The hum of rain falling sounded like distant applause, its rhythmic pattern growing more insistent with each passing second.

"Com'on, Raven. Ain't nuthin' ta see," he said, his voice low but firm, as if he did not want others to hear.

"Oh dear," Raven said, dropping Tucker's reins to run ahead.

"Wait!" Flint called out, but it was too late.

Raven charged straight for the water, sloshing into the

shallows until the current lapped against her thighs. Flint leaped off his horse and ran after her, gun in hand, eyes peeled and heart pounding. Raven lunged out, hands outstretched and fingers grasping. Another bolt of lightning split the heavens, this time forking overhead beyond the storm's borders, spreading in scattered directions. Daylight faded behind the cliff wall and brewing sky, but not enough to keep Flint from witnessing Raven's plight.

"What are ya…" Flint's voice dropped, his jaw tightening as he realized he was too far away to do anything but shout. "Raven!"

CHAPTER TWENTY

29.7057° N, -95.5495° W

A mix of earthy aromas filled the one-room apartment—caramelized garlic, fresh ginger, warm cumin, star anise, and the sharp bite of Sichuan peppercorn. Steam swirled above a large rice bowl centered on a small, round table in the kitchen of apartment 4C. Fish scales, a shimmering mash of color, littered the counter beside a knife, its blade flecked with iridescent hues. On the stove, flames flared beneath a seasoned frying pan in dazzling blues and oranges, where the outstretched carcass of a massive carp lay, braised in soy sauce and herbs. Its mouth hung open, its large eyes staring ahead, frozen in that final moment where life and death collided. A *shāguō* of Jasmine tea bubbled beside the fish, its floral note escaping the traditional clay pot. Together, the entirety of aromas filled the apartment with a warmth that drifted across the ocean, past the East China Sea, beyond the towering modern buildings of Shànghǎi, to a small village west of Wuhan. There, in a modest home shared by generations, similar dishes simmered, with recipes and secrets passed down over the years, filling the surroundings with the familiar taste of home.

A television hummed in the living room. Its volume remained muted, but words flashed along the bottom of the screen in a mix of English and Chinese characters. The walls were bare, save one scroll hung near the front door. The artistic brushwork flowed from top to bottom as if written as poetry beyond the meaning of its characters. Long strokes, delicate twists, and black ink danced on the page above a *yìn zhāng*, the artist's signature carved in bone and pressed in red ink, where meaning flowed as much as did the scrolls message. 谋事在人，成事在天，*Móu shì zài rén, chéng shì zài tiān, Man proposes, Heaven disposes.*

Images on the television showed smoke billowing into the sky behind a young local news reporter, who stood just beyond yellow police tape in a zone safe from the swirl of emergency lights. Her account of the disaster in Southeast Houston, the top story and breaking news, caused the man watching the segment to pull a cigarette from a fresh pack of Pandas, placing it between his lips as he stood and nodded with quiet satisfaction.

A woman's voice called out from the kitchen. "*Wèi, chīfàn le!*"

The man watching the news raised a Zippo in front of him, flipped open the lid, and used his thumb to spin the flint wheel. A sharp flame burst forth, and he eased the tip of his cigarette into its path, taking a long drag before pulling the lighter away. Smoke filled his lungs with a tantalizing combination of burn and tantric pleasure before escaping through his nostrils like a fire-breathing dragon.

"*Nǐ zài tīng ma?!*"

The man turned to the kitchen, an irritation growing

across his face as much in the way the woman had delivered her message.

"English!" his voice commanded. "Only English!"

A petite woman with shoulder-length hair stepped out of the kitchen, her eyes sharp and squinted, her jaw tightened. The man stared back at her, his head encircled by smoke, and removed the cigarette from his mouth without speaking further. Biting her lip, the woman spoke again.

"The food...is ready."

"Very good," the man replied.

The woman retreated to the kitchen, her pearl-smooth cheeks turning red as an exploding firecracker.

The man, dressed in black pants and a white button-down shirt, adjusted his glasses and turned his gaze back to the news.

"Very good, indeed," he whispered to himself, his English fluent yet accented. "Everything is falling into place."

CHAPTER TWENTY-ONE

NEWGULF POWER SUBSTATION, NEWGULF, TEXAS

The crunch of gravel ricocheted off the truck's undercarriage, a steady beat of clinks against the steel skid plate as we rolled down the deserted country road toward the power station gates on the edge of Newgulf. The sun, inching closer to the horizon, painted the sky in broad strokes of pink and orange that brushed across billowing clouds like pastel islands adrift in an endless blue sea. For a fleeting second, I could almost picture myself somewhere else—a beach lounger under those cotton candy clouds, a piña colada in hand, with nothing but time to drink in the view. But the rumble of the engine and the looming silhouette of the station's towers were a stark reminder, this was anything but a vacation.

"You drew the short straw this time, Cass," Ray said, looking out the front window. "We are in the middle of nowhere-Texas. I bet Sharp was just waiting to send you on a wild goose chase."

I pulled off the gravel road and onto an access road leading to the facility's secure entrance. A chain-link fence stretched over ten feet high, topped with spirals of razor wire that circled the entire compound. Massive gantries stood in precise rows, their thick high-voltage power lines swinging from steel arms. In one direction, the lines fed into lower substation equipment. In the other, they connected to outgoing platforms fitted with large, high-voltage protection relays before continuing on to connected towers beyond the station. Like giants in marching formation, the transmission towers stretched across the landscape in a diminishing line, their silhouettes shrinking against the horizon.

I stopped the truck short of the gate and scanned the immediate area. Mast lighting towers, each outfitted with opposing HID (High-Intensity Discharge) fixtures, stood watch over various sectors of the yard. The lights remained unilluminated, waiting for dusk to fall. A cluster of elongated buildings filled the nearside of the substation. Their older façade and dirty exterior made them look like ancient homes in a rural trailer park. Two beat-up pickups and one dusted over Chevrolet Caprice were parked in front of a building marked with a rust-edged sign that read *OFFICE*.

Letting my foot off the brake, the truck rolled forward to a call box. I lowered my window and pushed a button next to the grated speaker. A steady hum like a distant swarm of bees hovering overhead and a hint of ozone consumed my senses. The sound did not bother me, but the metallic, almost chlorinated tang in the air was an acquired taste I could have done without.

A sudden *beep* sounded through the speaker, followed by the clink and pull of the chain-link gate as it opened in front of us.

"This place looks like a ghost town," Ray muttered.

As we drove past the gate, a man wearing khaki pants, a dark polo, and loafers emerged from the office. He paused, raised a hand to shield his eyes as he looked our way, then descended the three wooden steps where he stood and waited as I pulled over and parked. I cut the engine and got out.

"Skeleton crew, huh?" Ray said, joining me next to the truck. "Lead the way, Short-Straw."

I ignored his jab and walked over to introduce myself.

The man watched us, his gaze indifferent yet expecting of our arrival. His greeting confirmed my thoughts.

"Y'all the FBI guys we've been expectin'?" His voice did not fit my first impressions, rather it seemed like the man dresses for a role to keep up appearances but would feel more comfortable in boots and blue jeans. On some level, I related. "Our T&D said y'all'd be out here. Just didn't know exactly when. Been waitin' a while."

"T&D?" Ray said.

"He's the Director of Transmission and Distribution for our sector. I guess ya could call him the go between fer us an' Centerpoint."

I produced my wallet and showed him my identification.

"I'm Agent Cass Callahan. This is Detective Ray Tucker."

"Clyde Morrell," the man said. "Newgulf Substation Supervisor."

"Well," I said. "Let's get to it. Tell me what happened."

"It's better if I show an' tell ya at the same time. It's always easier fer civvies that way. Maybe won't take as long, then we kin all git outta here before dark."

I sensed irritation in his tone but disregarded the notion.

"All right, Mr. Morrell. Make it easy for us."

We walked together, passing between the office and an adjacent systems building, emerging on the far side in front of a small security hut. Morrell pointed ahead as we veered left.

"Just up here. Ya kin see the burn marks where the guy got flashed."

As we drew closer, I spotted the scorched earth and rock, warped in an amoebic pattern near the base of a large bank of transformers. Junction boxes, relays, incoming and outgoing high-voltage transmission lines, busbars—all clustered together in a chaotic mass of electrical tech. It looked like something a mad scientist might build in a secret lab. The low hum of residual current seemed to pulse from the boxes, a reminder of the lethal charge still running through the setup.

We stopped fifteen feet from the scene. Morrell turned around, his lips curling just enough for me to notice. What was he thinking?

"Okay. I can see the damage to the ground and unit. Mind filling in the blanks?"

"First of all, ya should know that we"—Morrell circled his fingers in the air—"ain't have nothin' ta do with it. All our people were accounted fer this morning. Even them that weren't on sight when the incident happened. S&C, that's safety an' compliance, determined that whoever the fella was that got flashed was in the wrong place at the wrong time."

"Flashed." I looked at the blacked ground and char-stained steel legs at the base of a platform labeled *Transformer Six*. "You've used that term twice now."

"Means burnt to hell," Ray said.

Morrell nodded. "Technically speakin', an arc flash happens under certain conditions," he explained, his tone emotionless and routine. "Ya got a high voltage difference between conductors, or sometimes 'tween a conductor an' ground, an' it leads to what we call ionizin' the air gap. Basically, that air turns into a conductor—kinda like a shortcut for the current to jump through. Now, if there's enough fault current in the system, and somethin' like a loose connection, a tool, or even a bit of conductive dust gets in the way, that's when ya get an arc."

He pointed toward the scorched earth by the transformer. "That's what y'all are lookin' at right there. Coulda been a fault in the equipment, coulda been someone makin' a mistake, possibly tamperin' with somethin'. But when all the pieces line up just right, that arc flash don't just happen—it blows up." Morrell gestured to Ray. "Like ya said, it's hotter hell."

"Tampering. You think someone was trying to sabotage the grid?"

Morrell laughed. "The *grid*. Agent Callahan, this is just a small part of a larger system."

"What I meant was..." I tried to continue, but Morrell waved a hand in front of me.

"I know what ya meant. There's more to it, an' far too much ta explain in one sittin'. What ya want ta know are two things. Who got flashed so bad he'd be canceled fer wearin' blackface, an' did they do anythin' that might affect the power station security."

I looked at Ray, speaking in a low tone. "Sharp said explosion. Somewhere in his briefing the information must have gotten crossed or embellished." I turned to Morrell. "So, if I'm hearing you correctly, this was just a case some local yokel trespassing for whatever reason, and had a stroke of bad luck?"

"If ya want ta put it that way. Ain't the first time we've had someone jump the fence. Usually, it's kids on a dare or drunks doin' the same. About a year ago we had a disgruntled employee hop the fence. Jimbo Duggars. He's livin' in Arkansas now. Took off when his probation lifted. That, an' every time he ran inta someone from the plant, he'd near got himself beat. Anyway, Jimbo got so bloodied by the razor wire, he passed out at the base of transformer seventeen. He had a bag like just like guy last night had, tools an' all, the works, but never laid a hand on the RTU where we found him."

"Hang on. What tools did you discover on the body? And what is an RTU?" I asked. For a moment, I was ready to dismiss everything Morrell had said and agree with Ray that this had been a wild goose chase ordered by a misinformed Special Agent in Charge, dumbass Sharp, but learning that the man who had been killed carried a bag of tools meant he was here for a purpose. This was not a dare. Maybe it was a similar situation to the last attempt at sabotage, but with Jimbo Duggars out of state and the rest of the employees safe and sound, there were no leads to support my theory.

You know there is something deeper. My gut twisted.

"RTU? Yeah, that's our Remote Terminal Unit. Fancy name for the lil' box that keeps tabs on everythin' in the yard," Morrell explained, tapping the side of his head like he had it all up there. "Basically, it watches all the equipment—voltage, current, temperatures, you name it—and sends all that info back to the folks in Houston. Let's 'em see what's goin' on here without ever leavin' their cushy control room."

He nodded toward the substation. "That RTU also lets 'em flip switches, open breakers, cut power—pretty much run the place from miles away. An' if somethin' ain't right, it'll trip an alarm, so they know they got a problem. Keeps 'em in the loop, saves us a trip out here every time somethin' blinks."

With a smirk, he added, "So yeah, that lil' RTU—she's

the eyes and hands of the folks who ain't out here gettin' their boots dirty."

"And the tools?"

"Sheriff Deputies took what was left with 'em when they left earlier. Weren't much ta speak of. Couple warped adjustable wrenches, a wad of melted plastic cased meters, pliers, wire cutters, pole dancers. Typical tools we carry on the job."

Ray chimed in. "Pole dancers?"

Morrell glanced at Ray, "Strippers. Wire strippers. Just a little nickname among us blue collar types."

"Anything else you can share with us?" I asked.

Morrell thought for a second, then added. "There was one other thing. The guy had some kind of bag slung around his neck. Looked like he was carryin' a laptop or somethin'. Everything was destroyed that it was hard ta tell what exactly it was once the body was moved an' the bag removed. The deputies took it when they left. Probably at the department right now. But I'll tell you, it looked like a sack full of melted tar. Took all day for my nose to clear out once everyone left. Can you imagine the smell? Melted plastics. Burnt flesh. Mix that in with the standard electrical stank we have around here, an' ya won't be welcomed home fer a week. Better off sleepin' in a skunks den."

I did not have to imagine. The hint of the scent lingered in the air, but also in polluted memories from abroad during the Gulf War. I squeezed my fingers together, feeling the ends of my nails dig into my palms. The smell was a trigger I was not about to let overpower me.

Out of the corner of my eye, I saw Ray glancing my way. A slight lift of his chin told me that he saw my reaction, and probably had the same visceral moment.

I took three steps forward, stopping when I heard a crackle overhead.

"Might wanna not git so close. Lines an' equipment are stable, but ya just never know. Arc Flashes aren't what ya might call, predictable."

Before turning around, I closed my eyes and took a deep breath. The air did not taste fresh, but I needed an extra jolt of oxygen to right the ship.

Walking back, I had more questions, but Morrell was not the person who would have the answers, except for maybe one.

"Do you know where they took the body? I assume the county morgue but would need an address to follow up."

"Nope. Morgue's down in La Marque. The local funeral home in Wharton was called out when the county said they wouldn't be able to make the run right away. Easy ta find, hard ta forget."

Ray huffed. "Does this place have a name?"

Morrell cocked his head and gave Ray a what-the-hell-do-you-think look.

"Of course, Detective."

He paused, goading him a bit.

Ray glared back, then turned to me, restraining himself for once.

"Boots 'n' Blessings. Off state road sixty," Morrell said. "Ya can't miss it."

I nodded at Morrell, then turned and walked with Ray, unaccompanied to the truck.

"Anything back there seem off to you?" I said, pulling out of the substation and back onto the gravel country road.

"Plenty, but you're looking for confirmation of something. Spit it out."

My fingers flexed around the steering wheel. My mind

raced, but that was not unusual, especially in recent events.

"Not yet. Let's pay a visit to the funeral home first. Maybe the body will provide the answers I am looking for."

A familiar feeling began burning deep inside of me.

Don't look now, but your gut wants back in the game.

CHAPTER TWENTY-TWO

THE FLYING H RANCH, WEST TEXAS

Clinging to the body, Raven waded backward through the current, her fingers disappearing beneath layers of soaked fur.

"Help me, Flint."

Standing at the river's edge, Flint watched as Raven rescued a medium-sized dog from a snag of reeds in the water.

"It's alive," she continued. "And it's bleeding."

"Just let it go, Raven. Ain't no animal worth the trouble in that condition."

Raven swiveled her neck around as she slid her feet through the muddy bottom of the Rio Grande toward the shore, shooting Flint a cutting glare. She bent over, cradling the injured dog using the water's surface as a buffer, but the river's relentless current pulled at her, trying to claim them both. She staggered, knees buckling as the water surged harder, until she fell, losing her grip on the animal.

"Flint!"

Grumbling under his breath, he held his rifle in one hand, then stepped into the cold, running water and hooked his fingers around its tail like the dog was a tangle of wet rope, and pulled. The dog did not put up a fight, nor did it even seem alive once Flint dragged it onto the shore.

Raven sloshed her way out of the river, dropping to her knees next to the dog on the soggy banks of the Rio Grande. She laid a hand on its side, pressing her palm against its matted, wet fur.

"She's alive."

"Raven." Flint's voice was void of emotion, more bent on irritation that she had made him retrieve a wet and dying, strange animal from the river than anything else. He shook his head and raised his rifle. "It may be alive, but let's be realistic. Only humane thing ta a do is put 'er down."

Raven looked up at him wide-eyed and mouth agape. Her face tightened into a hard frown when she saw the rifle in his hand.

"You put that away, Levi Flint. Maybe out here the law of the land guides your decisions but it doesn't govern mine."

Turning back to the dog, Raven's gaze lingered on its side, watching the faint rise and fall of its ribcage. Blood darkened its coat in slick trails. Its pink tongue lolled from its mouth. Its head lay still. With deepening concern, she peered into its one visible eye, watching it flutter and roll in a weary, half-conscious struggle to hold on. Raven stroked the dog's matted fur, her fingers sifting through the damp layers as if her touch alone could anchor it here, keep it breathing. She looked up at Flint, her gaze unyielding. Deep down, she hated that part of her agreed with him, but today had seen its share of brutality, and she had enough of it.

"I'm taking her back to the CR. If she dies on the way, we can bury her, but I won't leave her here or let you shoot her without giving her at least a chance."

"Raven..." Flint tried again, but her fierce, unyielding tone cut him off.

"Either help me or get the hell out of my way."

Flint turned and walked to his horse, shaking his head as he stowed his rifle in its saddle sheath before returning to Raven at the river's edge. Positioning herself with one knee sinking into the softened soil, the toe of her other foot digging into the sludge for added balance, Raven slid her arms beneath the dog and tried to lift it. Her muscles strained, but the size of the dog and the added water weight soaked into its fur made it difficult to move.

"All right," Flint said, taking a knee next to her. "Let me in."

Raven removed her arms from beneath the dog and sunk her backside onto her heel as a seat.

"Thank you."

Flint stretched his arms out and scooped the animal up as easily as if he were carrying a load of dirty clothes to the wash. He stood, pulling the dog into his chest, feeling the wetness on its fur soak into his shirt and sleeves, and at the same time, the surprising warmth of Raven's hand as it rested on the back of his neck.

Flint felt the weight of the animal, its body limp in his arms, and swallowed the grumbling words on his tongue. He glanced down at Raven, her gaze locked on the dog, her face a mixture of raw worry and determination. Against his nature, he kept his thoughts to himself and simply muttered, "If this nasty, wet thing is half as tough as you, maybe it'll pull through."

Raven's hand moved to scratch the dog's ear, but her eyes shifted upward, meeting Flint's. Her smile was small, beginning with a soft gaze on the furry face in his arms and landing on Flint's own, rougher one—his jaw set tight, eyes hidden behind a hardened squint.

A flash overhead turned the land and sky white beneath clouds that were now cresting the tops of the nearby cliffs. An immediate clap of thunder shook the banks, echoing along the long corridor of rock that ran the length of Mexico to the north and south for miles. The air smelled of rain, sharp and metallic, as the horses fidgeted under the darkening sky.

"We've overstayed our welcome, Raven. Git ta the horses, an' let's ride."

Flint led the way with Raven right beside him. She mounted up first, then positioned herself in the saddle so Flint could lay the dog across the leather in front of her. Tucker's ears pricked up as he turned his head to smell his new, additional passenger.

"Give us a smooth ride, will ya?" Raven whispered, rubbing the side of Tucker's neck.

Flint was in the saddle and leading the two of them toward the distant fence line beyond the small grove on the Flying H ranch as the first sprinkles of rain started to drizzle down on them. In rhythm, the horses rocked their riders, whose eyes were set on home, but under the cover of lengthening shadows and falling rain, two figures emerged from behind a riverside mesquite thicket at the foot of the Mexican cliffs.

One lifted a pair of binoculars, tracking the riders, while the other pressed a damp, bloodstained rag to his shoulder. They exchanged murmured words, then disappeared back into the brush.

CHAPTER TWENTY-THREE

BOOTS 'N' BLESSINGS FUNERAL HOME, WHARTON, TEXAS

"Well, isn't this quaint." Ray opened the door and stood on the footrail of my truck, looking around at the simple buildings within range of the Boots 'n' Blessings Funeral Home. "Looks like 1950 arrived and decided to stay a while."

I hopped out and walked around to the front grille. Its new chrome trim and metallic black paint was flaked with farm road dust and the dangling carcasses of mosquitoes, mayflies, and lovebugs. "You have a problem with small-town living?" I asked.

Ray eased himself down from the truck's lifted body and joined me at the front bumper. "Nope. Just feel like we've entered *The Twilight Zone*. Next thing you know, the mouthless man will be waiting for us at the door of this *creepatorium*, or we'll find ourselves on a slow train to Dachau after stepping inside. You've seen the show. One minute everything is fine and dandy. The next, you're in the fight of your life. Just glad we stopped to switch cars before driving out here."

"Anyone ever compliment you on your positive personality, Ray?"

The entrance to the funeral home swung open like a pair of batwing doors in an old-west saloon, causing us both to stiffen and look.

"I hate it when I'm right," Ray said.

A man wearing a cloth facemask and a tan Open Road Stetson over a pearl snap shirt, blue jeans, and boots stepped outside and hailed us with a wave. "Evening, gents."

"See." Ray leaned closer, muttering. "The fucking mouthless man."

"You must be Agent Callahan? I'm George Henderson. We spoke on the phone just a short time ago."

We shook hands, and I regarded his voice as less nasally than when it came through the speakers in my truck. I had not given him much warning about my heading to see him other than a call while on the way, but he seemed more than happy to accommodate our after-hours arrival.

"Yes, we did. This is Detective Ray Tucker," I said, gesturing to Ray.

George was quick to offer him a hand. "Pleased to meet you. To meet you both, really." Ray managed to smile, pocketing his hand as soon as they released from their shake. "Sure is strange what happened last night. Can't say we've come across anything like this before."

"Strange?" Ray said, giving me the side-eye.

"Whelp, what I mean is that we haven't ever had anyone expire quite like the John Doe you two are interested in. Follow me, and you can have a look. It's why you came all this way, am I right?"

We headed for the entrance.

"Thank you, Mr. Henderson," I said.

"Please. Call me George. Everyone around here does. You should too."

I could not hold back the smile that etched my face as a thought of Chance crossed my mind. It was exactly what he had said the first time we met. Sheriff Chance Gilbert, Brewster County's finest, invited most everyone he met to be on a first-name basis with him, just as George was offering now.

George held the front door open, and as we passed through, a rush of cold air hit me like an unexpected norther blowing across the CR at the beginning of fall. The chill sent goose bumps crawling along my skin. Ray felt it as well.

"Shriveling," he whispered.

A faint, tinny chime sounded when the door closed behind us. Looking around the foyer, my first thought was that this was the strangest receiving room I had ever seen in a funeral home. A gallery of western paintings hung along the walls, each with its own cowboy Christian theme. My eyes passed from one to the next until it dawned on me that each work portrayed a Bible story set somewhere out west. A pair of iron wall sconces cast as horse's heads hung on either side of a varnished barn-wood counter where a feathered pen and a closed signature book rested upon a thin burlap table covering. In large, flowing cursive and sculpted in metal filling the space between the sconces were the words *Boots 'n' Blessings Funeral Home*. A familiar tune from ages past drifted into my ears. "He Stopped Loving Her Today" by George Jones played through hidden speakers, adding a soft, old-fashioned tone to the room.

"Walk this way," George said, leading us through the rustic foyer.

Ray followed, hunching his back and dragging one foot behind him where George could not see.

"Detective Tucker," I said, breaking him out of his lurch through the building. "We have any further info on the ten thirty-three?"

Ray straightened up.

"Ten thirty-three, my ass."

"Just ahead, gents. We'll avoid the main hall. Suzette is finalizing things ahead of tomorrow's service."

"Oh, yeah?" Ray said. "Who died?"

Damn it, Ray!

"Local rancher. Well known around these parts." George stopped and turned to face us. "Can you believe he lived to see one hundred and four years?"

"That's unbelievable," I said. "And who is Suzette?"

George's eyes squinted and the mask on his face rose and fell over a hidden smile.

"Purtiest girl in the county, and my wife."

Pride swelled from George, or was it love? Whatever it was, it made me want to call and check in with Raven.

We continued ahead as he filled us in on the deceased man's local fame and how he and Suzette turned Boots 'n' Blessings Funeral Home into the eye-catching business it was today.

Passing through two sets of doors and descending one short stairwell into a sealed and even colder basement, we arrived at a set of metallic swinging doors. The deeper we dove into the belly of the building, the more it felt like the lead-up to an old horror movie. Incandescent bulbs flicked overhead, casting shivering shadows. Behind me, Ray hummed *The Twilight Zone* theme beneath his breath. "Do-do-do-do."

"If you fellas get too cold, I've got a couple jackets in the closet." George placed a hand on the metal door, then turned and glanced at Ray. "Probably even one big enough for you, Detective."

"I'll be fine," Ray said.

George nodded. "You know what they say—a warm soul fends off the coldest of times." I could see a sincerity in his aged, brown eyes as he spoke. In a line of work such as his, my guess was he lived every word he spoke, which meant he was the warmest of us all.

He held the door open so Ray and I could pass through. Three incandescent bulbs dangled from wires in a straight line down the center of the room. Along the far wall was a bank of refrigerated storage units standing three levels high with square, latching doors making the wall look like a grim grid of Hollywood Squares. Each door had a magnetic dry-erase plaque with the deceased occupants name written in fancy script and blank marker. On the left wall was a rack holding metal gurneys, folded in wait for their net passengers. A counter ran along the opposite wall supporting a small sink in its middle, a bevy of drawers beneath and tall cabinet doors above. Near the handle on one of the doors was a small circular, yellow happy face sticker with the caption, "Have a nice day."

"Here he is," George said, releasing the latch and pulling the handle on a mid-level hatch. "Mind stepping to one side while I pull him out?"

Ray and I stepped together as George opened the door. He reached in and slid a long, stainless-steel tray between us holding the body of our John Doe. A hint of burned flesh wafted from the unsealed compartment, reminiscent of charred brisket fresh out of a refrigerator. Hanging with that smell was a sweeter aroma that made my stomach grumble like it was hungry until logic overpowered my senses, identifying it as an early onset decomposition.

"Remind me again why we are here, Cass?" Ray whispered.

"Must warn you fellas, what's under this sheet is not a pretty sight."

George corralled us with a glance, his eyebrows tilted, his pupils swirling.

"Go ahead," I said.

Using both hands, George leaned forward and pulled back the sheet draped over the body.

"Jesus," Ray said. I could hear the gurgle in his throat as he spoke.

Laying before us were the charred remains of someone, purportedly a man, but the extent of the burns across the entirety of the body made it hard for me to tell for sure.

"Someone had a bad fucking day," Ray said.

"Detective." George's voice was firm, like a father chastising a child. "Please refrain from such obscenities. While grotesque in nature, this soul is at rest. I will not allow anyone to disparage the departed under this roof."

I sensed the message caught Ray off guard. He cleared his throat, shifting his glance to look anywhere but at our host. The room was already cold, but the momentary silence between us felt like the chill touched bone.

"Tell me, George," I said, breaking the ice. "Have you seen anyone in this condition before?"

He shook his head and placed a hand on the edge of the tray. He squeezed his fingers around the concave rim as if internalizing a layer of hidden emotion. He let out a breath that caused his face mask to puff out and fall with the pressure.

"Can't say that I have. Most of the time, bodies like this end up down in La Marque at the county morgue. Looks like there was no room at the inn, so he was brought here for the time being."

I nodded, listening. Wondering.

"The guys at the substation say he wasn't one of theirs," he continued. "A mite bit strange if you ask me."

"How do you know that, George?"

"Word gets around in a small community. Plus, every employee was accounted for. Even the ones who weren't on shift at the time."

I glanced at the blackened form lying on its waist high body tray.

"Can you tell me anything about the body? Possible background?"

George stroked his chin with his thumb, thinking.

"Best I can say is the fella isn't from around here. Probably some drunk so-and-so caught up in a dare. Maybe had—"

"That's all right, George. We can speculate all night. I just need to know who he is, where he came from. Facts beyond the town gossip."

"Understood," he said. "Your guess is as good as mine."

I leaned over the body, taking in the injuries that engulfed him. His skin looked like leather, blackened in most places from head to foot. All the hair on his head and face had burned away. His ears and the end of his nose were a charred mess that looked more like melted marshmallows dripping on the end of a campfire stick. Teeth shone through where his lips should have been.

I swallowed, shifting my gaze to his legs, my eyes needing a break from the scorched image of his ruined face. While dark red and raw, the lower portion of his body below the thighs was less impressive, though one glance at his midsection, charred and hairless, caused my testicles to ascend into my lower gut.

Damn.

George and Ray stood by as I continued my examination of the body. The burns to the victim's arms, like his legs, grew more significant moving from hands to shoulder. I took a quick glance at both sides, then centered myself on the chest, my gaze freezing on a detail on the upper left quadrant of his torso.

"George," I said, my eyes fixed on the body. "May I borrow a pair of gloves?"

"Top drawer behind you. Help yourself."

I pulled two latex gloves from a box in the drawer and slid my hands into them.

"What is it, Cass?" Ray asked when I turned around.

My mind raced as I leaned back over the body. Placing my index finger on the victim's left breast, I swirled the surface of his skin like I was buffing a blemish from scratch on my new truck's paint.

"Cass?"

I leaned closer.

Is that what I think it is?

I reached into my pocket and removed a small knife. With a flick of my thumb, the short blade on my Microtech Troodon-M deployed.

"Whoa there," George said, raising his hands in protest. "What do you think you're doing?"

I focused on the area of skin I had rubbed. "Just need to scrape away a thin layer of char is all."

"Agent Callahan." George's fatherly tone returned. "I cannot allow you to desecrate the body."

I glanced at him through the tops of my eyes as I bent over the body.

"George." I kept my tone friendly. "I assure you, my regard for the victim is honorable."

I looked down at the victim's blackened, leathery skin and scrapped the blade across the burned surface in slow, surgical motions.

Come on. Show me something.

On the fourth pass, the top layer of charred skin

peeled away, revealing what looked like a moist, sticky undercoating as if I had punctured the smooth surface of an aloe vera leaf.

"Son of a bitch," I said, my words low yet revealing.

I swiped three more times, cleaning a one-inch area of subdermal skin.

There you are.

Satisfied, I straightened up, wiped and retracted my knife blade before slipping it back into my pocket and noticed differing glances from Ray and George. Ray looked puzzled. George seemed mortified, edging on curious. I could tell he was uncomfortable by my actions, but at the same time wondered what was so important about my findings. I chose to ignore them both and reached for my cell phone.

The room remained quiet. The cold air did not feel as frigid anymore. The fire in my gut took care of that. If what I had discovered proved true, my investigation was far from over.

I pressed the camera icon and centered my phone over the scraped skin. Each silent click grabbed another angle from the deceased man's chest, each press of my finger registering a wave of concern and determination. I captured more images than I would need before locking and putting away my phone. Peeling off the latex gloves, my hands felt powdery. I wiped my palms on my pants and addressed the elephant in the room.

"George, I need you to hold on to this body. Whatever it takes. Do not release it to the county morgue."

"Please forgive me, Agent Callahan, but do you mind telling me what this is all about?"

Spotting a trash can near the door, I walked over and placed my spent gloves in the hamper. "I appreciate your cooperation, George, and I hope that I can continue to count on it. Right now, I am not in a position to share information about the case with you. I hope you understand."

George's facemask twitched. His eyes closed, then opened to glance at Ray and then the body.

"I suppose you're all finished here?"

"I am."

George covered the body with the sheet, then slid its tray back into the dark, refrigerated cell, and secured the door. Ray remained uncharacteristically quiet as we were led out of the basement to the receiving hall and out the front door.

"Not sure I completely understand," George said, rubbing the back of his neck. "But I supposed it's not my place." He removed his mask and for the first time I saw his smile. "Isaiah 55:8-9— 'For my thoughts are not your thoughts, neither are your ways my ways,' declares the Lord."

Sincerity beamed from his face, reassuring me that our visit would not remain objectionable in his view. I offered my hand.

"Thank you, George. I'll be in touch."

We shook. Ray offered a hand as well, shaking and nodding without a word further.

George watched us walk to the truck and load up. With a final wave, he turned and disappeared through the swinging batwing doors.

Ray let out a long, exasperated breath. "Now that we're alone, you mind telling me what the hell was so important that you had to play Dr. Quincy back there?"

The engine roared and the headlights blasted the purple haze of twilight falling around us as I turned the key.

"There was a marking on the corpse's chest."

"Yeah. So."

"It was the same coloration with ink lines similar to the tattoos on our Chinese."

"Good ole dead Dong. You think he's linked to the stiff inside?"

"Possibly. Li from the ranch and the dead guy from the camp out, too."

I pulled out of the Boots 'n' Blessings parking lot and mashed the accelerator. "If he is, and there is a connection between them, we may have a Texas-sized problem on our hands. That little incident at the power substation may be only the beginning."

CHAPTER TWENTY-FOUR

29.7057° N, -95.5495° W

The door to apartment 4C opened with a creak causing the two occupants to glance from their seats at the kitchen table, then return to their bowls of rice and fish without concern. Thudding closed again, a man wearing blue jeans and a black turtleneck emerged in the kitchen entryway. He took a moment to inhale the tantalizing aroma before addressing the room.

"*Dragon Fire* and *Veiled Falcon* were a success, as noted by the images on the television just now. Are we set for phase three?"

"Sit, *Miào Wén-Kē*." The man said. "Eat. We are waiting on Sūn Tiān."

The woman glanced again, meeting Miào Wén-Kē's gaze as he entered the kitchen.

Miào Wén-Kē took a seat next to the woman and served himself a helping of food, pondering aloud his thoughts on their missing comrade. "He is irresponsible..." He took a bite, filling his mouth with rice and bits of fish, but continued speaking. "...and too young. I told you that before we left Xi'an, and again in Shànghǎi. Sūn Tiān was unprepared for this mission. Now we have to wait?"

Beneath the table, Miào Wén-Kē felt fingers grip his knee, then slowly move up his thigh in short, gentle circles. He stopped talking and looked at the woman next to him. "You have a different perspective, *Líng Líng*?" Her hand stopped, her fingers squeezing the meat of his leg. She gave a curt smile but did not answer. Looking to the other man at the table, Miào Wén-Kē tilted his head, expecting an answer. "What about you, *Zhàn Huǒ*?"

Sitting back in his chair and pulling his pack of Pandas from his shirt pocket, Zhàn Huǒ tapped the pack until a fresh stick popped away from the others. He leaned forward and pulled the cigarette from the pack with his lips, then repeated the process before offering one to Miào Wén-Kē.

"Do not grow impatient with Sūn Tiān. It is in our youth that we will look when you and I are too old and gray. He will arrive shortly, and I am confident that he will bring good news."

Miào Wén-Kē waved off the cigarette and instead, picked up his bowl and scooped another helping of rice and fish into his mouth.

Zhàn Huǒ's chair squealed as it scooted across the linoleum floor as he stood up. He looked at his two comrades, then lit his Panda and took a long, slow drag. The end of the cigarette pulsed a deep orange then receded to a slight burn once Zhàn Huǒ pulled it from his lips. Smoke filtered out of his nose. He smiled, enjoying the pleasure in his mouth and lungs while silently lamenting on subtle clues that transpired between Líng Líng and Miào Wén-Kē since his arrival. Masking his thoughts on the matter, he turned and walked out of the kitchen.

Alone in the kitchen, Líng Líng removed her hand from its precarious hold and reached across the table for a jar of pickled mustard greens when Miào Wén-Kē grabbed her by the arm.

"*Nǐ gàn shénme ne?*"

Líng Líng flashed him a glare, her eyes narrowing like a tiger on the prowl.

"In English. You know what is expected."

Still grasping her arm, Miào Wén-Kē began pulling her closer.

"What are you doing?"

Her lips parted, and she inhaled a quick burst of air as if caught by surprise. Upon exhaling, she aimed her breath at his face and blew a steady stream across his skin. Miào Wén-Kē took in her scent, her breath lingering within his own, and mirrored her look with narrowed eyes.

Dishes clanked and food spilled on the floor when Líng Líng yanked her arm away before sliding her chair back and jumping onto his lap. Her legs squeezed his hips like a constrictor paralyzing its prey. Her nails, like claws, dug into his back as she pressed her lips to his.

Sitting in the living room, not fifteen feet from the kitchen, Zhàn Huǒ grabbed the television remote and unmuted the feed. Sitting back, he focused on the screen and the determined voice of the Channel 2 news reporter delivering an update on the blaze in Southeast Houston while trying to ignore the disruptive noise spilling out of the kitchen.

"*...Firefighters are still trying to gain control of the blaze while investigators work to learn the cause of this disaster. Forty-five thousand homes and businesses are currently without power in the area, but that number may still grow as more reports come in. A spokesperson with Enterprise Products Partners will address the media within the hour as fears of a much larger explosion loom within the oil, gas, and power* *transfer facility. A shelter-in-place order has been announced for residents in the immediate area."*

CHAPTER TWENTY-FIVE

Rain soaked their clothes and flashes of lightning marked their path as Raven and Flint trudged through the downpour across the CR. The dog's body rocked back and forth as it dangled across the saddle. With one hand holding the reins, Raven rested the other on the dog's soggy ribcage, keeping time and counting the breaths between each rise and fall of its labored hold on life. In her mind, each clomp of hoof brought them closer to a saving grace, but only time would tell, and there was not much to spare.

Come on, pup. Hang in there.

The soil was saturated, making the ground softer than usual. Rain was not uncommon for the area, but with spring just settling in, a storm like the one pounding the CR made the terrain difficult to navigate. On a clear night, Flint and Raven could easily spot the warm glow emanating from the barn and house, but under the cloud-choked sky and relentless curtain of rain, it had grown too dark and disorienting to see home. Even so, the horses knew the way. With slow, purposeful steps, the horses moved forward, their instincts guiding them through the storm.

Raven shivered as drops of water ran down her back. It had been a scorcher of a day, but high above, the rain had thrashed about at lofty altitudes, becoming small bits of hail before growing too heavy in the clouds and falling to the earth. Their quick descent from colder air into acrid humidity beneath caused them to melt into frigid drops on the way down.

"How much farther?" Raven yelled to Flint, her voice drowned out by the rain.

Flint could not see much through the downpour, but he did not need to. Years spent traversing these paths had taught him every rise and dip of the land. The subtle slope beneath the horses' hooves, the way the terrain shifted, the direction the wind and rain whipped at their backs— these were his markers.

"Only a bit," he called back, trusting his instincts. "We can pick up the pace, but yer friend may not like the added jolts in the saddle."

She stroked the dog's side and for a brief moment felt its muscles strain beneath her palm as if it was attempting to shift positions. Raven leaned forward and whispered.

"Now, now. You stay settled until we get to the barn."

Please, make it to the barn.

The dog's chest rose and fell as if in distress, causing Raven to lose her breath, but the sudden shudder did not last more than a few seconds. She moved her hand to brush away the water from the dog's face, then called out to Flint again.

"I'll risk it. Let's get home as quick as we can."

"Raven…"

"I'm sure, Flint. Just go, and I'll do my best to keep up."

Flashes of lightning cracked the sky, casting bursts of white across the land like an ancient projector bulb sputtering in a darkened theater. The low moan of thunder followed, though sounded more distant than its previous roars.

As the whitewash faded, Raven saw Flint look back and nod. With a swift nudge of his heels, he urged his horse into a trot. Raven gripped the reins tighter. Water ran over her knuckles, the raw rub of saturated leather grating against her skin. She squeezed her legs and supported the dog's body with her free hand, pressing it closer to her thighs, then clicked her cheek.

"Move it, Tucker. We gotta keep up."

Raven felt an immediate jolt followed by a rhythmic bounce as her horse fell into a steady trot. The rain stung her face at first, but as they settled into a steady stride, she noticed the drops thinning, their sharpness fading.

It's letting up.

Pulling next to Flint, Raven caught his attention.

"Thank you, Levi." She never called him by his first name, but she knew that doing so would reflect genuine gratitude.

"Don't thank me yet, Raven."

Flint pointed ahead, gesturing to the fuzzy glow from the light post near the back of the barn as it faded into view.

"Besides. I should be thanking you."

The rain thinned to a sharp drizzle.

"Curly had me dead to rights if ya hadn't jumped in when ya did."

The thrum of rain lessened. The rumble of thunder remained but was not as intense as before.

"Well, I kinda put you in a bad position."

Flint chuckled. "Maybe. If ya don't mind me sayin' so, somethin' I've learned these past few months about ya is that even when ya act without thinkin', it's usually the right move." Flint paused to lift his head and let the pooling water on his hat drain across his back. "Curly woulda drawn on me either way. You shootin' like ya did, saved me."

"I got lucky."

"Nope," Flint said, shaking his head. "Ya've gotten good. Maybe we should start callin' ya Calamity Raven."

"What? Why?"

"'Cause," Flint glanced her way, and smiled. "Yer as tough as Calamity Jane, an' crazy ta boot. Plus, she never turned away from a fight, and that was sayin' something back then."

"Calamity Raven." She let the compliment soak in, then burst out laughing.

"What's so funny?" Flint said, his head tilting with curiosity.

"Calamity Raven. CR? That's a little too much. Cass would laugh me off the ranch."

Flint smirked. "I s'pose. But maybe we should run it by him. He may take to it."

Cass...you need to be here. You need to be home.

Raven let out a chilly breath, her body bouncing in rhythm to the horse, then found herself feeling the icy pang of dread as the dog began wheezing violently as if its shallow breathing had grown intolerant of its condition.

"Crap!" Raven tugged the reins, bringing Tucker to a sudden stop. "What do I do?"

Flint reined his horse around and pulled close to her.

"Give'er ta me."

"What? I thought..."

"Just do it, Raven. It ain't got much time."

Raven loosened her grip on the dog as Flint leaned over and scooped it out from in front of her. With one motion, he spurred his horse, and took off at a gallop toward the barn.

Raven looked on, stunned by Flint's quick actions, and watched as he charged on ahead of her.

Feeling her stomach knot and the stomp of hooves beneath her, Raven snapped out of her daze.

"Go, Tucker. Go!"

She whipped the reins and kicked her heels harder than intended. Tucker tossed his mane, then sprang forward with a burst of speed. All Raven could do was hold on. Hold on to the reins, hold on to hope.

Fearful tears mixed with the misting rain, her world blurring into a moist fog as they ran to catch up with Flint.

Don't die. Don't die. Please...don't die.

CHAPTER TWENTY-SIX

HWY 59 N, FORT BEND COUNTY, TEXAS

Lights from the city pulsed over the northern horizon, their ambiance flooding the night sky with a gray luminesce that snuffed out the black, speckled ocean of stars above Houston. For as many years as I could remember, I never paid much attention to things that were not right in front of me, but having spent the better part of a year in West Texas, there was no way of avoiding the hypnotic pull of the constellations cast within a certified black sky. Some nights Raven and I would turn off all the lights in the house and barn, plunging the CR into a cloak of darkness, and walk beyond the corral to sit between the house and not-so-far-off Mexico to gaze upon the heavens. The solitude of the western frontier and the hushed interminglings of nocturnal animal chatter lent the night a mix of mystery and paradise the likes of which we never could experience in the city.

I listened to the truck's tires humming as we cruised back to the city on Highway 59 and a thought popped into my mind. It started as a peaceful wonderment that transformed into a nightmarish scenario better suited for an episode of J.J. Abrams, *Revolution*.

"Shit."

Ray had been playing Candy Crush or Royal Match, one of those brain-draining mobile phone games, and had been locked into his digital addiction when he heard my muttering.

"Shit, what?" he said, eyes still glued to his tiny screen.

I tapped the steering wheel with my thumb and contemplated my response. What I wanted to say would sound crazy, but the more I pondered the thought, the more I found validity in its absurdity.

"That news report from earlier. The one about the explosion in Clear Lake."

"What about it?" Ray tapped his phone, then grunted as he lost another round of his game.

"Remind me...what was its location? A refinery? Look it up, will ya?"

Ray's finger danced along the touch screen, the light from which flashed across his face with each swipe.

"Here it is."

"Read it to me," I said, my interest growing exponentially.

Driving past Richmond, the highway split into multiple lanes, the blacktop thoroughfare marked by intermittent high-mast lighting. As soon as we sped past one, we approached another. The patterned bursts and momentary fades into darkness felt like I was driving through a firefight where tracer rounds lit up the sky overhead. It felt like synapsis firing behind closed eyelids. I squeezed the wheel tighter.

"Come on, Ray!"

From the corner of my eye, I saw him look up from his phone, then slowly twist his neck and head to glare at me.

"Keep your panties on, Cass. I'm reading it already."

The CR, black sky, Houston lights, power station, mysterious corpse, illegal Chinese, dead detainees…what was I thinking? Looking ahead, the white lane lines seemed to blur together. I glanced down at the truck's instrument cluster and read the speedometer.

Eighty-seven.

I let my foot off the gas as Ray began to read the headlines and noticed headlights gaining on me from behind. I shifted my gaze from the rearview to the side mirror.

"Says there was an explosion at the Enterprise Products Partners this afternoon. Eyewitnesses say a drone from a local high school demonstration event malfunctioned and crashed into the facility causing the disaster. Officials speculate the drone hit a solenoid valve—a highly sensitive piece in the pressurized labyrinth of metal and gas—which sparked the explosion."

"Enterprise Products Partners?" I repeated, watching the headlights behind us draw nearer.

"It's some kind of electrical, gas transmission hub. Bunch of word salad in that report but seems like a pretty big deal. It's still burning and thousands in the southeast Houston area are currently in the dark."

In the dark.

"I gotta make a call," I said.

My mind raced, piecing together half-baked ideas into worst-case scenarios.

What was our mystery corpse doing at the power station? The Newgulf Substation Supervisor, Clyde Morrell, said that Center Point ran a full system assessment resulting in zero irregularities. How deep did they search? Was I overreacting?

"Not calling our buddy back at the FBI shack in El Paso, I hope."

"Nope. Scoots Faraday."

"The computer nerd?"

"Try whiz kid."

I had met Scoots years earlier by coincidence at a local coffee bar. He was just shy of twenty years old, and busy rattling computer keys in the booth adjacent to mine, which made no difference to me except as he worked, he talked to himself. What he thought was a hushed whisper, or maybe a voice inside of his head, resonated in my eardrums the moment I heard him say, "I am a hacker god!" Needless to say, I turned around and caught his attention one keystroke before he pissed ten to fifteen years of his young life away for illegally accessing his ex-girlfriend's bank account. When I called him out, he took me for a true-to-life spook and has been in my back pocket ever since.

All in all, he is a good kid. Loves fast cars, thrives on his own eccentricities, and thinks faster than any human I know. Before cashing in his lone get-out-of-jail-free card, we sat and talked for over an hour. I would argue that Scoots's intelligence should not only be weighed by his jaw-dropping results from the Wechsler Adult Intelligence Scale (WAIS), the Torrance Tests of Creative Thinking (TTCT), or by a perfect SAT score, but that he needed only two things with which to think, create, and destroy—1's and 0's. His ability to see the world through binary thinking made him one of the most gifted kids I had ever met. Give the kid a computer and an access point, and he can hand you any bit of information your heart desired.

"I need him to dive deeper into the SCADA system at the power station. See what he can dig up, if anything."

"So, you wanna give access like that to a hacker? You're playing with fire, Cass."

"Doubtful. Give him a box of Hot Pockets and a couple Mexican Cokes, and he'll be good to go."

I activated my blinker, signaling my intent to exit as the car behind me closed the gap. Ray leaned forward, picking up the reflection of headlights as they fell in line.

"You have insurance on this beast?" he asked.

"Yeah."

On cue, the car behind us chirped its horn and bright flashes cut the night, illuminating the cab of the truck with swirls of blue. Ray slapped his armrest, his eyes reflecting the pulsing strobe.

I pursed my lips and cursed under my breath as I eased the truck off the highway and onto the shoulder preceding the exit ramp.

"We don't have time for this shit."

CHAPTER TWENTY-SEVEN

THE CR, WEST TEXAS

Rain pelted the wood slats and pinged against the metal roof, its intensity rising once again as Raven and Flint examined the injured dog inside the barn. The animal's drenched fur stuck to the workbench surface, their makeshift examination table. Fresh blood mixed with the pooling patches of wetness, creating a reddish ooze. Raven held her cell phone to her ear with one hand and pressed a shop towel over the dog's wounded thigh with the other. Its wheezing had subsided, but its breathing became shallower than before. Each breath left Raven wondering if it was the dog's last. The line rang and rang, causing Raven's anxiety to rise to new heights.

"No one's answering, Flint? Is there another vet we can call?"

"Out here? Nah. Colt Rawlins is the only animal doc fer miles around. If he ain't answering, he's probably holed up avoidin' the storm, or elbow-deep in another issue."

Raven looked at the helpless animal dying before her eyes.

"What are we going to do?"

Flint stepped next to Raven and looked down at the dog. He knew what he would do, but that suggestion had already been shot down. He knew of one option left, but it was risky and could cause more harm than good.

"Flint?" Raven's voice wavered. Her vulnerability was at its peak, which was uncharted territory for Flint. The Raven he had come to know was gritty, determined, and one verifiable bad ass. This version of his friend was not something he had expected to see.

Shooting a person was okay, but not dogs?

"Run to my truck and bring me the black box under the back seat."

"Your truck? What do you..."

"Go." Flint whirled around. "Or do you want this dog to die?"

Air rushed from Raven's mouth in a high-pitched huff —a wounded response to Flint's bluntness. Flint turned away, leaning over the dog as he rolled up his soaked sleeves. His gut twisted; he knew Raven did not deserve his harsh tone, yet the urgency pressing on him felt undeniable.

Without looking back, Flint spoke again. This time his voice was soft and low. "I will do everything I can to help the dog, but I need that black box."

Flint heard Raven's quickened footsteps as she hustled to the garage at the rear of the barn. Laying a hand on the dog's neck, he ran his palm over its side, his hand collecting every loose hair on the way. He wiped the mess of fur on his wet jeans then used his fingers to peel back the dog's eyelids and inspected its pupils.

"Yer one lucky dog," he whispered. "Yer gonna owe Raven near 'bout everythin' if'n ya pull through."

In less than a minute, Raven returned holding the black box. She coughed as she caught her breath and tried to speak.

"What's in there?"

Flint flipped the plastic latch securing the box and opened it.

"Hope," he said, removing an X-Acto knife.

Raven's eyes bulged.

"What are you..." she stammered. "Do you know what you're doing?"

Flint stepped aside and reached below the workbench, pulling out a first aid kit and set it next to the dog's head. Without answering, he opened the kit, removed a small plastic bottle of isopropyl alcohol, and doused the blade. Satisfied with its cleanliness, he removed two square swatches of gauze from the kit and folded the blade inside of them before setting it down.

"Gonna need ya ta hold 'er down. Take the shop towel an' use it as a swaddlin' blanket. I ain't got anything fer the pain."

"Flint?"

"Raven, the dog's been shot. If the bullet stays in, she'll bleed out. If I can find it an' remove it, maybe..." Flint paused. He did not want to offer false promises but what else was there to say? "...maybe it'll help. She's lost a ton of blood already."

Raven's hands trembled, but she took the towel and draped it over the top half of the dog, leaving only its snout uncovered enough to breathe. It did not resist. Its exhaustion and injury had teamed up against itself, but Raven held on to hope.

Leaning forward, she whispered, "Fight through this. Everything is going to be okay."

Flint glanced at Raven. Her hair was a mess, wet and tangled. Her clothes were dirty and as soaked as he was.

Goose bumps riddled the back of her neck, a combination of the chills of cold rainwater on her skin and trepidation in her veins was his best guess.

Laying his left hand on the dog, he found the entry wound on its thigh. The skin around the opening was raw. Blood seeped in dark rivulets. He picked up the blade, unwrapping it from the gauze, then folded both squares together and soaked them with the antiseptic, creating a spongy alcohol wipe. He cleaned the area around the wound with deliberate, gentle movements. Setting the wipe aside, he looked back at Raven.

"You ready?"

Her voice trembled as she nodded. "Ready."

Flint pinched the knife between his fingers.

"Here we go."

He lowered the blade to the wound, his focus narrowing to the task at hand.

The rain outside hammered harder, a pounding rhythm that drowned out everything else. Raven looked on, lifting silent prayers as she held the towel in place. Feeling the faint rise and fall of the dog's shallow breaths, she whispered, "Hold on...just a little longer."

CHAPTER TWENTY-EIGHT

HWY 59 NORTH, SUGARLAND, TEXAS

Badges were flashed, explanations given, and in the end, I was issued a warning along with a reminder that if I had official business that made it necessary to exceed the speed limit, I should coordinate with Sugar Land P.D. or the Fort Bend County Sheriff's Office before disregarding traffic regulations in a civilian vehicle.

"Freaking Johnny on the spot, if you ask me," Ray said as the ticketing officer walked back to his patrol car.

"It's fine," I said, reaching for my cell phone.

Scrolling through my list of contacts, I found one marked Wunderkind and tapped the *text* icon. My fingers flew through the message:

8:58 P.M.

Callahan: Scoots. Meet me at House of Pies on Westheimer. Need your expertise. Sev1.

I set the phone in its cradle on the dash and smirked.

"I see that look on your face, Cass."

"Oh, yeah? Which one?"

"The one that says, 'I may have to start some trouble to find what I'm looking for.'"

I shifted the truck into drive, checked my mirrors, and pulled off the shoulder, bypassing the exit ramp.

"You know me too well, old friend."

Ray sat back in his seat and resumed playing games on his phone, muttering, "Who the hell are you calling old?"

CHAPTER TWENTY-NINE

Thunder shook the barn as Flint wiped his bloody fingers on the shop towel and looked down at his furry patient. He had performed many procedures over the years, most of which his role was assistant to the vet, but this was the first time he had done more than what he considered necessary to save a dog's life. A dog. A strange, wandering mutt from the wilds of West Texas. What was Raven thinking?

A glance at his side and a brush of her arm against his body was the only answer he would ever need. Raven was the queen of empathy. Emotion encircled her like the warm embrace of a feather blanket. She carried a look in her eyes that spoke of wonder, excitement, and genuine awe that could only originate in a heart of gold.

"Bullet's out. May have a broken hip 'er leg. You'll want ta take him to town in the mornin', but Raven..."

She turned and wrapped her arms around Flint and squeezed. With her face buried in his chest, she replied before he could finish what he was saying.

"I know. She still might not make it, but we had to try." Raven leaned back, her hair dangling in wet, crusty strands. "You didn't have to, but you did anyway."

Flexing to her tiptoes, Raven kissed Flint on the cheek, then let go. Flint's body turned rigid. A shooting warmth raced from his face to his feet. For a brief second, he held his breath and stared straight ahead.

"Thank you, Levi."

Reviving from his daze, Flint turned to the dog.

"Let's git 'er off the table an' somewhere more comfortable."

"Can you carry her to the house?"

The steady drum of rain on the metal roof and a well-timed clap of thunder decided the next step of their plan for them.

"May be better off if I prepare one of the stalls. Pile a hay'll do just as good as a couple towels on the floor."

Raven stepped to the side door and propped it open with her boot. Rain blew in through the cracks as she looked across the yard, now a mud-puddle minefield all the way to the house. Closing the door, she called out to Flint.

"I'm staying out here with her." Across the barn, Raven saw a smirk grow across Flint's face. "What?"

"It's how I figured."

"Meaning?"

Flint walked to the first stall at the beginning of the row and talked through the slats.

"Raven, as long as I've known ya, which ain't really been that long, you've always been the kind of person that sees things through from beginnin' ta end, no matter the circumstances. The second ya run inta the river ta save that dog, I knew exactly what we were in fer." Flint moved to a haymow tucked between the stalls and tossed an armful of fresh hay over the rails. Grabbing a rake hanging on a nearby wall hook, he returned to the stall.

Raven walked over and folded her hands across the top rail and watched Flint form the pile of hay into what looked like a soft, fluffy bed on the ground. "You think I'm crazy? Out of touch with reality, maybe?"

"Already said ya were crazy, but yer more in touch with how things are than most. Ya've become a mix of city an' country." Flint stood straight, balancing his hands on the rounded end of the rake's shaft, and drew her gaze to his. "Yer kickin' ass an' takin' names but still have the wherewithal ta do more fer others than fer yerself at times."

Raven smiled and bowed her head.

"Com'on. That pup of yers may stir itself right off the workbench if'n it comes around while we're camped over here jawin' at one 'nother. Let's git 'er squared away." Flint's eyes gave Raven a once over. "I'll watch over it while ya run ta the house an' collect whatever ya think you'll need for the next few hours."

With a delicate touch, Flint lifted the dog from the workbench and carried it to the stall. Raven followed, watching the dog's face. Its tongue lolled from its mouth, swaying with each of Flint's hefty strides. Easing to one knee, Flint laid the dog on the bed of hay, then rotated his body and sat in the dirt, back propped against the wooden stall slats.

"Go on, now," he said.

Thunder rumbled directly overhead, reminding Raven that her jog to the house would be like the Muddy Dash she and Cass ran last spring, the summer before their entire world was flipped upside down.

"K...I'll be right back."

Raven disappeared through the door, entering the stormy fray, while Flint sat listening to the pattering of raindrops echoing through the barn. He leaned his head back and shut his eyes, finding solace in the moment when all things went dark and the sounds of God and nature consumed him. Three deep breaths were all it took before he drifted off, dozing next to the wounded dog, one hand resting across his lap, the other plopped in the hay, his thumb stroking the underside of its ear.

CHAPTER THIRTY

HOUSE OF PIES, HOUSTON, TEXAS

The smell of warm pies fresh from the oven was an olfactory gift, the aromas stirring memories and activating hypothalamic sensations that had me yearning for Grandma's home-baked goodness. The scent overtook me the moment we walked through the door. It must have lured Ray as well, its pull leading him over to a display case that shelved an assortment of crusted delights.

A sign on the host stand read, '*SEAT YOURSELF (but only if you're hungry)*.' I scanned the restaurant for an empty booth and found Scoots sitting against the far wall, his laptop out, his eyes flicking back and forth across the screen. Only two other tables had seated customers and one of them seemed to be squaring up the check.

"Ray," I called out over my shoulder.

"You go on, Cass. I'm gonna stay awhile and inhale some more heaven."

A middle-aged waitress approached Ray from behind the counter. Her hair was pulled on top of her head in a

1960s-style beehive, and she wore enough makeup to outfit a small theatrical company. Yet, what her overdone cosmetics did for her appearance was balanced by a sweet southern drawl and a sparkle in her eye that softened her bold look, making her seem both endearing and effortlessly charming. The beehive and makeup might have seemed excessive to some, but her warm southern drawl and the lively twinkle in her eye turned her into a character you could not help but like. She reminded me of a modern-day Flo from *Alice*, the sitcom that ran during the late '70s and early '80s.

"See somethin' ya like, sugar?" the waitress said with a smile.

Ray straightened and rubbed his hand over his mouth. "I, uh…"

"Aw…cat got yer tongue? Happens at least five times a day." The curve of her lips was as provocative as the deliciousness filling the pie trays. "Ain't no rush. My name's Belle. You go on and find a seat. I can always bring ya somethin' at yer table, hon."

Belle gave a wink, then twirled around and disappeared through a pair of double-hinged, swinging doors. I caught him staring.

"Detective," I said, my voice sarcastically firm. "You're one step from a restraining order. Come on. He's here."

Like a kid being dragged from a candy store, Ray shuffled his feet behind me, grumbling beneath his breath. We weaved our way past the tables, drawing a smile and a nod from an older woman sitting two booths away from Scoots. Her white hair and blue-gray eyes gave her an air of sophistication, each well-earned wrinkle a roadmap of a life well lived. I returned the friendly gesture, wiping it from my face once I stopped next to Scoots.

"Using community Wi-Fi to fix a few traffic tickets?"

Without looking up, Scoots replied as if he had been in

the car with us earlier. "No, but I got you covered if you've had a run-in with the locals."

Ray leaned in with a grin. "The kid's a smart-ass. I like him."

I slid across the seat in front of Scoots. Ray took the aisle, stretching his longer legs into the walkway.

It had been a while since I had seen the kid face to face, but it seemed little had changed since we last met. His styled hair suggested this was a detour on an otherwise on-the-town kind of night. He wore a long-sleeved, paisley designer shirt with a single gold cross chain around his neck. A small diamond stud pierced his left ear, and I noticed a flashy thumb ring on his left hand as he closed his laptop.

"This is Detective Ray Tucker," I said, introducing Ray. "Looks like you're doing okay for yourself, Scoots."

"Yeah. I try. I'm working for a tech company that just relocated from San Fran to H-town. Cyberdine Solutions. Ever hear of it?"

I shook my head, but there was a familiarity about the name. "Noted. I'll keep an eye out for terminators while I'm at it."

Scoots grinned. "Well, the building's crawling with Golden Staters, but they're pretty chill. Meeting a couple of them for drinks later tonight."

"That's great Scoots. It sounds like you're on the up and up."

Scoots paused, allowing time for Ray to be Ray.

"Up and up? You can't talk to the natives like that, Cass. The kid doesn't know it's a compliment. You gotta use words like *legit* or *grinding*." Ray snapped his finger. "*Glow-up*, that's even better. Tell him, 'Big things, Scoots! You're totally glowing up.'"

"Oh, my god." Scoots flashed two open palms at Ray. "You need to stop right now before you break a hip."

Ray cocked his head, his mockery defeated.

"Y'all decide on what ya want?"

Belle's quiet approach caught us all off guard, causing us to jerk our heads toward her like a parliament of surprised owls. She placed a hand on Ray's shoulder.

"What about it, darlin'. See anything that ya like?"

Scoots and I shared a glance, enjoying the flush in Ray's cheeks and his ability to speak evaporating at Belle's intentional double entendre.

With reluctance, and wanting to see how long Ray remained muted, I swooped in for the save.

"Please bring us some coffee and three slices of your freshest pie."

Belle shifted her look to me, smiling.

"Coming up, hon. Three coffees and some fresh pie."

She nudged Ray with her hip before returning to the kitchen.

"Lady killer," Scoots said. "Way to go, player."

"Cut it, kid. Show's over."

It was well within Ray's bag of tricks to act the role of flirt or flirtee, but circumstances being what they were with Ruth Ann, that part of him had become understandably extinct.

"Sure. Sorry, man."

Leaning forward, my folded hands on the table signaled a shift in our conversation. Scoots noticed right away.

"So, what's the need for such a *sub rosa conference?*" he asked, his voice taking on a more serious, game-time tone.

I pursed my lips, considering my words before spilling my plan all over the table.

"I need you to use some of your special skills to help me look for something."

Scoots looked at me, then Ray, then me again, his face becoming more curious by the second.

"My *special* skills, huh."

"Look, Scoots. I need you to get into ERCOT and dig around. See if you can find anything abnormal."

"Whoa, Cass. That's some serious play. Systems like that don't just step aside and let anyone in for a peek."

Ray chimed in, folding his hands to mimic mine.

"I thought you said he was a whiz kid genius or something, Cass. Sounds more like a pussy if you ask me."

Scoots sat back, pinching his lips into a wry twist. He eyed Ray, then shot forward and opened his laptop. A clatter of keys popping sounded like the snap of Black Cat firecrackers exploding beneath his fingers. Tap after lightning tap, Scoots's fingers blazed a trail to somewhere...*but where*? After a few moments, his keystrokes slowed until he left his finger hovering over the keyboard, a deliberate motion for his amusement and our amazement.

"Flashy," Ray said. "Remind me to have you take dictation when I decide to write my walking papers."

"But Ray...Officer Ray Tucker, isn't that correct?"

Scoots rotated the computer so we could see the screen.

"What I mean to say is, the moment I push this key, your rank, pension, years served, everything you've worked for over the past however many years, goes away and its back to beat work or directing traffic."

"Pretty funny," Ray said, his tone and expressions not buying it one bit.

"Oh, one more thing. Got your social security number right here," Scoots said, pointing to a small pop-up window on the screen. "Also, you bank at Regions but have a secret account stash at a local Prosperity branch, something you wouldn't want anyone to discover, even though, based on your transactions, everything lines up as *legit*."

Ray's eyes bulged. What blood had rushed to his face

when our waitress Belle teased him, now ran for the hills like wolves being chased from the flock.

"You little shit."

Ray started to stand up. I threw an arm out to restrain him. Scoots never flinched.

"Look, Detective. We don't know one another but look at what I can do with such limited information."

"Fix it, now!"

Ray fumed but held his volume low enough so as not to concern the few customers or staff in the restaurant that he was about to lose his shit.

Scoots shifted his attention to me.

"Come on, Scoots. Show and tell is over. I need you for the big game."

Twisting the computer around, and with another few, less anxious taps of the keys, Scoots flashed a sardonic look at Ray, then turned the screen so he could see that nothing in his work profile or bank accounts had been altered.

"Done. You are still a detective, though there was not a keystroke that nullifies douchebag."

Ray settled into his seat. A small rumble vibrated in his throat. It grew exponentially until he burst out laughing. He leaned back, laying his arm along the back of our booth bench, and shook his head.

"You're my kind of smart-ass."

Ray's tension breaker came with perfect timing. Belle arrived with a tray holding three mugs of piping hot coffee and three dessert plates with steaming apple pie. The heat licked at scoops of ice cream perched on top, coaxing them into rich, dripping trails that hugged the contours of the flaky crusts.

When the coffee and pie were served and Belle retreated to the front counter, replaying her coquettish role with two new customers who had just walked in, I finished what I'd started to say to Scoots.

"You're right about ERCOT, but I believe two things: One, you're the only one I know who can get in and out undetected, and two, if there are any anomalies in the system, you're the only one I trust not to exploit them ex post facto. We won't be running to the paper, or Channel 2, and I don't need a whistleblower getting in the way of what I think may be a dark storm brewing over Texas."

I hated asking him to cross this line, but I did not see another option. If anyone could find a threat in the system, it was Scoots.

Filling his mouth with pie, he mumbled between chews, "What do I get out of this?"

"There it is," Ray said.

"Look, Scoots. I know it's a big ask. You'll be doing me a huge favor. Think of it this way, when we first met, I had you by the balls. You do this for me, I'll owe you one."

Scoots took another bite of pie. He nodded, looking around the restaurant as if having an internal debate about how he should reply. He forked what was left of the ice cream and popped the whole glob of sloppy, frozen vanilla into his mouth and swallowed. Opening his mouth, he stopped short of answering, pressed his hands to his eyes, and groaned. "Brain freeze!"

Ray and I waited for our young genius to come around. Scoots slugged the rest of his coffee, and after pounding his seat a few times, survived the pain and returned his attention to us.

"Fine. I'll do it, but I need three promises."

"Spit 'em out, Scoots," I said.

"I need your assurance that if by or some technological miracle I do get caught in the system that you will have my back and keep me out of handcuffs."

"I wouldn't be asking you to do this if I wasn't prepared to protect you."

"Good. Two. I want complete access to ERCOT's data sets. I'll be responsible, but I want the freedom to innovate security measures that can be used to prevent future hackers from breaking the system."

"Hackers like you?" Ray quipped.

"There's no one like me. I'm an elitist. Should I find anything, there will be a trail to follow with a wealth of information I can use to revolutionize their security. Think of it this way, Ray. You walk into the forest and leave breadcrumbs behind and you'll never find your way out because all the little animals will have eaten them up. Leave pebbles instead, and even the dumbest hack on the planet won't get lost. Here's the thing, even the savviest black hat bandits think their work is untraceable, but they're wrong. There's always something to find, even if that means killing the forest animals and ripping it out from them."

"Gross," Ray said. "So, what? You're Scoots the Ripper?"

"No. I'm the guy that knows how to do it all without leaving breadcrumbs, pebbles, or even a hint of code behind. I'm the ghost in the machine, detective."

I stirred my coffee. "Can't authorize you to poke around in places you shouldn't..."

Scoots opened his mouth to speak, but I beat him to the punch.

"...all I can say is that I won't be looking over your shoulder while you work."

"Fine. Don't tell Dad. Got it. The last thing, and this is really a small request..." Scoots stopped midsentence, his eyes dancing back and forth between me and Ray like he was trying to decide who might be better suited for the task he was about to say.

"What is it, kid," Ray said.

"I need a wingman."

Ray huffed. A puzzled feeling overtook me. "A wingman?"

"Yeah. Tonight. Those Golden Staters, the ones I told you about, well, I kinda..."

Ray interrupted.

"Girls?"

Scoots nodded.

"Both of them?"

"Yeah."

"I see," he continued. "You wanna slip your USB into one of their ports, but you don't know if the connection will fit so you need an expert like one of us to come along to size up the ticket?"

"Funny, Ray. It's just...I'm better with computers than people, okay?"

Scoots looked away. His last request was not a deal breaker, but I could tell the kid needed a little moral support, though I could ill afford the time.

"How about this," I said, drawing his attention. "You find something out of place, something you think poses a danger or threat, and I'll see to it that you have a more suitable wingman than a couple guys old enough to be your father."

Scoots nodded.

Ray's cell phone buzzed, signaling an incoming call. He ignored the phone and took a bite of pie. It buzzed again. Scoots folded his hands and began twiddling his thumbs. When the phone buzzed a third time, the kid looked like he was unraveling, caught in some kind of *Zeigarnik Effect* spiral, the unanswered call clawing at his nerves. Before a fourth tone sent him off the deep end, Scoots pounded the table and blurted out.

"Come on, Detective. Aren't you going to see who it is?"

With minimal effort and a tortuous grin forming across his pie-encrusted lips, Ray reached for his phone and finally answered the call. With the receiver pressed to his ear, he listened as the caller spoke. He nodded. Glanced at me, then without saying a single word, ended the call, put the phone on the table, and resumed eating his cream-soaked pie.

It was more than Scoots could stand. Was it any of his business who was on the other end? No, but that did not matter to him. A person like Scoots, whose life was predicated on beginnings and endings, logic and resolutions, 1's and 0's, it was as though an inner drive to know had seized control, overpowering him like a glitch in his programming.

His mouth hung open, his eyes bulging as though they might pop out of his skull.

"Well?"

Ray chewed what was in his mouth, took a sip of lukewarm coffee to wash it down, then crossed both arms on the table and leaned forward. He ground his teeth. The subtle *clicks* in Ray's jaw sent fresh jolts of discomfort through Scoots, but he was drawn in anxiously awaiting the buffer wheel to finish downloading.

"Dead Dong is airborne," Ray said flatly, his delivery so straight-faced it felt like he had just announced a missile launch. Scoots's cocked his head, his eyebrows arching with puzzlement.

"Dead...dong?" he said.

"Cass," Ray said, scooching out of the booth. "We better get moving."

Though I knew there was no rush to go, I played along at Scoots's expense. He was as gullible as he was smart, but Ray was right, we had more to do and it was already growing late. Before sliding out of my seat, I snapped my fingers in front of Scoots.

"I need you working on this ASAP. There is a lot at stake, Scoots. I know I can count on you."

I left a twenty-dollar bill on the table to cover the check and followed Ray out of the restaurant.

Still muttering from the booth, Scoots's voice trailed behind us, the warm scent of pies clinging to the air as we left.

"What the heck is a dead dong?"

CHAPTER THIRTY-ONE

THE CR, WEST TEXAS

Raven stomped her boots on the porch, leaving muddy footprints as evidence of her dash through the puddled yard in the rain. Her tromping about also stirred interest from inside the house. The patter of tiny feet running within drew closer to the door until the slow squeak of the hinges creaked and the rush of clean air burst out through the crack. Peeking out with eyes wide and curious, then squinting above an innocent smile, Miguel welcomed her home.

"Mami Raven," he called. "You are all wet?"

Raven used her heels to remove her boots, her sock already drenched causing the skin on her feet to wrinkle.

"That's what happens when you're a cowboy. A little rain doesn't get in the way of a hard day's work."

Miguel giggled. "You're not a cowboy?"

Raven knelt and opened her arms, inviting Miguel for a hug. "Oh? What am I then?"

Miguel opened the door fully, his expression a blend of childish wonder and sincerity.

"You're a cow-*girl*," he said, scooching out the door and into her soggy embrace.

The two shared a tender moment, a comfort Raven had not felt in years since Spencer, her only son, was so small. The life of a child is innocent and fragile, and Miguel's had been the epitome of instability and uncertainty. It was luck that brought the two of them together, and chance that allowed Miguel to stay, though every day Raven wondered about their future.

She squeezed him tighter, drawing a playful squeal before releasing him. Charlotte Huckabee, appeared in the doorway, her long hair and slender, younger curves silhouetted by interior lighting. She was the niece of their southern ranch neighbor, Floyd Huckabee of the Flying H, and was Miguel's babysitter while Raven and Cass were away at work. She was also the object of interest by Spencer, though his time away at college prevented any chance of a long-standing relationship from heating up.

"Hi, Charlotte."

"Mrs. Callahan. You're soaked. Let me grab you a towel."

Charlotte turned and disappeared into the house, returning quickly with a bath towel. "Here," she said, handing it over. "Sure is ugly out. Can't remember it raining like this in forever."

"Yeah," Raven said, wiping her face as she stepped indoors. "I feel like I've soaked up half the sky myself."

Miguel squatted on the porch behind Raven drawing pictures with his finger in the clumps of mud stuck to the decking.

"Charlotte, I have a huge favor to ask." Raven stepped closer, her voice dropping to a near whisper. "Can you stick around tonight? There's...something in the barn I need to watch over."

Charlotte tilted her head, her curiosity clearly piqued.

"Something?" she echoed, the single word heavy with questions she did not ask.

Raven gave a small, tight nod but did not elaborate.

On the porch, Miguel had paused his muddy finger drawings. He looked up at Raven, his head cocked slightly as though he were piecing together a puzzle. Then, with all the subtlety of a curious four-year-old, he stood and tugged at her jeans.

"What's in the barn, Mami Raven?" His tone was quiet but insistent, his dark eyes wide and searching hers for answers.

Keyed into Raven's unspoken discretion, Charlotte reached down and picked up Miguel, resting him on her hip.

"How about you come with me and make some mac and cheese?"

"But..." It took a moment, but his curiosity shifted from what was in the barn to what he could be in charge of in the kitchen. "Can I pour the milk?"

"Sure," Charlotte said.

"And stir?"

"Of course."

"And lick the spoon?"

Raven laid a palm on Miguel's head. Her heart growing full just by being in his presence.

"You are a demanding little thing, aren't you?"

Filling his face with a toothy grin, Miguel nodded enthusiastically, then wriggled out of Charlotte's arms. He skipped to the kitchen, his voice rising in a jubilant chant like a stadium crowd cheering on their star player. "Mac and cheese, mac and cheese."

"Sounds like a yes?" Raven said, her voice tinged with hope.

Charlotte smiled faintly, though it did not quite reach her eyes. "Yeah," she said. "Not much for me except a room and a bed back at the ranch anyway. Uncle Floyd's been nice letting me stay, but it's just so..." Her words trailed off, the weight of her unfinished sentence hanging in the air.

Raven reached out, her voice soft but firm. "Say no more, Charlotte. We love having you here. If you can stay, it would mean a lot. I promise it's just for tonight."

Charlotte hesitated for a moment, then stepped forward and pulled Raven into a hug. It felt less like a gesture of gratitude and more like a silent acknowledgment that, for now, they both needed each other—each doing the other a favor in their own way.

"Thank you," Raven said.

The two parted. Charlotte hurried into the kitchen acting like a sneaky monster as she rounded the corner, fingers spread like claws and walking on tiptoes. A gentle roar and a boyish shriek echoed through the house as Raven entered the bathroom and stepped out of her wet clothes.

By the time the water was boiling in the kitchen, Raven had dried off and changed into fresh jeans, one of Cass's Astros t-shirts, and her favorite flannel. He was not home to object, so she took and wore whatever clothes of his that she wanted. The baggier top would feel more comfortable overnighting in the barn. She grabbed a pillow and a throw blanket from a closet and set them by the front door. Entering the kitchen, a warm beating in her chest accompanied an awe-inspired sigh for before her, Miguel stood on a step stool stirring a pot of noodles with Charlotte's careful guidance, his little face lit up with pride.

"Look Mami Raven. *¡Esta noche yo soy el cocinerito!*"

Raven walked over, pretending to inspect his cooking.

"*Sí*, and what a good little cook you are."

She kissed the top of his head and shared an

endearing glance with Charlotte as she stepped away from the stove.

"You know," Charlotte said softly, her voice careful. "He is such a good boy. He is very lucky you took him in. I can't imagine, not that I want to, what it was like...you know."

Raven did know. Miguel had been deserted during an overnight illegal crossing. Coyotes, likely cartel associates, had led a small group of migrants across the Rio Grande toward what at the time had been the Double SS ranch. She and Flint had been riding on the opposite side of the CR at the time, when they heard gunfire. By the time they rode over to investigate, they came upon a gruesome scene where the Coyotes were shooting the migrants as they tried to flee. It was not until the next day that they found him—a helpless, injured little boy, frightened and alone sitting at the base of a tree overlooking the river.

Raven and Flint brought him home, and Brewster County Sheriff Chance Gilbert, a close family friend, arranged for her and Cass to watch over him. The legalese had been beyond her comprehension, but she had been determined to keep the boy they now called Miguel safe.

"Listen, I'll be in the barn if either of you need anything. Let's just hope this storm passes before we all float away."

"Sure thing, Mrs. Callahan."

Miguel parroted her, giggling as he struggled to pronounce all the syllables. "Sure thing, Mrs. Callahan."

"Stinker," Raven said, ruffling his hair. "You be good for Charlotte."

As she walked out of the kitchen, Raven considered herself the lucky one. She felt that at last the CR was becoming a home, not just a new place to live. She grabbed her pillow and blanket, stuffed them in a bag from the closet, and donned a raincoat and rubber boots for the trek back through the muddy slosh to the barn.

The clinking of pans and the soft, playful tune of Charlotte and Miguel singing one of the *VeggieTales'* silly songs about pirates comforted her. She glanced around the cozy house, a faint smile tugging at her lips as a thought slipped out aloud.

"All this place needs now is a little furry friend."

She peered through the door, the rain blanketing the CR in rippled sheets of darkened gray. The lights between the house and the barn flickered in the downpour, casting shifting shadows. Across in the other direction, Flint's tiny house remained black, but the front window of the Six M barracks glowed yellow. She could only imagine what Gilly and the others were up to—gambling and drinking, no doubt.

The wind bit at her cheeks as she stepped off the porch and into the steady rain. Her boots squelched through the thick sludge, the storm quickly swallowing the warmth of the house behind her. The barn loomed ahead, and her thoughts shifted to what waited inside.

She quickened her stride, pulling her raincoat tighter against the biting wind. It would be a long night, but there was no other choice. She had to hold on to hope.

CHAPTER THIRTY-TWO

HOUSTON, TEXAS

"What a fuckin' day," Ray said, kicking off his shoes and slumping back into the well-worn cushions on his living room couch. A crisp crack followed by the soft, soothing hiss of his beer can filled the silence between us. The sound was almost refreshing, a stark contrast to the whirlwind of today's events I was replaying in my mind.

"Haven't had to keep up this pace in God knows how long," he continued, tilting his head back with a sigh. "You're wearing me out."

My thoughts churned relentlessly, a grid locked mess of what-if scenarios ranging from improbable to outright absurd. But beneath the chaos, a gnawing sense of unease lingered. Something was brewing. Something big. Yet all I had were extravagant tattoos linking a small group of Chinese nationals scattered across Texas from opposite ends of the state. No paper trail. No plausible connections. And no doubt in my mind—they were up to no good.

"Grab yourself a beer and take a load off, Cass."

"What? No. I'm fine."

Ray turned his head and belched, then leaned forward, placing his elbows atop his knees.

"Bullshit. I can see it in your eyes. You're running on overload. Now, go grab a beer. That's an order, private."

I shot Ray a sideways glance. "Private? That was a long time ago."

"But not so long that you have forgotten what happens when you don't follow orders."

The muscles in my legs and back ached as I forced myself to stand, protesting every movement after finally finding some semblance of comfort and release.

"And grab me another as long as you're up."

I could hear Ray snicker from the kitchen. Yellow light spilled into the dim room as I opened the refrigerator door, its faint hum reverberating from deep within like a subtle growl. Aside from the beer and a Styrofoam takeout container, the shelves were bare. A few ketchup packets and a lone ranch dressing cup huddled together in the dairy slot reminded me of my days in college scraping by on a shoestring budget.

I pulled two cans of *Shiner* from the top shelf and closed the door, plunging the kitchen back into a dank solitude for dimness, pausing for a moment before returning to the living room.

"Damn it, Ray."

My lips formed the words, their meaning usually reserved for moments when Ray's crassness burned too bright, too inappropriate. But this time was different. They echoed in my mind like a gong crashing to the cobblestone floor of an ancient temple—a warning, sharp and unmistakable, that life was veering dangerously off course. Living here while Ruth Ann fought for her life was clearly taking its toll, no matter how hard Ray worked to keep up his tough-guy act.

Cold sweat from the cans dribbled over my fingers. There was nothing I could do or say tonight that would change a thing, but when was the right time to tell a friend they were failing at some aspect of their life? No, what I wanted to say, what I needed to say could not wait. I inhaled a breath of fresh air through my nose and mustered up an opening line to confront Ray about his overall welfare, and reentered the living room.

"Ray..."

I stopped short, letting both arms and handfuls of wet beer cans drop at my side. Ray's head tilted back on the couch, his eyes closed and his mouth open and taking deep, chugging breaths. I stood looking at my friend, watching him drift deeper into an overdue slumber, or maybe it was an escape that his subconscious knew he sorely needed. Except for the slow rise and fall of his chest and the occasional snore, the room felt still, like even time had paused to give him this moment. The empty chair next to him seemed to beckon, pulling at me with an almost magnetic weight. Easing myself into its folds, I adjusted the reclining mechanism until it let me kick back at just the right angle, my legs stretching out across from my friend. For the first time in what felt like days, I let all things be. I cracked open one of the beers, savoring the momentary *whoosh* from opening the can, then looking to see if it had disturbed the sleeping giant, and took a swig.

The cold, effervescent swirl of Texas-crafted goodness tantalized my lips and slowly glided deeper within, causing both a chill and a heat to radiate throughout my tired limbs. Its familiar taste dug up memories, winding its way through thoughts and time until I found myself imagining sitting on the front porch of the CR house looking out across the wide open plains of West Texas with Raven.

My eyes, heavy from the day and lost in seclusion, popped open with a start.

Raven.

I pulled my phone from my pocket, tapped the favorites tab, and found her number, *Little Bird*, at the top of the list. Without a second thought, I hit call.

CHAPTER THIRTY-THREE

29.7057° N, -95.5495° W

Orange-tipped cigarettes glowed like fireflies in the shadows of the Hong City apartment parking lot. The crackle of pop-tuned engines and aftermarket exhausts marked a pack of street racers flexing, their blips and barks polluting the late hours along the east end of Chinatown. The air hung heavy and thick, causing Miào Wén-Kē and Zhàn Huǒ to sweat as they stood across from one another. Smoke hung in the air around their heads, encircling the white van next to them like a ghostly shroud draped over a casket. Miào Wén-Kē glanced at his watch.

"We have a problem, Zhàn Huǒ."

Still incensed by his comrade's illicit behavior earlier, Zhàn Huǒ grimaced, speaking to the rows of foreign cars more than to Miào Wén-Kē.

"It is late. I know we have not yet heard from Sūn Tiān. Give him time."

"Time? We have little as it is, but that is not the problem."

Miào Wén-Kē pulled a key fob from his pocket, pressed the button, and unlocked the van. The headlights flashed, causing Zhàn Huǒ to straighten, his eyes firing, his voice low and grumbling.

"What are you doing?"

"Showing you this," Miào Wén-Kē said, sliding the door open. He reached in and pulled back the flap of a tarp covering a bulge in the van, revealing the head of an old woman, her vacant eyes and pale face frozen in a rictus of terror. "Sūn Tiān's absence is a problem, but what should we do about her?"

"*Kào!*" Zhàn Huǒ cursed, tossing his half-finished cigarette to the ground. "This is unacceptable. Cover her up, immediately!"

As if the body were nothing more than an inconvenience, Miào Wén-Kē pulled the tarp tight, once again hiding the corpse beneath its folds.

"Go now! Get rid of it." Zhàn Huǒ stormed away from the van but stopped short, spinning on his heel. Running his fingers through his hair, he retraced his steps with the coiled energy of a man ready to fight. "You have put the entire mission at risk. What were you thinking, killing an old woman?"

Miào Wén-Kē stood motionless, calm and unremorseful, though his irritation with Zhàn Huǒ grew steadily, swelling like a wasp sting. "She was becoming a threat, so I neutralized the problem." He took a drag of his cigarette, his serpentine eyes squinted as if ready to strike back at his superior.

"You should not have brought that here. Find somewhere to dump it," Zhàn Huǒ snapped, stepping nose to nose with Miào Wén-Kē. "If you do get caught, you know what must be done."

Miào Wén-Kē exhaled smoke through his nose, its sharp, acrid stench bit at Zhàn Huǒ's senses. He removed his cigarette and dropped it at his feet, crushing the glowing embers while glaring at his superior.

Maybe I come back and take care of you as well, he thought.

Without another word, Miào Wén-Kē stepped inside the cargo area and slid the van door shut. Zhàn Huǒ backed away, the side mirror narrowly missing him as the van roared to life and jolted into reverse. Like the street racers staining the asphalt, the van's tires screeched, leaving angry black marks across the cement in front of apartment 4C.

Zhàn Huǒ watched the van disappear out of the complex, the growl of its V8 engine and the high-pitched squeal of tires lingering in the night. A low, guttural sound escaped his throat, the kind of noise that fills silence when words have not fully formed yet. He turned and cupped his hands behind his back as he strolled toward the apartment, talking to himself with measured finality.

"Sūn Tiān has no excuse for his absence, which means he is probably dead. But you, comrade, yours is one of irrevocable dissonance. I will not allow further disrespect with so much at stake. We will see, but you may be the first of us to join him."

CHAPTER THIRTY-FOUR

HOUSTON, TEXAS

The glow and buzz of incoming text messages were lost to the fold of the recliner, the phone slipping into the seams of the leather chair and nestling on a foamy ledge just out of sight.

> 3:17 A.M.
>
> ScootsF: Cass. Entry confirmed. Their firewall is outdated—Cisco ASA 5500, open ports on 22 and 443. No IDS alarms, but I'm chaining proxies to stay clean. Pulling SCADA traffic from the historian now.

A faint vibration jolted the phone, but it remained unseen, tucked away in the recliner's depths.

> 3:43 A.M.
>
> ScootsF: Control logs look clean so far, but the Newgulf facility south of Houston isn't reporting to PUCT. No compliance data, no logs. It's a ghost. Digging deeper.

Another buzz rattled the phone against the chair's leather. Cass, sprawled in the recliner, remained oblivious, one hand draped over his face, the other clutching an unopened beer.

4:24 A.M.

ScootsF: Bombed with the girls, btw. >:/
Too many White Claws for my liking.

The phone's light flickered once more before being swallowed by the shadows.

4:39 A.M.

ScootsF: Found something weird. Looks like dormant code masking as Modbus/TCP traffic. The headers are fine, but the payload's malformed—too clean to be an accident.

The text went unanswered, its importance buried beneath exhaustion and the late hour.

5:07 A.M.

ScootsF: Damn, Cass. CALL ME ASAP. That code is a trigger that acts as digital dynamite. Looks like it creates a virtual backdoor through the SCADA system. If this thing activates, it could bypass everything, putting the entire substation at risk or worse—it could sweep the system and take down the entire grid!

The urgency of Scoots's final message seemed to fill the room, its weight heavy enough to wake even the deepest sleeper. But the phone lay silent in the folds of the recliner, unnoticed and unread.

CHAPTER THIRTY-FIVE

A warm sunrise over the CR ushered in clear skies and gentle breezes, a golden spark drying the soggy terrain left behind by the storm. Raven had spent a long night watching over the dog, her ears still ringing at times from thunderclaps that rattled the barn. An unexpected late call from Cass had helped take her mind off the storm, though his voice left an impression that lingered long after the line went silent.

It felt good to hear him, but something in his tone tugged at her. Was he in trouble? Causing trouble? Both? When he and Ray got together, the two of them were unstoppable. Unpredictable, but unstoppable. He had not given her much, just a few words, the sound of his voice. But it was not just what he had said. It was what he did not say. She could feel it, like a steady pulse just beneath the surface. Insistent. Unshakable. Something was wrong, even if he did not share it.

She shook the thought away, deciding to reach back out to him later, and turned her attention to the dog. It was alive. Its breathing had improved overnight and the bleeding on its hind leg had stopped. She laid a gentle hand across its head, scratching its ears and rubbing down its neck to the bumps of its ribs. Its skin felt warm. Before removing her hand, she embraced the rhythm of the dog's heart, pounding in strong, patterned beats. A gurgled moan trembled in the dog's throat, rippling through its body and up Raven's arm. Its eyelid fluttered, then parted revealing a deep brown eye, the color within like the swirl of dark roast coffee mixing with cream.

Raven noticed. "Shhhhh. You're safe, but you still need to rest."

As if understanding, the dog closed its eye and let a long, weary sigh escape like the air slowly receding from a balloon.

Rising to her knees and then to her feet, Raven winced at a dull ache in the small of her back, a stubborn reminder of a restless night spent propped against the stall slats. Stretching slowly, she laced her fingers together and cracked her knuckles, the sharp sound echoed by a satisfying pop as she arched her back. She rubbed her eyes and leaned against the stall railings, letting the sounds of early morning barn life—the scuttle of mice in the rafters, the soft chitter of an owl fresh from a night of hunting echoing from the deep shadows, the shuffle of hooves as the horses down the row stirred, knowing it would not be long before their riders arrived—and the lingering scent of last night's rain, faint yet sweet, like a waft of fresh morning dew, settle over her.

Blood flowing and lungs full, Raven's attention drifted to the soft glow slipping through imperfections in the wooden walls where streams of golden light pierced the shadows like shooting stars streaking across the horizon at dusk. As she gazed at the light, a piercing flood of brightness filled the main room of the barn from the workbench to the stall where she stood as the tall barn door slid open. Chattering voices filled the once peaceful space, but their familiarity brought a smile to Raven's face.

"Well, lookie here," Gilly said with a grin. "Cass ain't even home, an' still here ya are, sleepin' in the barn anyways?"

She walked over, dressed for a day on the ranch. Her leather boots, scuffed from years of wear, struck the perfect balance between comfort and practicality, their soles already caked with mud from her trek to the barn. Gilly wore a blue-and-white paisley shirt, its intricate pattern almost perfectly matching the streak of dyed blue hair peeking out from beneath the brim of her hat. Her belt buckle gleamed like a beacon, oversized and bold—at least to Raven, though all the hands from the Six M ranch seemed to favor buckles like that.

"What'd ya go an' do that for?"

"Take a look," Raven said, opening the stall door and stepping aside.

"That's a dog," Gilly said, tipping her hat back and cocking her head.

Raven laughed. "What were you expecting?"

"Dunno." Gilly squatted close to the dog and placed a hand near its wound. "Looks like a Sheperd. Where'd ya find it?"

"Flint helped me pull it from the river yesterday, just before the storm."

"Flint? And he didn't tell ya ta shoot it?"

Raven's lips flattened. "Actually, he did say that, but I couldn't. Yesterday was hell enough. You hear what went down on the Flying H?"

"Yeah. That's some crazy shit. Heard ya had a hand in stoppin' Curly before he killed anyone."

Anyone that we know of, Raven thought, but said, "Yeah. I couldn't believe what I was seeing."

"An' we heard a rumor that yer the one who shot Curly. Blew the gun right outta his hand?"

Raven bit her bottom lip and turned to look at the dog. She had no interest in reprising the events from yesterday, but her silence seemed to be answer enough.

"Damn, Raven," Gilly said. "How'd—"

Raven cut her off, steering the conversation back to the rescue. "Anyway, long story short, we tried to save the dog. Flint removed a bullet in her leg and helped me patch her up when we couldn't reach the vet last night. I've gotta bring her in this morning. Still hopeful she makes it."

Gilly nodded, catching the hint.

"Well, I'll be hopeful fer ya, too." Gilly stood, brushing her hands on her jeans. "She's got good colorin', considerin' how dirty she is."

"Gilly." Cody's voice echoed through the barn. "C'mon."

The two girls flashed a look in his direction.

"I guess ya ain't headin' out with us," Gilly said, stepping out of the stall.

"No. I may catch up after I get this furball settled, but we'll see."

Gilly gave a nod and clicked her cheek, then hurried over to join Cody and the rest of the Six M crew. Raven stayed behind, watching from the confines of the stall. She wondered how much longer the Six M hands would be staying at the ranch. It had been weeks since they arrived with their cattle following the destructive fires that scorched so many acres in the Texas Panhandle. Cass and Flint were quick to agree that we could offer the CR as a refuge for the cattle, but the Six M ranch was beginning to recover. With spring closing in, Raven guessed it would not be long before she was the lone hand working with Flint on the CR again.

Flint strolled into the barn as Cody and the others huddled near the workbench, hashing out their plan for the day. Instead of joining the pow-wow, his gaze shifted to the stall where Raven stood. A wry grin tugged at his lips, growing with each step as he closed the distance between them.

"Guessin' yer patient made it through?"

Raven looked down and away, glancing at the dog before answering.

"Yes, she did."

Flint bypassed stopping to chat at the rail and walked into the stall.

"Why don't ya run in the house an' get cleaned up. Then we'll take yer critter inta town ta see the doc."

"Do you think he's..."

"Already spoke with him. He's expecting us in any time this mornin'."

"Us?" Raven said, her eyebrow drawn in a curiosity.

Flint huffed. "Like I'm gonna let ya drive my truck?"

Smirking, Raven leaned over and stroked the dog's fur. "Hear that? Flint's looking out for you."

"I'll hang here until yer ready. Go on," Flint said. "Afore I change my mind."

Raven stood. "Thanks, Flint."

As she walked out of the barn, she gave a wave to Gilly and the rest of the Six M crew. She knew they would miss having another hand on the job, but Raven was essentially the boss, though she never once played that card when working with them. She strived to be one of the bunch, regardless of her family position on the ranch. A quick glance at her phone showed it was almost six thirty, a late start for work on the CR. Still, knowing the Six M crew, they would make up for it on the back end.

Her legs still felt stiff as she crossed the yard. Stopping on the porch, she slipped out of her boots before stepping into the house. She eased the door open, cringing at the squeaking hinges, and hoping she did not wake anyone up. The house smelled clean, a combination of the rain cleansing the exterior and what looked like someone had been straightening up inside. The hall leading past Miguel's room to her bedroom where a hot shower and fresh clothes awaited her caused a sigh of relief to escape her. She made her way across the living room, stopping abruptly and whirling around at the sound of clanking metal coming from the kitchen. She paused to listen, then tiptoed across the house to see what was causing the noise. Her hot date with a hot shower would have to wait.

Stopping at the kitchen entryway, she saw Charlotte standing with her back to her while at the counter stirring something in a mixing bowl. Raven smiled, somewhat relieved, but realized her lack of sleep and overprotective nature may have gotten the best of her this morning. She stepped onto the linoleum floor, trying not to startle Charlotte, but a misplaced toe and a biting chair leg had other ideas.

Raven's foot stubbed the chair with her little toe, causing her to lunge back and kick out at the same time while trying to swallow a high-pitched screech. The chair toppled across the kitchen to the window. Charlotte spun around and screamed as batter flew from the mixing bowl like a wave crashing into shallow waters. Raven hopped on one foot while bending over to grab her injured toe.

When the two finally caught each other's gaze, the screaming stopped and the uncontrollable laughing began. The kitchen was an instant mess. Batter was every-where—glopping on the tabletop, running down Char-lotte's apron, clinging to strands of her hair. The chair had knocked over an aloe vera plant near the window ledge scattering potting soil across the floor. Raven's toe throbbed but did not appear to be broken. Lost in delirium, the girls gravitated toward one another, falling together in a laughing heap on the floor.

"Care for a pancake?" Charlotte said, her voice bumbling. "They're fresh."

Raven reached out and scooped a glob of batter from Charlotte's hair and let it drip between them.

"Don't mind if I do."

Tears streamed down their cheeks before they finally regained control, but that was short-lived. As they stood, they both noticed the small audience member looking at them as if they had just lost their minds. Miguel stood in the entryway, his Elmo pajamas wrinkled and clinging to his body, the legs of which scrunched halfway to his knees. His hair looked like Gene Simmons after a KISS concert. A runway of dried mucus crusted his upper lip. Looking at the girls, he put his hands on his hips, cocked his head, and looked on with childlike concern.

"What is happening? All the noise woke me up?"

The girls shared a glance, then burst into laughter again, as if they had just failed to pull off a TikTok prank. Seeming to have had enough, Miguel turned around and walked out of the kitchen.

As the laughter settled down, Raven pulled Charlotte in for a hug.

"I'm so glad you're here," she said.

"Me too," Charlotte answered.

They parted and stood and surveyed the kitchen, each scanning the mess they had made.

"Don't worry about this, Charlotte. Why don't you go home early. I'm taking today off. After the long hours you put in last night, you should, too." Raven stepped through the laundry room and into Cass's office. When she returned, she handed Charlotte a wad of twenty-dollar bills. "Go shopping. Get your hair done. Make it a girl day."

Charlotte looked at the money. "It's too much, Mrs. Callahan."

"Nope. It's just right. You go spoil yourself..." Raven said, smiling. "...and we'll see you tomorrow?"

"Absolutely. Thank you, Mrs. Callahan."

Charlotte skipped out of the kitchen, gathered her things, and peeked in on Miguel for a goodbye hug, but he had fallen back asleep on the floor in front of a racetrack full of Hot Wheels, one of which was still cupped in his little hand. Drying mud crackled and squished beneath her tires as Raven watched Charlotte drive away.

Hot water never felt so good. Ten minutes was her usual indulgence in the shower, but today, she doubled her pampering, having grime emerging from more places than she would ever care to mention. Not wanting to keep Flint waiting more than she thought necessary, she dressed in what felt like the softest fresh cotton shirt, clean blue jeans, and dry socks. As a peace offering for overextending herself, she brewed fresh coffee for her and Flint and returned to the barn with two cups and a piping hot pot.

The barn was quiet, save for one odd thing—Flint was talking to the dog. She had heard him do something similar before, but that was with foals with which he was trying to form a bond.

"The funny thing is," he said with a tenderness summoned from deep within his hardened grit. "Ms. Raven ain't never met a person or a thing she didn't consider a friend. Hell, ya know the feelin' already. There ya were, bleedin', floatin', prob'ly givin' them mud cats below somethin' ta consider, an' yet ya done won the lottery the moment she splashed out ta git ya."

Raven moved slowly through the barn, feeling guilty for eavesdropping, but also not wanting Flint to stop.

"Ya fight hard enough, ya might pull through, but ya 'member one thing above all else. That woman who pulled ya from the water, that watched over ya all night long, the one that'll care fer ya 'til ya die is the one person yer charged with returnin' the favor."

Raven crept to the side of the stall.

"Ya hear me?" Flint stroked the dog's head, then stopped and looked straight ahead as if something before him had caught his eye. "You been standin' there long?"

Behind Flint, Raven rested her arms on the top slat.

"What? No. Just walked up."

"Yer a terrible liar, Ms. Raven. That, an' the coffee done gave ya away."

Flint stood and turned around. Raven handed him an empty cup. Flint tilted the cup and read the large, swirly red letters written on the side. "World's Greatest Mom." He chuckled and held it out for her to fill. "That how it is?"

Raven began to pour his cup when a car horn blared in the yard, startling her and causing her to spill hot coffee on Flint's hand. He quickly withdrew and wiped what was burning his skin on his pants.

"Shit. Sorry Flint."

"Who the hell is that?" he said, unconcerned by the slip-up.

He stepped out of the stall and power walked to the door. Raven followed close behind him.

Morning had arrived, and with it a glaring sun and bright blue sky with nary a trace of storm clouds in sight. It was a postcard-type day, yet beneath its beauty, a small car sped onto the property, kicking up mud-crusted gravel and rumbling over the cattleguards.

"Stay behind me, Raven."

Flint's voice was firm, his body language poised to attack and protect.

The car skidded to a stop. Flecks of mud flew into the air. The engine continued to rumble as the door slung open and Charlotte stumbled out. Her face was pale and streaked with tears, a stark contrast to the moments she spent dying of laughter on the kitchen floor only a short time ago. Now she looked terrified. She staggered ahead, arms shaking. She wobbled like a newborn fawn, every step a struggle.

Raven and Flint rushed to meet her, but before they could reach her, she lunged forward, screaming in hysterics. She crashed into Raven with a force that sent them both stumbling back, though Flint was there to catch them. Charlotte's body shook violently, tears streaming down her cheeks as a torrent of incomprehensible words spilled from her lips.

"Shhhhhh. Charlotte. Honey. What is it? What's wrong?"

Charlotte clawed at Raven's back, clutching her as though holding on for dear life.

"Are you hurt? Please. Settle down and tell us...what happened?"

With spit clinging to her bottom lip and eyes bloodshot and wide, her terror shifted to a chilling stoicism. Trembles racked throughout her body, and Raven gently pushed her back, cupping her cheeks in her hands.

"What's wrong, Charlotte?"

At first, she stuttered, her words choked and barely audible. Then, in a voice rising to a desperate scream, she cried out.

"Th...they...oh, god...They're all..." Her sobs overtook her once more, but in the midst of her convulsive wailing, she forced out the one word she seemed most terrified to say. "...dead."

CHAPTER THIRTY-SIX

A dull ache in my temples and a crick in my back were nothing compared to the dry, clinging taste of cotton stuck to the roof of my mouth stretching down the back of my throat. It was early and having tossed and turned in Ray's recliner for most of the night, I felt like I had been hit by a truck. Mornings like this were usually reserved as hapless reminders of the previous night's events where booze and buddies took center stage and regrets were for later, laughed off or lauded depending on the occasion.

I rubbed my eyes and found the handle to lower the chair's leg rest and noticed that Ray was no longer on the couch. Empty beer cans stood like forgotten tombstones on the coffee table. Some remained intact, others mangled and off-balance, crushed by frustrated fists. Condensation rings stained the wood surface, their smudgy white circles eating away at the varnish like rotting flesh.

Standing up, I took a deep breath and cleared my throat with a violent rumble. I stepped into the kitchen and spat into the sink, then ran the faucet, using my fingers to herd the mess into the drain. The water brought a refreshing calm as the coolness flowed over my fingers. I closed my eyes, and Raven's voice echoed in my mind.

It was late when I called, but after such a grueling day, I needed to hear her voice. It had been far too long since I had checked on her. She sounded tired. She talked about Miguel, and about finding some dog that she had been insistent on saving. Flint thought otherwise. Figures. I could picture her face, smiling and proud, yet I also sensed a subtle tinge of fear mixed with her joy. She mentioned that there had been trouble on the Flying H, but then did not elaborate. I should have asked for details. Thinking back, she wanted me to. Raven always loved telling a complete story, but the late hour and my scattered thoughts let that obvious clue slip past.

Our call drifted into quiet moments when words fell away, leaving only the soft sound of her breathing on the line. I missed her, but more than that, I missed being there *for* her. That was why we had moved to the CR, to focus on us. And yet, as much as I loved her, I could not escape the truth: I was failing to keep up with my one mission in life. I was failing to put family first.

I splashed my face, the abrupt shock disturbing my senses but not revitalizing my feelings.

"I should go back," I whispered, the words slipping out before I could stop them.

Bowing my head, droplets of water dripped into the sink and onto the front of my shirt. I drew in a deep breath, but its stale weight settled in my chest, offering no relief.

From the kitchen, I heard the buzz of my cell phone and instinctively reached for my pocket. It was not there. Shutting off the faucet, I followed the sound back into the living room. The buzzing continued as I zeroed in on its location. Sliding my hand into the recliner's crease, I searched, burying my arm to the elbow. Brushing the hard plastic case, I pinched the phone and pulled it free.

The buzzing had stopped, but a ribbon along the screen read: CALL FROM RAVEN.

I swiped upward, preparing to call back when I noticed a series of missed text messages. One from Dr. Frannie, and lengthy thread from Scoots.

"What the hell?"

Diverting my attention from the call to the text thread, I scrolled through the messages from Scoots, each hitting harder than the last. The more I read, the more the hairs on my neck felt like stiffening cactus needles. My pulse quickened, and my pounding head only worsened. When I read the last lines of text, my hand fell to my side, the phone dangling in my fingers.

"Son of a bitch!" I snapped, whirling around and taking a second look at the empty couch and graveyard of dead beers. "Where are you, Ray?"

CHAPTER THIRTY-SEVEN

THE CR, WEST TEXAS

"Take her ta the house an' lock the door. Call the Sheriff. Tell 'em I'm headed over ta the Flying H now." The world spun before Flint's eyes, but a man like him had a way of controlling the chaos. It was like riding a bull blindfolded, being forced onto its back by surprise. Charlotte's grim news was chilling to say the least. "And, Raven. Don't do somethin' stupid like followin' me this time. Stay here and look after Charlotte."

The firm cadence in his voice was both frightful and comforting.

Charlotte shook in Raven's arms. Her face buried in Raven's shoulder, her muffled sobs an unrelenting stream of grief.

Wrapping both in a wide embrace, Flint coaxed them toward the house. "Come on. We gotta move on this."

Like a tugboat guiding a ship away from the docks, Flint released the two girls at the porch steps, spun heel, and made his way to his tiny house. He slung open the unlocked door and rifled through the room, reappearing in a matter of moments with a shotgun in his hands and his Colt 1911 tucked inside his belt.

He glanced at the house and saw Raven lead Charlotte through the front door, catching a glimpse of Miguel looking up at both of them before it closed.

Rounding the back end of the barn, Flint tapped a switch mounted on the siding and stood back while a garage door raised. As soon as he had room, he ducked beneath the rising door and loaded up into his truck. With a roar from its 6.6L Duramax Turbo-Diesel V8 Engine and a blast of black exhaust, Flint reversed out of the garage with a stomp of the pedal, tires chewing at the ground. Skidding backward and shifting, rock and mud soared, clinking in the wheel wells and firing off like tiny rockets behind the rampageous truck.

Flint sped past the barn, rounding the corner by his tiny house, and shot straight for the dirt road at the head of the CR. The cattle guard burped like controlled bursts from an automatic weapon, and the dirt road outside the ranch seemed to flinch and scream under the assault. Flint's truck fishtailed across the dusty surface until its toothy tires finally bit into earth's gritty meat.

Gripping the wheel, Flint used his free hand to scroll through the contact list on his phone until he found and pressed the number for Harvey Oglethorp. Known as Harv by most, he was one of Huckabee's men. Flint and he had shared a fractious past, never passing up a moment to tussle over something. Still, ranchers around these parts knew how to get in touch with one another in case of emergency.

The phone rang through the speakers of the truck until voicemail answered the call. As Flint prepared to record his message, an announcement came over the line.

"The person you are trying to reach does not have a voicemail box set up. Please try your call again later."

He tried Floyd Huckabee next. Like the previous call, this one went unanswered. Flint tapped the steering wheel with an anxious thumb, each ring sharpening his frustration. He knew Huckabee had two other hands on the payroll, but they were off the grid for more reasons than one. Reaching one of them would be a longshot, if they were not already dead.

Flint's foot pressed harder onto the accelerator. With matching intensity, his finger ended the call and scrolled to a contact number he had nearly forgotten—Greaser MacFarland. He hesitated, his thumb hovering over the name, weighing the ramifications this call might stir. Still, Greaser had insight and connections that ran deeper than most.

Greaser MacFarland was an old acquaintance of Flint's former boss, Stewart Callahan, and lifelong *brushlander* with a wealth of knowledge and deep connections spanning both sides of the Rio Grande.

During the 1970s, Greaser had made a name for himself riding broncs in the rodeo circuits, raking in top prize money from 1972 to 1976 at the Southwestern International PRCA Rodeo, held annually in El Paso. He was on the brink of making the leap from amateur to professional status, his reputation growing with every ride. But in 1977, a fateful misstep during the Charro Days Fiesta in Brownsville—fueled by lost tempers and bad decisions—derailed his trajectory and set his life on a very different path. Starting a fight with a small group of locals in a border town was a bad idea. Bringing a knife to that fight and slicing the ear off someone who turned out to be the only son of Matamoros, Mexico's *Síndico*, the deputy to the mayor and a clandestine liaison to the *Jefe de Plaza*, or Plaza Boss of the dangerous Gulf Cartel, was disastrous.

Greaser never backed down from anyone, but when he learned that the cartel had green-lit a brutal retaliation, he fled The Valley. In his rush to disappear, he left behind his chance to cash in on a big-money ride, and his reputation, once solid as a championship buckle, unraveled into nothing more than a busted loop. After that, he drifted from ranch to ranch, working whatever jobs he could find, keeping one eye on the horizon and the other over his shoulder. Years later, he finally settled down—but only after his one-eared adversary was killed by the same cartel who had marked Greaser for death.

With the truck barreling down the road and Flint closing the distance on the Flying H, he tapped Greaser's contact and set the phone into its cradle on the dash. The phone rang once before being picked up on the other end of the line.

"Greaser. It's Levi Flint."

"*Yeah. What do you want? Ain't neared finished my coffee yet an' I...*"

"Listen...there's trouble at the Flyin' H. Looks like Floyd Huckabee and some of his men were killed last night."

"*Sum Bitch! Ol' Floyd's dead, huh?*"

"Looks like it. His niece discovered 'em just a bit ago. She'd been out at the Callahan's last night an' went out ta the *Flyin' H* just this mornin'. Poor girl raced back ta the CR in hysterics. Sheriff's been called, an' I'm on the way over now."

"*Why ya callin' me, Flint?*"

Flint pulled the steering wheel right, sliding the rear tires of the truck around, and turned down the gravel access road that ran parallel to the Flying H.

"Ya hear anythin' worth mentionin' that might be goin' on cross the brown soup?"

The line went cold except for the nasal harassment of Greaser's heavy breathing.

"Greaser? Ain't got time ta..."

"*Let me git back ta ya,*" Greaser interrupted, then ended the call.

"Shit." Flint pursed his lips, his teeth grinding beneath.

The front gate of the Flying H loomed ahead, coming into view through the dusty windshield. Flint eased off the accelerator, letting the truck roll to a slow crawl as he lowered the window. The familiar crackle of gravel under the tires mixed with the steady hum of the diesel engine. The silence beyond those sounds was a good sign, but it did not guarantee the ranch was safe. Charlotte's discovery had left her in a state of shock, and Flint knew fear had a way of blurring details. She might have missed something, or someone, lurking just out of sight.

Flint turned onto the property, stopping the truck under the iron archway at the head of the ranch. Its welded western artistry displaying the name Flying H in large bold swirls, flanked by large stone columns crowned with cast iron horse sculptures rearing with wild aban-don. Huckabee was a small man with a larger-than-life appetite for opulence.

The early morning sun poured bright rays across the ranch, the crisp light gleaming as though it too was searching for something hidden. The lingering wetness from the storm clung to surfaces, catching the light in tiny droplets that shimmered like scattered diamonds before evaporating. Under different circumstances, Flint might have paused to admire the fleeting beauty of it all, but there was nothing beautiful about the task of uncovering death.

Tapping the accelerator and with his head on a swivel, Flint eased the truck ahead. From the entrance road, the porch looked still and the windows on the house were dark. The corrals were empty, but that was not abnormal as workers should have already been riding beyond the fences. Floyd Huckabee's truck was parked next to the barn with a horse trailer hitched to the rear. Another older model Ford truck stood in the shadows on the opposite side, but the barn doors remained closed. A few stray cows watched the truck, bellowing loudly as if chastising Flint for not bringing them their scheduled feed. As he drove on, their eyes followed and they moved along the fence line, mooing their discontent about not yet being turned out to pasture.

He turned his attention to the barn, then slammed the brakes. The truck slid across the crushed rock, its tires digging into the saturated earth beneath. Taking the shotgun, he jumped from the truck, leaving it to idle like a growling dog made to stand guard. Pulling the stock to his shoulder, he advanced on the front of the barn.

The large sliding door was shut, but a smaller access door to the side swung back and forth on its hinges. Flint quickened his pace, reaching the barn wall and pressing himself against it. Keeping his back to the wood, he edged toward the open door, stopping just short of its frame. Frozen in place, he strained to listen, attuned to the tiniest movements or irregular sound. Seconds dragged into what felt like minutes. His heart pounded, not from fear but anticipation. Charlotte's voice replayed in his mind, "...they're dead." He could only imagine what lay beyond the threshold, though every fiber of his being prayed he was wrong.

Life on the border came with its dangers. Flint knew that all too well. But the threats here carried a weight that was darker, deadlier. When they struck, the consequences were not just tragic, they were unimaginable.

Taking a deep breath, Flint steadied himself. He

brushed his hand across the pistol in his belt, returned it to the shotgun, then crept up to the door and peered inside. With the shotgun leading the way, Flint ducked into the belly of the barn.

CHAPTER THIRTY-EIGHT

The overgrown grass in Ray's front yard looked like a bad combover after a rough night's sleep. Weeds overpowered the flowerbeds, settling on top of the graying mulch, its once-black appearance and fragrant stench cozying up to the colorful fauna Ruth Ann had watched over year after year. Patches of clovers intermingling with buttercups stretched along the curb. Two houses down from Ray's, a small, two-door truck pulled up to the curb, windows down and Tejano music blasting its infectious beat and folksy Spanish lyrics. Two men hopped out wearing neon yellow, long-sleeved shirts and oversized straw hats. They unloaded yard tools and a lawnmower from the bed, jumping into their work with a hop in their step. Work was what a man makes of it and these two seemed happy to have a job. I had a mind to walk down and hire the crew to care for Ray's yard, but a shrill tap of a car horn pulling into the driveway yanked my attention back.

Damn it, Ray.

I walked over to the car, my mind reeling from the string of text messages Scoots had sent, frosted with a hint of frustration by Ray's temporary disappearance. Grumbled thoughts nearly spilling into words were immediately swallowed when Ray exited the car holding a small white paper bag and two Styrofoam cups.

"Didn't wanna wake you. The bakery on the corner makes donuts that'll hook you like crack, Cass. And I got us some coffee. I'm all out."

He handed me one, the warmth within seeping through the cheap, disposable cup.

My annoyance tempered, I lifted my drink. "Thanks, Ray."

He closed the car door, then shot me with a curious, near accusatory look. "You're pissed about something." He stepped closer. "Sleep with the TV remote jammed in your back?"

I pulled my phone out and showed him the messages from Scoots. His eyes darted back and forth across the screen. He hemmed and hawed, nodding, then handed me the phone.

"By the look on your face, we're hittin' the beat early today. Am I right?"

He took a sip of coffee, still standing close as if we were huddling in wait of the next play to come from the sidelines. The aroma from his cup smelled delicious. I turned to look at the yard guys down the street, the pop of their mower firing up drowning out their music and took a sip of coffee. It had the same smell as Ray's, its dark flavor and strong Columbian scent filling both my nose and my mouth with a jolt of instant vitality.

"Yeah," I said. "The sooner I get into this, the better. We'll call Scoots in the truck."

"You're driving...again?" Ray sipped, his eye arching

over the rim of his cup. "Something wrong with my car?" he said, wiping his mouth with his wrist.

"No," I said. "Same reasons I drove you all over the Middle East. Same reasons I drove during our shared shifts on the force."

Ray smiled. "You always did show respect for seniority, Cass."

"That's not it at all, Ray," I grinned, my sucker punch winding up. "Your driving sucks."

He squinted at me, his expression caught between indignation and amusement. Finally, he gave a slight nod, conceding defeat.

"Ass," Ray muttered, but there was a trace of a smile.

We were on the road before the lawn crew down the street finished the front yard, and on a call with Scoots before leaving the neighborhood.

"You know what time it is?" Scoots's voice sounded rough over the speakers.

"Don't care," I said. "I need more details, and in layman's terms. We caught the gist of your messages. Concerning, to say the least. But I need specifics. What are we dealing with?"

I could hear Scoots yawning over the line before he collected himself long enough to answer.

"Meet me at Sam's Deli on Kirkwood. I'll bring my laptop and give you a beginner's class on Cyber Warfare. I'll be there in fifteen."

Scoots ended the call before I could object. It was closing in on seven thirty, and Raven's call notification remained pinned to the top of my phone's screen.

Can't right now, Little Bird.

I swept my finger across the ribbon, removing it from view, then noted our location on the truck's GPS.

"We're not that far from Sam's," I said.

"You hear from your West Texas doc?" Ray asked.

"Just a brief text confirming receipt of the body late last night. Once we're done with Scoots, I'll give her a call."

Twenty minutes later, we pulled into the parking lot beneath the shadows of Interstate 10. The Katy Freeway, one of the world's widest thoroughfares, stretched over twenty lanes wide at times and saw more than two hundred and fifty thousand cars travel across its concrete sprawl every day. I sat for a moment and watched the endless stream of vehicles. Each driver, stuck in the pack or jockeying for position trying to shave off what would amount to mere seconds of their commute, had no idea the problems looming over the city this morning, let alone the state. Maybe that was for the best. Ignorance, dangerous as it is, may be the one thing that keeps our sanity in check.

Ray's voice cut through my thoughts. "We just gonna sit here?"

I killed the engine, and we got out of the truck, my mind stuck in a commute of its own. I spotted Scoots through the window at Sam's Deli and waved Ray to follow. Behind us, traffic shuffled along like mindless cattle crammed together in a citywide slaughterhouse chute. It was a grim start to a day already heading in the wrong direction.

The door chimed as we walked in and we were greeted by a friendly face behind the walk-up counter.

"Morning," a young lady wearing an apron and a cheery smile said from behind the register. "You fellas hungry this morning?"

Ray answered for both of us.

"Lily," he said, reading her name tag. "We'll take two number ones, eggs scrambled, bacon extra crispy please."

"Coffee with that?" she asked.

Ray reached for his wallet. "Absolutely."

Scoots eyed us from a table near the window. He was in the same clothes as last night but wore a more disheveled look about him—shirt untucked, hair a mess, and eyes puffy from extended screentime and lack of sleep. I walked over and took a seat across from him. His laptop took up most of the room between us. The rest of the tabletop was scattered with empty sugar packets and spent single serve creamer cups. His hand jittered when he raised his mug and finished what I guessed to be a second or third cup of coffee so far.

"This is crazy, Cass." Scoots's voice carried beyond our table.

Ray joined us, setting down a steaming mug in front of me, then took a seat.

"Might want to keep your voice down, sport," Ray said. "Or should we invite everyone over?"

I glanced around the restaurant, exchanging nods with a group of old-timers huddled around a nearby table. Their easy camaraderie filled the space with a sense of familiarity. Toward the back, another group sat deep in discussion, their heads bowed over well-worn Bibles, the quiet murmur of their morning study weaving into the hum of the diner.

"Fine," Scoots said, his voice low and discreet.

"Lay it out for us, Scoots," I said. "What are we dealing with here?"

Scoots took a deep breath, then shifted his chair closer. Turning his laptop toward us, he tapped a few keys, his fingers flying across the keyboard, bypassing layers of ERCOT's robust cybersecurity like peeling an onion. "Here, take a look," he said. The screen split into multiple panes, each running a different analysis. ERCOT's system showed nothing out of the ordinary—lines of code and status readouts scrolling in serene blues and greens, oblivious to the lurking danger.

In a smaller, separate window—the one Scoots had custom-coded for deep packet inspection—something far more sinister emerged.

"ANOMALOUS CODE FRAGMENT IDENTIFIED" flashed in muted orange, invisible to ERCOT's native detection algorithms. Scoots zoomed in on the string, his custom scanner isolating a buried payload hidden in the system's encrypted logs.

```
/* Embedded Code - Anomaly */
function SilentTrigger () {
if (GridState == "Normal") {
InjectPayload();
Sleep(86400); // Delay Activation for 24
Hours
}
}
```

"See this?" Scoots said, tapping the screen. "Smart, real smart. The virus wasn't designed to strike right away —it's camouflaged, waiting for specific conditions to activate."

A secondary window opened, showing ERCOT's system topology.

Scoots pointed to a faintly glowing node on the map. "To anyone else, it'd look like a perfectly functioning grid. But not to me." He tapped the screen again. "Here. Node TX-Grid48. The glow pinpoints a deviation so subtle even ERCOT's best analysts would miss it."

I leaned in closer. "This is good work, but what does it all mean?"

Scoots turned to me, his eyes bloodshot and exhausted, but his glare bore a seriousness that cut to my core. "This isn't just a virus—this is custom-made sabotage."

He faced the screen again and typed rapidly, launching a diagnostic program. Lines of green and white code scrolled in the terminal as his algorithms ran checks against known malware signatures. A deep red string appeared at the bottom:

"Unknown Code Variant - No Match Found in Database"

He opened a final window. A map of Texas's power grid appeared, unmarked save for a faintly glowing trace line snaking from Node TX-Grid48 toward other critical substations.

"The virus isn't active yet," Scoots said, his voice grim. "But it's poised to create a cascading failure that could cripple the grid in and around Houston. And that's just the beginning."

He leaned back. Ray grumbled something under his breath, but I paid no attention. I was too absorbed by the weight of Scoots's discovery and the catastrophic possibilities if he was right.

"This thing's a ghost," he said. "And ERCOT doesn't even know it's haunting them."

A sharp *tick, tick, tick* echoed in my head like a time bomb counting down the seconds to detonation. My pocket vibrated with the buzz of an incoming call. Needing a momentary distraction, I pulled it out and read the screen.

Raven.

Answering this call would not be momentary. I closed my eyes as I tapped the red *decline* icon and slid the phone back into my pocket.

Taking a deep breath, I forced myself to recenter my thoughts, opening my eyes when Ray spoke up.

"We should get on the horn. Let the tech jocks at ERCOT know what we've found."

"Bad idea," Scoots said. "The second any one of those

click monkeys attempt to remove it, it could activate. A hard patch at the original access point is the only option. They'll tell you otherwise, but they'd be wrong."

"Well, we can't just sit around holding our dicks," Ray protested.

"You're both right," I said. "Not only do we have to stop the virus, we've got to catch the fuckers that planted it."

"I'm way ahead of you, Cass," Scoots said, mustering a grin. "I've already embedded a temporary sandbox around the existing code to stall any activation sequence. It won't prevent it from spreading, but it should buy us some time if things go south. On top of that, I've injected a monitoring program into SCADA to act as an early-warning system. It scans for similar code patterns, flags anything suspicious in real-time, and sends us an alert."

"What kind of alerts?" I asked.

"Realtime location data—GPS coordinates of the upload's origin, timestamps for when the code was injected, and the IP address or node ID of the compromised system. Maybe we get lucky and catch the hacker red handed."

"Yeah, lucky," Ray repeated, his tone sharp with sarcasm. "Because that's the foundation of every great investigation. Luck."

CHAPTER THIRTY-NINE

29.7057° N, -95.5495° W

The van idled, its steady vibrations rattling the frame from the engine to the rear cargo doors. Air blasted through the dash vents, whistling as it blew into the cab mixing with the stale remnants of a night eradicated of cold flesh and slow decay. In the payload bay, two cardboard boxes sat beside a large, lumpy trash bag slumped on its side. A discarded tarp lay crumpled against the van wall, no longer needed to conceal things better left unseen.

Standing next to the passenger door, Zhàn Huǒ glanced at his watch. The second hand's rotation around the dial seemed like the only thing moving smoothly for him. He lowered his wrist, pulled his last Panda from the crumpled pack, and tucked it between his lips. He let the empty wrapper fall to the ground, nudging it beneath the van with a careless kick. The cigarette's dry paper teased his lips, sparking a craving for its bitter taste. With a practiced flick of his lighter, the first drag spilled over his tongue, curling into his chest and spreading a tingling warmth before he let the smoke escape in a slow, deliberate exhale.

Pulling the Panda from his lips, he looked at his watch again, then glanced at the door to apartment 4C.

What is taking them so long?

He took another draw, his patience beginning to wane. A third puff and the initial rush felt deadened, swallowed by the grip of addiction and his mounting frustration with a mission not running as planned. With Sūn Tiān missing, his team was down to three operators, which made today's task riskier than he would have liked.

"Enough of this waiting!" Zhàn Huǒ grumbled. He tossed the spent cigarette into the grass and began to storm back to the apartment when the door opened and Líng Líng stepped outside followed by Miào Wén-Kē. Glaring, he stabbed a finger at both of them. "You do not take this seriously. There is much at stake, and still, you treat our being here like a vacation."

Líng Líng squinted her eyes like an alley cat ready to pounce on a gutter rat. She took a stormy step forward, but Miào Wén-Kē grabbed her shoulder and held her back. Leaning close to her ear, he whispered.

"Do not let the old man get under your skin. His dutiful ways and regimented thinking are not like ours."

Zhàn Huǒ growled. Miào Wén-Kē's gaze fell upon him, his calm, insolent voice deepening canyons of malice already separating the two.

"You see, Líng Líng," he continued. "He is at the mercy of the *Zhànlüè Zhīyuán Bùduì*, as we are, but there is one thing he faces that you and I will most certainly avoid should this mission fail. A punishment far beyond the sting of dishonor."

Zhàn Huǒ's face reddened. With surprising speed, he pulled a silver-plaited Norinco Type 59 pistol tucked between his belt and the small of his back and leveled it with practiced precision. Líng Líng's eyes fluttered, now staring down the end of the deadly barrel. Pressed close behind Líng Líng, Miào Wén-Kē did not flinch. His thin lips curled at the corners, a sinister look that was neither a smile nor a sneer.

Zhàn Huǒ held steady, his finger resting on the trigger.

"Go ahead," Miào Wén-Kē said, his words hissing like a snake.

Zhàn Huǒ stepped forward, closing the gap between the three of them. The bitter aftertaste of tar and nicotine clung in his throat. His grip on the weapon tightened, but his finger eased its pressure on the trigger.

"He won't kill either of us," Miào Wén-Kē said, his voice low and taunting as he leaned closer to Líng Líng's ear. "He may wish to do it, but he knows he cannot." His lips brushed her ear in a mockery of tenderness before his hand slid deliberately up her waist, each movement calculated to provoke.

A muffled whump and the sharp stench of burning gunpowder quietly dissolved in the morning breeze as Zhàn Huǒ dropped his weapon, clutching his stomach. Disbelief and anger twisted his features into a grimace of absolute pain. Blood spilled from his gut, seeping through his fingers even as he pressed desperately against the gunshot wound. Gasping, he staggard forward, his free hand reaching out but Miào Wén-Kē yanked Líng Líng aside, escaping Zhàn Huǒ's futile attempt to strike at them. He fell to one knee, blood now reaching his mouth and mixing with the aftertaste in his throat, dripped from his lips.

"Líng Líng, get the door," Miào Wén-Kē said.

She moved quickly, opening the door while scanning the complex for watchful eyes. Miào Wén-Kē stepped in front of Zhàn Huǒ and knelt. Using one hand, he pulled his head back by the hair, locking eyes with the older man's turbulent gaze.

"Do not worry. The Americans will see their world crumble into darkness and disarray, but unfortunately Zhàn Huǒ, you will not."

Zhàn Huǒ opened his mouth as if to speak, but instead of words flowing over his bloody tongue, Miào Wén-Kē slipped the suppressed barrel of his gun into this mouth and pulled the trigger. A violent jolt preceded a sudden limp slump as the bullet tore through Zhàn Huǒ at an angle ensuring the evidence remained buried deep within while sparing any additional eternal mess.

With no sense of urgency, Miào Wén-Kē walked to the door and handed Líng Líng his gun. He smiled at her as if he had just won their freedom, then returned to Zhàn Huǒ's body. He grabbed both wrists and pulled the dead man into the apartment. Blood smeared the walkway and began soaking into the carpet once Miào Wén-Kē pulled him inside. He returned to the door, reclaiming his weapon from Líng Líng. It felt warm in his hands.

Seeing the dark stain bloom across the concrete, Líng Líng stepped outside. She grabbed a garden hose coiled beside the building, her fingers twisting the spigot to release a sharp stream of water. Pivoting, she aimed the spray at the bloody mess. With gentle, sweeping motions, she rinsed the concrete as though tending to a garden or watering flowers. The warm, fresh blood trickled into the grass bordering the walkway, leaving behind only a faint crimson trace.

In the parking space just beyond her, the van continued to idle, its rumble providing a mundane back-drop to an otherwise brutal morning. Miào Wén-Kē walked over. He opened the door and killed the engine with a simple flick of his wrist. The clattering of water against the sidewalk was the only sound left that might draw interest from a nosy neighbor, if one had not already become alerted by the swift and deadly altercation. Miào Wén-Kē turned, his gaze tracing Líng Líng with unhurried intent, his thoughts slipping to unmentionable places where darkness and desire intertwined.

When their eyes met, a heat passed between them, ignited by their shared chaos. Miào Wén-Kē walked past her to the apartment, adrenaline pumping, feeling the cool mist from her spray, and stood in the open doorway. He watched her, devouring her every movement.

Líng Líng washed the water across the concrete path one final time before shutting off the spigot and tossing the hose aside. Her shoes and the front of her blouse were damp, though she did not seem to notice. Without a word, she stepped into the apartment, brushing her knuckles across Miào Wén-Kē's midsection as she passed him. By the time the door clicked shut, she had already turned to face him, her fingers deftly unfastening the buttons on her blouse, her eyes blazing with desire and the unspoken promise of what was to come next.

CHAPTER FORTY

THE FLYING H, WEST TEXAS

Stepping into the dimly lit barn, Flint was struck by a scene so haunting it carved jagged scars into his mind—a nightmare no passage of time could ever erase. He lowered the shotgun and wiped his mouth with his hand, his breath caught in a chokehold of disbelief. Before him, bodies dangled from the rafters, each one swaying in sullen silence, their lifeless forms twisted into awkward backward arches, held fast by the ropes that bound them.

"Jesus."

One word, then silence reclaimed the space around him. That was all he could manage in that moment. Neither a call for help nor exclamation of faith, it was a resignation to the grim tableau that crashed over him with unimaginable force.

With eyes glued to the bodies, Flint made his way to the main barn door. He undid the latch and slid it open just enough to let in more light and fresh air. It was a good and terrible idea. The light illuminated every gruesome detail, sharpening the nightmare into something almost unbearable.

Flint was as tough as they come, had faced death from the natural to the gruesome, and had a hand at times of sending someone to meet their maker but the sight before him, accentuated in all of God's glory, was the most harrowing of his life. His mouth and throat dried up as if he had swallowed a shot glass full of sand. Heat rose to his neck and ears. Each heartbeat pounded his chest like a post-hole digger jabbing into packed earth.

The man dangling closest to him was one he recognized but had never met. Huckabee had a way of finding workers who needed to disappear into the land, men with more reasons to stay hidden than Flint cared to know.

The body hung limp, suspended in a grotesque display of cruelty. His boots had been removed, exposing his flesh to the raw teeth of the braided rope that wrapped around his ankles. His wrists were bound together behind his back and connected to his ankles in a synch that caused him to hang inverted. The skin around the bindings was raw and discolored, deep grooves cutting into the flesh where the weight of the body had borne down on the ropes. The hands were dark and swollen, and his feet looked as if he suffered multiple, torturous burns before being strung up.

His head lolled forward, but the contours on his face were clear. His skin was pallid and waxy, the lips tinged blue. His eyes drooped open, dull and unseeing, as if caught in an endless rift between sleep and wakefulness. A sticky pool of congealed blood spread beneath him, its darkened surface resembling the chaotic swirls of a dirty pour painting. Tiny droplets fanned out in hardened rivulets to one side having caught the initial spray from the man's throat once it had been cut.

The air hung heavy with the metallic tang of blood,

underscored by the faint stench of sweat and fear. The odor drifted toward Flint and the open door, as though pulled by an invisible force, desperate to escape the confines of the barn.

He bowed and shook his head knowing that when he raised it again, nothing would have changed, no matter how much he wished it to be. Reaching for his back pocket, he removed his cell phone and scrolled through his contacts until he found one labeled *Boss*. Deputy Marie Bostwick, one and the same that had hauled away Curly Yates yesterday afternoon. She was his best option, short of calling Sheriff Chance Gilbert who was still laid up in the hospital recovering from a serious car accident.

He pressed her contact icon and placed the call. He did not have to wait long before the line was answered.

"*This is Marie.*"

"Hey, Boss. It's Flint. We got a huge problem out at the Flyin' H."

"*Huckabee still in a fuss over his man going all Charles Whitman yesterday?*"

Flint took a breath, the fresh sensation filling his lungs yet not quenching the growing pit in his stomach.

"Ya need ta get out here. Bring everyone. Huckabee's dead. His whole crew."

The line went silent for a count, then erupted in a volley of descriptions by Flint and instructions by Boss for him to follow.

"*You hear me, Flint? Everything I said is important, but none more than the last. Do not approach the bodies. I know you knew those men and want to see them in any other way than how they are now, but don't. I'll be out there as soon as I can. Deputy Castillo is out on the road and will most likely be the first on scene. You can expect DPS and Border Patrol as well, just not sure of an ETA for them yet.*"

"Read ya loud an' clear, Boss."

Flint could hear Boss working in the background of their call.

"It'll be okay, Flint. Hang tight."

Flint disconnected the call and leaned against the frame of the barn door and looked inside. The ropes creaked as the bodies swayed in the fresh air that rushed into the barn—a sound as chilling as the sight itself. His voice was low and strained as he whispered to himself.

"Ain't nothin' 'bout this gonna be okay."

CHAPTER FORTY-ONE

HOUSTON, TEXAS

Scoots, Ray, and I gathered around my truck, mingling in the parking lot like teenagers hanging out at Sonic on a Friday night. "Maybe we get lucky," Scoots had said. That was like trying to catch a single raindrop in a downpour. Houston and its surrounding counties had a population of over seven million, and that data was in perpetual flux. More and more people were flocking to Texas, and not just from south of the border or overseas. Judging by the swarm of sleek Teslas and Subarus with West Coast tags, Houston was becoming a promised land for Californians fleeing their own golden coasts.

"So, we just sit around and wait for something to happen," Ray muttered. "Were fishing without bait this time, Cass."

I turned to Scoots.

"You said that a direct patch to the original upload point was our best chance of stopping or removing the virus, right?"

Scoots looked around the parking lot as if searching for something. He adjusted the backpack slung over his shoulder before answering.

"In theory."

"Shit," Ray scoffed. "We need hard evidence and definitive answers but all we have to move on is theory. You sure you're not cooked up top, Mr. Computer Genius?" Ray tapped his forehead, his eyebrows arching with doubt.

Scoots's face flushed red. I could not tell if it was embarrassment, anger, exhaustion, or a combination of all frosted with a defiant certainty that he knew what he was talking about, regardless of Ray's accusation. He pulled at the shoulder straps of his backpack.

"Look, Detective…"

"Can we," I snapped, my voice cutting through their bickering. Both of them turned to me, their attention startled. I calmed my tone and focused on Scoots. "Can you, Scoots, remove the virus without anyone knowing? And without activating its protocol?"

Ray's jaw was clenched, his patience dissolving by the second. Scoots locked eyes with him before answering.

"01011001 01000101 01010011."

As Scoots spouted off the series of numbers, I caught a flash in Ray's eyes, reminiscent of when he had grudgingly accepted Scoots's smart assery the night before. Ray was inherently skeptical—about everything—but his gut, like mine, told him the same thing: know when it's time to fold your hand.

Ray and I shared a look, neither of us understanding, which was Scoots's point. And then it clicked.

"Yes?" I said.

Scoots nodded.

"All that for a yes? Do you have to make everything so God damn complicated, kid?"

Scoots shrugged, a slight smirk tugging at his lips. "It's not complicated at all—at least not to me."

Ray snorted. "So, you're the one that's going to save us all from the Matrix, then?"

"No," Scoots said, his voice calm and even. "I'm the architect."

The color returned to Scoots's face, his bravado restored.

If getting lucky was the only option, then we were damn sure going to have to make our own luck.

"Scoots, you have wheels?"

He cocked his head, eyes narrowing and full of questions. "Yeah, but I gotta get to work soon."

"Not today," I said. "I need you to take Ray and do what you do best. He'll get you where you need to go, and you'll work your magic. Just keep me in the loop."

"Cass, I can't just—"

"Scoots," I interrupted, placing a firm yet reassuring hand on his shoulder. "Yes, you can." His reluctance hung in the air but I could see the gears already turning behind his eyes. "Bring your car around. Ray'll pay for the day."

Ray shot me a sharp *WTF* glare, then huffed and rolled his eyes in defeat.

"Go on, Mr. Wizard," he said, gesturing to Scoots.

Scoots sighed, pursing his lips as if to say something, but instead, he reached into his pocket and pulled out a jingling set of keys. "If I get fired..." His voice trailed off as he walked away, the sound of the keys echoing through the parking lot.

I stood with one foot on the running board. Ray leaned on the bed rail and folded his hands.

"This could really be some shit, huh?" he said, the contemplation in his voice near tangible. "You think this hail Mary of yours is the answer? What if the kid can't do it. What if he triggers this massive collapse he's predicting."

"Hail Marys only happen at the end of the game, Ray. This is us going on offense. Maybe if we disrupt part of the other guy's plan, he'll show his hand."

"And if he doesn't?"

From across the parking lot, we heard the clean bark of a finely tuned engine, its idle settling into an ornamental growl. The exhaust crackled mechanically, like a machine ready for takeoff, before a smooth rumble filled the air—but only for a moment. With brisk precision, the engine accelerated, climbing into a high-pitched wail, the sound growing closer with every second.

"Well, I'll be a son of a bitch," Ray muttered.

Rolling to a stop behind my truck, Scoots pulled up in a vintage, candy-red Honda S2000. Its wheels glimmered, and the black treads of its street tires gripped the asphalt like Velcro on velvet. Scoots sat behind the wheel of the sporty convertible like a showman at an illegal street race, his eyes daring us to comment.

"Hop in, Detective."

Ray straightened, called to attention by the sleek classic and Scoots's casual invitation. He walked over to the car, the hood barely reaching his thigh, then turned and shook his head.

"How in the hell am I supposed to fit in that?"

Ray was a big man, built like a wrestler with a touch of sog around the middle, and at six-foot-five, his question was more than valid. But there was only one response.

"Figure it out, Ray," I said.

With a resigned sigh, he walked to the passenger door, leaning over to reach the handle. The car hummed patiently as he maneuvered into the seat, wiggling and adjusting until he was secured. The door pressed snugly against his outer thigh as he fastened his seat belt. Settled in, he glanced up at me, his expression pure Roger Murtaugh: *I'm too old for this shit.*

Scoots, one hand on the wheel and an elbow resting on the door, radiated a calm, cocky confidence akin to that of a fighter pilot. I approached the car, taking in its raw, classic charm, and peeked inside. The cockpit did not disappoint. Everything looked authentic, as if the car had just pulled off the showroom floor, but here we were, twenty years later, and it was just as pristine. The black leather seats had a soft, elegant appeal, their bold yellow stitching and Alcantara accents underscoring the finesse of the design. The instrument panel glowed with a digital cluster pulsating like a machine begging to be unleashed, ready to find redline and shift into lightspeed.

The only nod to modernity was the Kenwood audio system, its touchscreen display and built-in navigation just the tip of the iceberg in terms of sleek functionality.

Scoots wore his car like a second skin, every polished surface and fine-tuned feature reflecting the hours he had spent making it his own. Behind the wheel, he was not just the computer genius, he was something more, an alter ego brought to life by the power and presence of the car that fit him like a perfectly executed line of code, flawless and ready to run.

"Get him access to whatever he needs down in Newgulf," I said to Ray. "If Morrell puts up a fight—"

"I'll fight back," he said, finishing my sentence. "We won't have any issues with some small-town power station Supe."

I straightened, turning my attention to Scoots.

"You up for this?"

Without taking his eyes off me, Scoots reached into the center console, pulled out a pair of Ray-Bans, and slid them onto his face with the cool confidence of a Hollywood mogul.

"I got this," he said.

I nodded, then leaned close.

"Try not to give Ray a heart attack, will ya?"

Scoots grinned like the Grinch after having stolen a sleigh full of toys, jammed the clutch and shifted into first gear. The rear wheels spun, creating a cloud of white smoke before gripping the surface and shooting ahead. I saw Ray's arms flail as he grasped the side of the car, his hair blowing back in the sudden burst.

"Yeah," I said to myself. "I'm never gonna hear the end of that."

I hopped into the truck, leaving the door open in the breeze, and pulled out my cell phone. In the process of getting Ray and Scoots on the road, I had missed two calls. One from Dr. Frannie, the other from my friend, the sheriff, Chance.

My call back list was growing exponentially, but with Chance still in the hospital, I figured I needed to get back to him first.

I located his contact, and pressed *send*. The call rang once.

"*This is Sheriff Gilbert.*"

"Chance, it's Cass. Good to hear your voice."

"*You talk to Raven today?*"

His tone was abrupt, the kind of no-nonsense voice he usually reserved for emergencies. I set the phone in its cradle on the dash and closed the door.

"Not yet. She's next up."

"*Cass...*"

The pause in his voice triggered an immediate stir in my gut. Something was wrong.

"What about Raven?"

"*You need ta call her right away. She's fine. Miguel's fine. But the whole world is about to know where Brewster, Texas, is on the map, and it ain't good.*"

With Chance still on the line, I scrolled through my missed calls, her name staring back at me, blaming me for my disregard.

"On it," I said, ending the call.

My fingers moved fast, swiping to her number, and pressing *Send*. The silence on the line felt like an eternity before the first ring finally chimed.

Ring.

No answer.

Ring.

Still, nothing. My impatience grew, feeding the unease twisting in my gut. What was so bad that everyone knew except me?

Ring.

The line crackled, and then her voice—shaky and cold—came through.

"Cass, where have you been?"

CHAPTER FORTY-TWO

HOUSTON, TEXAS

Raven's voice trembled over the line, her breathing ragged and quick, as if she had sprinted to answer the phone. But there were more than just her words coming through. In the background, I caught the soft, haunting moans of someone whimpering, each labored huff and sigh rolling like waves on a distant shore. I had no idea what was happening.

"Talk to me, Raven."

The line remained silent for a beat, the pause stretching just long enough to make my chest tighten. Then, with a sharp sniff, as if slurping back tears, Raven tore the lid clean off my day.

"Floyd Huckabee and everyone at the Flying H are dead, Cass. Killed just last night."

A prickling tingle radiated across my body, its epicenter caving my chest, the blast pulsating into my limbs. Heat poured from my collar. I found myself gripping the truck's steering wheel as if locked in the drag race of my life, but I was not driving anywhere. I was still in the same parking spot in front of Sam's Deli, listening to Raven as her voice echoed through the speakers, chipping away at me.

"*It's been awful*," she continued. "*Curly Yates went crazy yesterday afternoon and started shooting at people across the river. Flint and I ended up stopping him, but Curly tried to shoot Flint too. I got him first.*"

"*I got him first.*" The words rang in my head, impossible to ignore. Did Raven kill Curly? The thought hit like a gut punch. Was this what she had tried to tell me last night? I had not pushed, too wrapped up in my own chaos to notice hers. Now, the pieces were falling into place, but now? What was I supposed to do with this?

"*Boss finally showed up with Huckabee and hauled Curly off*," she said, her voice heavy with exhaustion. "*Then, this morning, Charlotte—*"

Her words cut off as the whimpering in the background rose, swelling into sobs like a rogue wave crashing through the line. I heard the faint click of the phone being set down, followed by Raven's voice, muffled but still audible. Her words were soft, nurturing, doing her best to comfort someone. For a moment, I was left alone. And then it hit me, cutting through the fog like a stiff breeze: Curly was alive.

"Raven?" I said, my voice was low and anxious.

When the sobbing subsided, the speakers scratched with the sound of hair brushing the phone on the other end.

"Raven?" I said again. "Who is..."

"*It's Charlotte*," she eked out, her voice trembling on the edge of breaking. "*She stayed here last night to help out with Miguel.*" Raven's words caught in her throat, strangled by rising tears. "*If she had gone home...if she was at the Flying H...*" Her voice faltered, leaving the unspoken horror to hang heavily in the air.

I pictured the two of them, huddled together on the couch, afraid, confused, swimming in the rise and fall of relentless emotion.

"You're okay? Are you at home now?"

Collecting herself, Raven replied. *"Yes. We're both here. Miguel is still asleep. Flint drove out to see what happened, but I haven't heard from him yet."*

"Keep talking, Raven," I urged, though the words felt more like the practiced lines of an interrogation, drawing slivers of truth from a frightened informant. "How do you know what happened?"

The whimpers in the background grew faint, and Raven's voice dropped to a whisper.

"Charlotte drove home this morning and discovered every-thing. She came right back here in hysterics. This all happened within the last hour." Her voice rose, shaky and edged with accusation. *"I tried calling you, Cass. Where have you been? Why haven't you answered my calls?"*

Guilt clawed at me, sharp and insistent. My failings for her were starting to pile up again, but there was no time to dwell on that now. My only choice was to steady the storm before it broke. Of the many things I could have said, only one might inject the calm she needed to hear.

"I'm sorry. It sounds like you are both safe. Stay in the house and wait for Flint to come home. I'll call him after and get the details."

"I need you to come home, Cass."

"I know, Little Bird."

"Today."

The words "I can't" formed on my lips but never made it to the call. I took a deep breath, the weight of the world pressing down on me as I struggled in a tug-of-war I knew I could never win. Murders next door to the CR, computer hackers threatening the imminent collapse of the power grid, dead Chinese piling up—it was a multiverse of terror spanning the state of Texas, and I was caught in the middle of it all.

"Raven, I..." I started, but her sudden gasp interrupted me, sharp and full of dread, as if bracing for the worst. What I had to say was not quite that, but I knew it was not what she wanted to hear either. "Tonight." I pressed my eyes closed, knowing what I was saying and what I would be able to do might not overlap. "Tonight's the soonest I can make it. Can you hold on until then?"

A symphony of crickets could have played an overture in the span of time between my question and her answer. With each passing second, the silence pressed down harder, the weight on my shoulders growing heavier with the unspoken tension. Then, her voice cut through with three words. Three fragile, devastating words that broke the silence and crushed my heart.

"I'm scared, Cass."

I pursed my lips and inhaled a deep breath, letting it out again before answering.

"It's going to be okay. You're safe. I will do everything I can to get to you as soon as possible."

"Tonight, Cass. You just said, tonight."

"Yes, Little Bird. Tonight."

"Promise?" she whispered.

"Promise," I said, silently praying it was one promise I could keep. "Rave, I gotta go. I've got something going here I have to finish up. Call if you need me. I will answer, no matter what." I paused, waiting for her reply, hoping for a sound of acceptance or acknowledgment that I was doing the best I could.

"Okay, Cass," she said as trembles returned to her voice.

"I love you, Raven."

The line clicked, dropping dead without another word spoken between us.

I wiped my mouth, concern twisting into resolve. My mind raced, sorting through how I would get home to Raven with Houston unraveling around me. I fired up the truck's engine and headed for the highway, knowing I had to find a way.

CHAPTER FORTY-THREE

29.71028° N, 95.64308° W

"We should wait until it is dark. We risk too much going in now," Líng Líng said, her sharp eyes fixed on the Barker Substation from inside the van. The faint hum of highway traffic outside where unassuming motorists went about their day unaware of the danger lurking nearby did not shake her focus. Across the road, the small industrial complex sat, a squat and unassuming structure that housed the heart of their mission.

The substation was small, but critical, housing an RTU that linked every grid line from Houston to the Gulf Coast. It was a weak point in an otherwise formidable chain.

Miào Wén-Kē sat behind the wheel, rolling his neck until a sharp crack broke the silence. He looked ready, his fingers twitching as if already picturing the path they'd take.

"It must be now," he said. "If the intel Zhàn Huǒ gathered is accurate, there will be only one man in our way." He twisted his head toward her, sliding his sunglasses down his nose to meet her eyes with a piercing gaze. "He will not be a problem that you cannot handle."

Líng Líng exhaled through her nose, unimpressed. "And you are sure that when I patch into this RTU, I will have access to the entire system?"

"Yes." Miào Wén-Kē's voice was calm, his confidence unwavering. "The grid is centralized. Once you're in, it's all open."

Líng Líng's brows furrowed as she considered his words. She shook her head, her lips pressing into a thin, disapproving line. "Why would they design it this way?" Her tone was incredulous as she gestured toward the substation with a small motion of her chin. "To place such a critical access point here? Security is practically nonexistent."

Miào Wén-Kē leaned forward, resting his forearms on the steering wheel as he scrutinized their target.

"Americans think their technology is invincible," he said. "They believe complexity makes them untouchable. Layers of systems, layers of arrogance."

"Arrogance," Líng Líng repeated, her voice cold, almost mocking. She leaned back in her seat, arms crossed as her gaze shifted from the building to her comrade. "This is more than arrogance. It's incompetence."

"It is their way," Miào Wén-Kē said with a faint shrug. "Efficiency, ease of maintenance, cost-cutting. They prize convenience over caution. They've done this to themselves."

"Americans," she muttered, shaking her head. "They build fortresses with walls that reach the heavens, but the doors? They leave those unlocked."

Miào Wén-Kē smirked at the remark but said nothing. The silence in the van deepened, charged with the inevitability of what came next. Both of them waited, poised, for their moment to strike.

CHAPTER FORTY-FOUR

THE FLYING H, WEST TEXAS

The sun was still low in the sky, its bright beams casting a warm, golden hue that emblazoned the land and the buildings with a fine radiant crest. But just beyond those gilded edges, darkened voids filled the empty spaces where light had yet to touch. Shadows stretched long and deep, swallowing the recesses of the buildings and pooling in the dank crypt that was the Flying H barn.

Waiting was not in Flint's nature, but he had no other choice and was under strict instruction not to touch or even approach the bodies. With a hand propped on the open barn door, he looked upon the horrible scene better suited for a demented Wes Craven movie, a lump growing in his throat.

He liked Floyd Huckabee about as much as a Charbray bull hated wearing a flank strap, but like that bull, he would never wish him dead. Huckabee had been owner of the Flying H since Flint first began working for Stewart Callahan at the CR. He had spent a lifetime tolerating the man, never finding a reason nor a need to think anything further of him, but always knowing him as a man with a leathery visage and a bravado that seemed to stretch higher than the brim of his hat.

A cool breeze from the storm overnight drifted into the barn, its faint wafts nudging the hanging bodies into a slow, macabre dance on their ropes. He looked again at the first hanging man he had discovered, then let his gaze roam to the next, and the next. In the waning light, it grew harder to distinguish who was who among them. He cast a quick glance over his shoulder toward the Flying H's gravel drive, then leaned into the light wind, straining to catch any sound of approaching emergency vehicles. Both checks came up empty.

"Fuck it," he said to himself, wanting to see who each of the victims were.

He alternated between looking ahead and glancing at the ground, careful not to disturb any footprints or marking left during the deadly, near-ritualistic executions. The growing stench of blood and old hay filled his lungs as he moved deeper into the barn. Each man hung the same way—hands bound behind his back, ankles exposed and feet bare, both looped together to hang in an awkward, inverted position. As he took in each man one by one, the lump in his throat dissolved, replaced by a burning fury that felt as though it could erupt as fire if he opened his mouth.

"Don't know ya, friend. Ain't an ending fit fer a cowboy!"

He moved on to the next, recognizing this man right away.

"Damn, Harv! Sons a bitches got you, too."

Harvey Oglethorp's body rotated like a worm at the end of a hook, except there was one thing different about the way he had met his end. Walking up on the body, Flint had not noticed until standing just before Harv that his eyes had been gouged out, his raw, empty sockets staring ahead, yet blind to the world. Flint shuddered at the sight.

"Sure as hell hope they did that...after," he said, shaking his head.

There was one more body dead ahead. One more that needed to be identified. It hung in the deepest part of the barn, farthest from the door, cloaked in significant shadow that made it nearly impossible to see from where Flint stood with Harv. But he knew who it was, who it had to be. Still, despite everything his gut screamed at him, and against Deputy Bostwick's explicit instructions, Flint stepped forward, closing the distance to the final hanging man.

Each breath felt like Flint was sucking air through a straw, every exhale a forced effort. His heart pounded, knowing what he was about to see, yet he could not resist the pull of the dead man's presence, drawing him closer with every step. His eyes slowly adjusted to the dark, new details emerging, new horrors unveiling themselves. The lump that had faded now returned, not as a precursor to emotion but as a mental dam, holding back the rising wave of his stomach threatened to retch.

Flint's steps shortened, his heels dragging the final few feet. The limp body looked small like a child, but its weathered skin that showed around the bindings spoke of aged years and toil from long days on the range. A belt and buckle were slung on the barn floor, its discarded leather coil and brass craftmanship stained with sprays of blackened blood. His ankles looked the same as the others— scarred, abraded, raw, and bound, as were his wrist, but like the first man, he had been made to suffer further torture to his feet. They were burned, blackened at the heels, with bone exposed where the pads should have been, leading up to his charred toes. His left hand curled in a bony fist, clenched around a small golden pinky ring still fixed on his finger.

The man hanging before him had every attribute of Floyd Huckabee, enough for a positive identification, except for one thing. His head was missing.

"That you, Flint?" a low voice murmured from behind.

Flint whirled around to see the figure of a man standing in the open barn door. He wore a brown duster over a plain pearl-button shirt, jeans, and boots. A rodeo buckle fastened at his waist struggled to contain the forgotten gut of a cowboy who had long since left the range behind.

"Greaser?" Flint replied.

"A-yuh, it's me."

Retracing his steps, Flint walked back to the open door where Greaser MacFarland stood. He offered him a hand, and they shook.

"Haven't seen er heard from ya in ages. Yer callin' 'bout Ol' Huckabee near kicked the chair out from under me," Greaser said.

"It's a goddamn crime, Greaser. Ain't none of these men deserve what they got. Not Harv, not Huckabee. None of 'em."

Greaser leaned to one side, taking in the scene.

"Which one is he?"

"Huckabee?"

Greaser nodded. "A-yuh."

"Last one in. What's left of 'im anyways."

The faint wail of sirens filtered onto the ranch, growing louder as they sped closer.

"Before, on the phone," Flint said, leaving his words hanging. He locked eyes with Greaser, expecting some sort of reply. When none was given, Flint finished the question, his voice raised and demanding answers. "Ya said ya'd git back ta me."

Greaser turned his head and spat a string of tobacco juice into a swatch of hay.

"I'm here, ain't I?"

"Okay. Yer here, but fer what good? Come ta gawk at the slain body of a longtime local, or do ya have anythin' ta offer. I said it b'fore, I know ya got ties over'n the other side. If anyone can find out somethin', it's you."

Sirens wailed as they approached the entrance to the Flying H, their mournful song no promise of safety, but a warning of reckoning.

"Ya ain't wrong," Greaser said, looking over his shoulder as the first emergency vehicle came into view. "I'll put some feelers out, but I'm guessin' by the looks of things, we both already have an idea who ta blame."

Flint nodded as he stepped aside, gesturing to the lead patrol unit where the trouble was located. The siren cut off as the car rolled past and parked in front of the barn, its strobes still spinning. Red and blue lights poured through the open doorway, flooding the barn's interior. From where Flint and Greaser stood, the barn looked like a gruesome rave—bodies swaying in the dark as red and blue lights pulsed through the shadows.

CHAPTER FORTY-FIVE

NEWGULF POWER SUBSTATION, NEWGULF, TEXAS

Scoots jumped out of the car, waving his hands wildly in a futile attempt to divert the swirling dust cloud his arrival had kicked up. The gravel lot outside the substation offered no reprieve, and the haze began settling over his car like an unwelcome guest. Ray wobbled to his feet, steadied himself, and smirked as he watched frustration bloom on Scoots's face when his efforts failed. With a groan, Scoots ran his fingers through his hair, glaring at the fine layer of dust now clinging to his paint as though it had personally insulted him.

"Why the long face, hot shot? It's not like it won't wash off."

Ray slid a finger along the hood drawing the words *wash me* in the powdery grime.

"Whoa! Stop. You're gonna scratch the paint."

Ray looked up, dumbfounded. "What? My finger ain't made of steel wool."

Scoots pushed in front of Ray, leaned over to inspect the fresh graffiti on his hood, and blew a puff of air across the surface.

"This is a matte-based paint. Super expensive. Super sensitive. I use special microfiber clothes to wash this baby." He stood and faced Ray. "Please, just leave it alone."

Ray looked down at Scoots, his lip curled in bemusement.

"Fine. Keep the genius busy. Keep the genius happy. Seems to be my job today." Ray started walking to the entrance gate. "Come on, genius. A little farther and we could have parked inside."

Scoots grabbed his bag from the trunk and followed, casting pitiful glances over his shoulder at the car, as if bidding farewell to its once-spotless glory.

After a gruff back-and-forth over the intercom and a quick flash of Ray's badge to a small security camera, the gate buzzed open, and they were allowed inside the perimeter. No sooner had the gate clanged shut behind them than Ray's old buddy, Newgulf Substation supervisor Clyde Morrell, marched over to meet them.

"Something I can do for you, detective? I thought we had wrapped everything up yesterday?"

"Aw, come on, Clyde. I missed you, too," Ray said, dripping with sarcasm. "Look, the kid needs access to an RTU."

Morrell huffed. "That's funny. I thought you just said I should allow a strange kid who has no credentials access to one of my remote terminal units? You drove all the way out here for that?" He sized up Scoots. "You're both out of luck."

"Clyde," Ray said, doing his best to keep his cool. Under the circumstances—and the trajectory his life was taking at the moment—that lasted for a count of two. He stepped close to the substation supervisor, drawing the attention of two other workers making repairs across the complex. Scoots noticed the men approaching, one carrying a large spud wrench.

"Fellas," Scoots tried to intervene, but his words faltered as he caught himself staring. It was not the size of the men or the large wrench that unnerved him, it was the pointed end at the tool's base. The thing looked less like it belonged to a repair kit and more like it was made for killing vampires. "Hold on. Mr. Morrell, you're right. I don't have credentials like Detective Tucker does, but what I do possess is of much greater importance."

Morrell spoke without backing down from Ray.

"Spill it, kid. You've got about ten seconds."

Scoots straightened his shoulders, forcing a firm, calm voice. "You're right, Mr. Morrell. I don't carry a badge or a title, but I'm not here to waste your time either. Let me ask you something: how's the load balancing across your feeders been looking lately? You're running an RTU-based topology, I'd guess, probably an ABB or SEL platform, and if you've got intermittent faults or latency between your IEDs and the DNP3 master, that's something I can spot faster than most."

He gestured toward the equipment. "Take those capacitor banks, for instance. If your VAR compensation is out of sync with the grid's demands, you're risking voltage instability at your end nodes. And that's just the beginning. Fault isolation and restoration lag could cascade through your distribution network before you even know it."

Scoots glanced at the workers with the spud wrench, his voice unwavering. "You don't have to trust me, but when those relays start choking on misconfigured IEC 61850 schemes, or worse, harmonic distortion skews your current sensors, you'll want someone who knows what to look for. Someone like me."

He turned back to Clyde, lowering his tone slightly.

"You want me gone, fine. But if you've got a system that needs eyes on it, I've got the expertise to save you time and headaches."

Morrell spared a glance at Scoots, then nodded to Ray.

"Fancy, kid. So why is he here then?"

Scoots scratched the back of his neck, glancing briefly at Ray before turning back to Clyde. "Look, Mr. Morrell, the detective has his angle, and I have mine. I'm here because sometimes you need someone who knows how to talk to the machines when the humans can't."

He gestured toward the equipment. "Let's say, hypothetically, you had an anomaly in your power distribution. A relay tripping when it shouldn't or a breaker refusing to close. Maybe it's a software glitch, or maybe someone with sticky fingers found their way into the system. That's where I come in. I'm here to rule out the technical side so he can focus on his job."

Scoots met Clyde's eyes, his tone steady. "I don't ask questions about his work, and he doesn't tell me how to do mine. We're here to help, not step on toes. If you'd rather I not be here, fine. But when corporate comes calling, don't say I didn't warn you."

Morrell turned to Scoots, waving off the two men's advances.

"So, we have a problem out here that I am unaware of, and you're going to fix it, huh?"

Scoots looked around the complex. "Well, we didn't come out here for the scenery."

Morrell let out a long, exasperated sigh.

"What do you need from me again?"

"Two things. First, access," Scoots said, shooting Ray a sly wink.

"What's the second thing?" Morrell asked, sounding as if he were already regretting the question.

Ray stepped next to Scoots and answered for him.

"For you to stay the hell out of his way."

CHAPTER FORTY-SIX

29.71028° N, 95.64308° W

The city was alive, a living organism stretching out in all directions, engulfing everything within its reach, each vacuole a separate ethnic enclave or high-tension business center. Poverty did not discriminate, but the rock walls surrounding the many gated communities embodied that very sentiment of separation between wealth and welfare. Empty warehouses and crowded apartment complexes festered in the shadows of corporate industry, their downtown cityscape reaching the sky, disappearing into the mix of thick fog and smog as if lingering in the excretion of the very lives that struggled at their doorstep, yet all remained interconnected. The city, the American city, was, to Miào Wén-Kē and his superiors, a place that required a crushing blow, whether its population liked it or not. A dip into darker times, where the lowly and the rich would face off in a struggle for survival, drew nearer as foreign shadows approached.

Miào Wén-Kē and Líng Líng stepped out of the van, collected their matching leather satchels, the ERCOT initialism branded across the outer flap, and donned white hard hats and hi-vis vests. Miào Wén-Kē wore black chinos, Wolf & Shepherd shoes to match, a minimalistic black leather belt, a gray Carhart FRC button-down, and sunglasses. Líng Líng owned her subordinate role, dressed in functional Bulwark coveralls and high-laced Westco Highliners. The name Barbara Wu was embroidered in white threading over her left chest. Below the name was the ERCOT logo, a stylized graphic resembling Texas with a symbolic wave cutting through its middle, a representation of constant and reliable electronic flow made available across the state.

With practiced ease, they made their way to the Barker Substation security gate, walking side by side, their every movement an effortless display of confidence and poise.

Stopping at the gate, Miào Wén-Kē tapped the call button on the gate intercom affixed to a steel column to the left of its hinges and waited. His eyes shifted behind his sunglasses, surveying the switchyard, the control housing structures, the exterior doors of the operations building, and the perimeter fencing. Two dust-covered work trucks sat parked next to one another along the outer rim of the substation's lot. Suppressing a flicker of amusement, he shook his head when he noticed the dangling wires and the empty cradle meant for a missing security camera.

"A fortress with no eyes to guard it," he whispered.

Líng Líng remained emotionless, her face blank with indifference, but a subtle shift in her gaze and a slight nod of her head communicated her agreement.

When no one answered his call, Miào Wén-Kē pressed the call box button again, feigning impatience. As he reached to press the button a third time, a hollowed scratch followed a nasally voice echoed over the speaker.

"This is Jimmy Dikes."

An airy sound remained on the open line.

"Mr. Dikes," Miào Wén-Kē replied, his English perfect, his accent slightly Bostonian. "You're speaking with Daniel Wu, South Zone PGI. My colleague and I are here for inspections."

A new voice murmured in the background, then Jimmy Dikes came back on the line.

"What'd you say your name was again?"

Miào Wén-Kē sighed, his frustration cutting through the airwaves. "Daniel Wu." He spoke each name clearly. "Power...Grid...Inspector."

More murmuring, then Jimmy responded. "Thought you fellas came out last week."

Miào Wén-Kē shared a glance with Líng Líng before answering.

"Yep, you're right about that. Friesenhan and McCormick, right? I'm here now to follow up on a problem with their paperwork. You mind clicking the lock?"

"You know those two?" Jimmy asked.

"Mr. Dikes, I know them by name and by their lack of detail in what's become a series of shortcomings within their reports. They're about to be placed under review by the Superintendent of Power Grid Operations. Should I recommend your name be added to the list for noncompliance?"

The line paused. The lock clicked.

"I'll meet you," Jimmy said, his voice agitated.

The constant, vibrating hum from the power lines tickled the senses. A faint scent of ozone bit each breath like No-see-ums hovering, irritating, their swarm an unrelenting nuisance.

Miào Wén-Kē led the way, opting to bypass the operations building and headed straight for the row of control housing units buried within the switchyard. Leaning on the intel he and Zhàn Huǒ had collected, studied, and memorized, paved the way for expediency and credibility. At the halfway point, hurried footsteps approached from behind.

"Wait up, there Mr. Wu."

Miào Wén-Kē and Líng Líng stopped and turned around. The two studied the man intently, Miào Wén-Kē removing his sunglasses and narrowing his eyes, making it clear that he was being carefully appraised. Sweat trickled down the man's face beneath his blue hard hat. Dark patches of perspiration soiled his armpits, and he wore the sleeves of his shirt rolled over the elbows. Blue jeans and lineman's boots, both scuffed and in need of washing, completed the man's rough appearance.

"You must be Jimmy Dikes?" Miào Wén-Kē said.

"I am." Jimmy stopped, placing his hand on his hips, his body language betraying both uncertainty and agitation. "Your intent is all well and good, but I'm going to need to see some identification."

The two Chinese operatives reached into their pockets and produced viable ID cards and handed them over. Jimmy looked at both cards, then glanced at Miào Wén-Kē and Líng Líng. After a moment of silent scrutiny, he returned their identification.

"Daniel Wu. Barbara Wu. You two married?"

"Woo is a very common Korean name, but we are definitely *not* married. Are you married, Mr. Dikes?" Líng Líng replied, her lips curling into a seductive tease, her English practiced and perfect, her tone rich and deliberate.

"No ma'am, I'm not."

Miào Wén-Kē cleared his throat, drawing Jimmy's attention, then locked eyes with him. "We have a lot on our slate, and two more stops before we can call it a day.

Let's not waste any more time. I believe we are headed in the right direction for VoltGuard-RTU-3, are we not."

Jimmy dropped his hands from his hips, shifting his weight as he gestured to the control housing unit furthest from them.

"You are. It's the last one—"

"In the line," Líng Líng interrupted. She squinted, puffed her cheeks, and let a mischievous look play at the corners of her lips, just enough to stir Jimmy's imagination and keep him off guard.

"That's right," he said.

"Will you be joining us, Jimmy?" Líng Líng asked, her false eyes hopeful.

Miào Wén-Kē slid on his sunglasses.

Drawn into her trance, Jimmy contemplated the moment.

"If you must know what we are inspecting," Miào Wén-Kē began, his tone clipped. "Join Barbara at the RTU. She will explain everything in detail. I will head into operations and begin reviewing system performance reports, maintenance records, and incident logs." He turned to Líng Líng. "Run your list: check the RTU's firmware version, run diagnostics on its input/output channels, and inspect the redundancy systems. Let me know immediately if there are any issues." Switching back to Jimmy. "I'll need full cooperation from your man inside. Will that be a problem?"

Distracted by Líng Líng's quiet intensity, Jimmy shook his head, forcing a grin. "Nah. Edgar's a teddy bear. You'll see."

Miào Wén-Kē rolled his eyes behind his shades, a mental tip of the hat to *his* lover. Líng Líng was skilled in more ways than one and had the goods to back it up.

"Good," he said, turning and heading back as he answered.

Jimmy watched him walk away, then returned his gaze and childish grin to Barbara Wu, his faculties swirling into a professional-personal gray area.

"Well," he said. "I guess it's just you and me?"

Líng Líng formed her best Barbara Wu smile, a curl of the lips, a slight scrunching of her cheeks, a distant, vulnerable pool shimmering in her eyes. "It's better this way. I don't like when I have too many eyes looking over my shoulder."

She turned and walked, swaying her hips just enough to draw attention, her face wiped clean except for a calculated smirk and subtle arch of her eyebrow.

CHAPTER FORTY-SEVEN

Meandering through side streets to skirt the dwindling flow of harried morning commuters, I wrestled with my promise to Raven: Come home tonight. My affordable time in Houston was razor-thin, slipping through my fingers with every mile, and yet my direction was in limbo. Juggling my family's needs with the demands of my role on TITON, the *Texas Intelligence and Tactical Operations Network*, had become a delicate act. This time the stakes were unbearably higher. But higher for whom? Deep down, I knew that there was only one choice.

Next move, Cass. Work the problem.

I pulled into the parking lot of a retro-style Whataburger, its tall A-frame stretching stripes of white and orange to a sharp, skyward peak. The outside seating area was empty, but through the bay windows, I spotted a small flock of older men, some with ruffled ball caps, others sporting Vitalis-slick combovers. A few wore overalls; others leaned back in weathered denim or canvas jackets. This Texas original was a morning haven for seniors to trade stories and sip black coffee, much like my grandfathers had done at the soda fountain or pharmacy counter back in the day.

Walking inside, I stepped to the counter and ordered as if I were a golden-ager late to the party.

"One coffee, please. Black."

The young girl behind the counter smiled and handed me a cup as I paid.

"You're not one of my regulars," she said, her teenage charm shining through.

"Nope," I said. "Just needed a jolt of caffeine."

"I know what you mean, mister."

I smiled at her. "Call me Cass."

The coffee station stood on the outskirts of the cluster of old-timers. Their conversations drifted my way, a chaotic blend of words, punctuated by arguments over politics. It reminded me of one of Raven's elementary classrooms, where no one truly listened, each voice jock-eying to juggle which debate they wanted to join next.

I filled my Styrofoam cup, careful to avoid eye contact with any of them, knowing it could suck me into their conversational black hole. On any other day, I would have loved to sit and listen. Turning toward the exit, I froze when I heard a voice call out from behind.

"Mornin' young man."

My shoulders slumped as I let out a sigh, bracing myself before turning around to face my caller. A large man stood behind me, his overalls stretched taut over a faded Buc-ee's T-shirt, a red MAGA hat sitting slightly askew on his head. White stubble poked from his chin. The chatter of the group calmed as all eyes settled on me.

"Good morning, sir."

A welcomed grin escaped his lips revealing a line of

discolored dentures glued to his upper gum line. No telling where the bottom half was.

"Care to set a spell? We've plenty of room," he said, gesturing to an open spot at his table.

The men tilted their heads in unison, like a parliament of wise owls, silently approving the invitation.

I took a moment to regard them, tipping my steaming coffee in acknowledgment. Each seemed hopeful I would accept.

Eyeing the bunch, I relished the history woven into each of their lives. Veteran hats perched atop heads. Forearms etched with faded tattoos. Shining wedding bands wrapped some fingers, while pale scars circled others—marks of love once worn and lost. Their bony hands and weathered faces spoke volumes without the need for words.

These men bore wrinkles like clutches of time, each fold a pocket where stories had been tucked away, waiting for days like today to unfold.

"I appreciate it, folks. Just can't today."

A murmur of understanding swept through them. As I turned to go, one man from the bunch spoke up, his voice sage and deliberate, drawing my attention while gathering the quiet respect of those around him.

"Don't let life pass you by, son. You've too much to lose if you don't pay attention to what matters most."

He gave a knowing wink, then raised the ceramic cup in front of him, a subtle toast to my presence, his words landing with the weight of hard-earned wisdom. The advice, simple as it was, cut straight to my core.

I swallowed hard, exiting the restaurant to the returning banter of gentle conversations and timeless friendships. Resting my cup on the hood of the truck, I pulled out my cell phone, remembering I had missed a call and a text from Dr. Frannie. I scrolled to the message and read it.

5:57 A.M.

Dr. Frannie: Examination almost complete.
Waiting on skin sample comparisons and
confirmation of preliminary DNA analysis.
Call you when I know more.

Instead of replying to the text, I tapped her profile picture at the top of the thread and called her back. I stole a quick sip from my cup before she answered.

"Cass. It's about time, buddy." Frannie's voice was ragged, another soldier putting in the extra hours on my behalf.

"Good morning to you, too," I said.

"And it's going to get better," she said, the seriousness in her voice grounding me. "But you may not agree. You sitting down?"

CHAPTER FORTY-EIGHT

29.71028° N, 95.64308° W

Miào Wén-Kē removed his sunglasses as he stepped into the operations room, the quiet drone of cooling fans and distant electrical hum filling the space. Industrial lighting flickered, casting sharp reflections on the sleek rows of control panels. Monitors stretched across a central console, each screen alive with grids of fluctuating data: voltage levels, frequency readouts, and real-time generator performance graphs. To his left, a wall-mounted video display cycled through security feeds and grid flow diagrams, the images sharp but slightly muted by years of continuous use. One feed showed only static. *The security entrance*, Miào Wén-Kē thought.

Against the far wall, a rack of servers blinked methodically, their bundled cables neatly secured with color-coded ties. Below the panels, an alarm indicator panel stood silent, save for a single amber light blinking in steady rhythm, marking a minor fault waiting for acknowledgment.

The break area to the side seemed almost out of place in the otherwise sterile environment. A battered mini-fridge bowed under the weight of an aging microwave, its handle worn to the plastic core. Nearby, a folding table held a coffee machine that burbled, the smell of burned coffee lingering in the air. An old leather couch sagged against the wall, its armrests polished smooth from years of use. Sitting in the center of the couch, eyes fixed and judging Miào Wén-Kē, sat Jimmy's teddy bear of a man.

A thin line of smoke spiraled above his bald head like a lazy lasso loop. Bulging muscles stretched the short sleeves of his shirt, a sharp contrast to the rounded swell of his gut challenging the limits of his grease-streaked coveralls.

"You the inspector?" the man said, his tone unwelcoming.

"I am."

"Got any ID?"

"I do."

Miào Wén-Kē produced the ID and held it out for the man to see.

"Can't see that from here. Why don't ya bring it on over."

"Sir, I believe you are stepping out of line. I might caution you to remember that I am…"

"Don't need no warnings. Not from you." The man stood up, his head reaching heights well over six feet tall. "I ain't never seen you before. What'd you say your name was?"

"We haven't gotten that far yet, but, since you asked, my name is Daniel Wu. I am a South Zone PGI," Miào Wén-Kē replied with calm detachment.

The man walked over, his arms swaying out as if he wore a jacket five sizes too large. He glared at Miào Wén-

Kē, then reached out and swiped the ID badge from his hand.

"I didn't catch your name."

"Edgar Tully."

"Ah, that's right. Now I remember. Jimmy mentioned you as a…well, he said you'd be in here and assured me that I would have your full cooperation."

Miào Wén-Kē slid his right hand into his satchel.

"Now," he said, his gaze returning to the consoles. "I can already see you have an alarm indicator triggered. Why has it yet to be addressed?"

"Ain't got to it yet," Edgar said, still inspecting the ID. "It's just a cautionary alert."

"I see, and I know." Miào Wén-Kē slowly pulled his hand out of the satchel, pausing beneath its leather flap. "You mind handing me my ID?"

Edgar sneered before thrusting the card toward him.

"Still, you don't look much like any inspector I've seen before."

Miào Wén-Kē reached out to take the ID with his left hand, but Edgar held tight to it.

"No?" Miào Wén-Kē smiled, his eyes hardening like water turning to ice. He shifted his weight, twisting his body to face Edgar. "You know, Edgar. Now that I think about it, you're right."

With a fluid slash, Miào Wén-Kē thrust his right hand, knifing Edgar twice in the chest and once across the throat before the hulking man even knew what had happened. Stepping back into a fighting stance, arms poised and fists ready to strike again, he dodged the initial burst of blood, but could not move quickly enough to avoid the subsequent crimson spray.

Edgar clutched at his throat with both hands, his fingers slipping and fumbling over the slick, pulsing gash. His eyes widened, panic coursing through him as the dark torrent drained his strength, each gurgling attempt to breathe a futile plea against the inevitable. His legs buckled, folding under him as he swayed like a ship battered in a storm, his balance lost to the betrayal of his failing body. His hands faltered, falling slack at his sides before he toppled forward, striking the floor with a lifeless, final thud. Like a beached whale stranded by the tide, his bulk lay still, soaking in the dark, viscous pool that spread beneath him.

Miào Wén-Kē circled his prey, twirling the knife between his fingers, taunting Edgar even in death as the blade sent blinding starbursts dancing on the walls and the floor. Completing a final pass, he leaned over and wiped the blade clean on the dead man's clothing.

"Jimmy was right. I see that I have your full cooperation after all."

Stepping over Edgar's broad corpse, he eased into a chair behind a monitor displaying real-time readouts: real-time voltage levels, load distribution, and power flow from the Barker Substation to various points south and east. His eyes tracked the streams of data scrolling across the screen.

"Now," he murmured, his voice low and secretive. He placed the blade on the keyboard in front of him and laced his fingers together. "It is up to you, Líng Líng. I am standing by."

CHAPTER FORTY-NINE

THE FLYING H RANCH, WEST TEXAS

Flint leaned against the tailgate of his truck watching deputies from the Brewster County Sheriff's Office roll out yards of yellow tape making the Flying H ranch a bona fide crime scene. Two DPS officers conversed with Deputy Bostwick. A pair of Border patrol agents camped out on the road in their vehicles SUVs but had not entered the property. Flint had no idea nor gave a rats ass what role each of the civil servants played. What he did care about was what any of them were going to do about what he, or rather, Charlotte, had discovered.

Charlotte, he thought. *Raven. They both must be scared out of their minds.*

He dug his cell phone from his pocket and keyed in Raven's number but hesitated before pressing send. What would he say? He had no good news to share. No words of comfort. That was Cass's job, but he was gone, again.

Flint stared at his phone, then slid it back into his rear pocket. Surveying the scene, he decided there was nothing more he could do there. Greaser had slipped away shortly after the first patrol unit arrived. And Boss had already taken his initial statement. Rumor filtered around the ranch yard that Sheriff Chance might make an appearance, but he was still pretty banged up after rolling his truck into a ditch. His people were here doing their jobs. His presence would only be important to the victims or survivors, but there were none except Charlotte and she was at the CR.

An unstable breeze zigzagged through the ranch, mixing cool and warm drafts with the smells of manure, stale hay, and decay. None of it was satisfying. He took off his hat and brushed it against his leg, then turned toward the front of the truck. As he reached for the handle, a voice called out to him.

"Flint. Hold up, there."

Deputy Bostwick had broken away from the DPS officers and was waving at Flint to attract his attention. Flint lowered his hand and returned to the rear of the truck.

"What's on yer mind, Boss?"

"You said that Charlotte is with Raven over at the CR, right?"

Flint nodded.

"Are they there alone?"

"The Six M crew are out on the range. Far as I know, the girls are still at the house. So, yeah. Probably alone." Boss shifted on her boots, her jaw tight. Flint straightened, his fists clenching as unease rippled up his spine. "Why?"

His voice dropped low and sharper than he intended, but if Boss had concerns, he wanted her to spill it, now.

Boss glanced back toward the barn where the DPS officers were still talking, then lowered her voice.

"It doesn't take a genius to know what happened here. This is retaliatory, probably because of Curly's shootout yesterday. If they knew to come here, it's not a stretch to think they might..."

Flint's stomach turned cold, the implications snapping into focus. He stepped in close, cutting her off. "What are you saying?"

Boss pressed her hands on his chest, edging him back, unafraid but very aware of Flint's inner fire. One errant spark would be enough to set him off.

"Let's not jump to conclusions."

"Yeah, sure," Flint muttered, already moving toward the driver's door. White knuckling the handle, he slung the door open and looked back. "You comin'?"

CHAPTER FIFTY

"Wuhan? As in where the China virus originated, Wuhan?"

I sat in my truck, hands clamped on the steering wheel like it was the only thing keeping me grounded. My eyes fixated on the center console as Dr. Frannie's voice crackled over the speakerphone. She sounded calm, clinical, and notably exhausted as if she had not just dropped a bombshell. But how much could she have learned from a couple of dead bodies? Turns out, plenty. More than I needed. More than I wanted to know.

"Everything lines up, as crazy as that sounds."

"You're sure. I mean, what is the margin for error in these kinds of tests? My experience with anything that calls itself *rapid* suggests a degree of..."

"Fallibility? First of all, Cass, you're not wrong, but the Rapid DNA analyzers used at the WTHIL are state of the art. At two hundred and fifty thousand a pop, they better be spot on with their analysis."

"Hold up. You've lost me already. And I thought *you* performed the tests? What is the WTHIL?"

"I ran most of them, Cass, but I had to farm a few out in order to dig deeper. Ever hear of Bode Technology or the University of North Texas Center for Human Identification?"

"Should I have?"

"Probably not." Frannie's voice softened. "The WTHIL is the West Texas Human Identification Lab. It's a much smaller operation whose primary function is identifying remains, reuniting families, and supporting law enforcement in human trafficking cases, but primarily, it employs a team of forensic experts and collaborates with international organizations to track missing children and verify kinship across borders. Let's just say I have...a connection there. It helped expedite the results."

I rolled my neck, each pop a reminder of the stress and age wearing on me.

"I've worked with them before. In fact, last month Sheriff Gilbert had me working on something for..."

"Let's stay on target, Frannie. I know you've had a long night, and I owe you a big one, but, so I am clear, run it all by me again."

"Okay, but you're getting only the bullets. I'm three Red Bulls in, and a sixteen-ounce Mocha Frappuccino is calling my name."

I glanced at what felt like my umpteenth empty cup tossed on the passenger side floor mat. "Fair enough. Hit me."

"All the bodies. The John Doe from Big Bend, Mr. Li from the raid at the Bar S, and the guy y'all are calling Dong—I still can't believe that one," she murmured, half to herself. "Anyway, they all have markers that place them within a region west of Wuhan, China. Their ages are within five years of one another."

"That doesn't sound random," I said, frowning.

"It's not," she said firmly. "The DNA tells us they're not related, but they lived together long enough to share a strain of dormant tuberculosis. LTBI, Latent Tuberculosis Infection, Mycobacterium tuberculosis. Specific to that region. They had to have been kept in close quarters for a significant time. My guess? A controlled, confined space."

"You can get all that from their DNA?" I said, my grip tightening on the wheel.

"Yep," Frannie said. "But wait, it gets better. I found traces of industrial solvents, lead, and flux residues on their hands and nails. Those particles can embed under the nails and in the skin for weeks if not scrubbed out thoroughly. It's consistent with soldering and cleaning high-tech electronic components. Not factory-line stuff, Cass—precision work."

"Seems like a shot in the dark. You sure?"

"Positive. This wasn't some random shop in the middle of nowhere. It screams specialized tech. Communications, surveillance, maybe even weapons systems. That's PLASSF territory."

Her words hit me like a concussion grenade, but the last detail made it feel like I had swallowed the blast whole. "You're saying these guys were—"

"PLASSF operatives," she confirmed. "Fucking China's People's Liberation Army Strategic Support Force. The radiation exposure sealed it for me. Prolonged non-ionizing radiation. DNA damage, thermal lesions. It's from working near high-frequency devices like radar or electronic warfare systems. It all ties back to a PLASSF facility."

"And the tattoos?" I asked. That was what started this whole mess.

"A red-inked bird above bamboo poles wrapped in razor wire," she said, recounting the details. "Wings spread wide, every feather detailed like it was etched by hand. The bird's beak curved down, eyes glaring. In its talons, a limp serpent. Dragon-like. Hairy chin, big nostrils, horns, the works."

"I'm familiar," I muttered, the image forever burned into my mind.

"It's not just art, Cass. It's symbolic. The bird represents a predator. The razor wire, confinement. And the dragon? That's no coincidence. It's a broken serpent, stripped of its power. It represents the United States. This was their badge. Their oath. They were part of a unified cell, and their mission was overseas operations. They were targeting us."

"That's an impressive interpretation, Frannie, but I don't think—"

"Hang on," she interrupted. "Maybe this will prove my point."

My cell pinged with an incoming text.

"Take a second and look that over."

The message had no script, just an attachment with a web address: *CipheredInk.onion.* I clicked the link and waited.

A solid black page burst onto my screen with a simple line of red text. ****Content on this site is unverified and considered dangerous. Access at your own risk.****

Beneath the warning was a solid green access button.

"You see it?" Frannie said.

"How the hell did you find this, Frannie?"

"Keep going," she urged. "You'll understand once you're inside."

I hesitated, then shook my head. Against my better judgment, I tapped the button. The screen went dark, then pixelated, resolving into a shadowy gray background filled with scattered images, cryptic text, and links. A bold header stretched across the top: *Every Mark Has a Meaning. Decode the Shadows.*

"This is some dark web shit, Frannie, but I don't have time to—"

"You see the search bar at the top right? Type in P-L-A-S-S-F."

I chewed on the inside of my mouth. "Yeah."

I typed in the letters, tapped the search button, and waited. The page shifted instantly, loading dozens of images of men, women, even children—some alive, others unmistakably dead. They all bore tattoos ranging from faint outlines to intricate, vivid designs. My eyes scanned the thumbnails until they froze on one image three rows down. A man stared back at me, his gaze so intense it felt like he could see through the screen.

I clicked the thumbnail, and the image expanded.

The whites of his eyes blazed, illuminated by a red glow reflecting from his retinas. His nostrils flared, his shirtless chest flexed, and his fingers curled before him like eagle talons. My breath hitched as I instinctively reached out, tracing the tattoo inked into his skin—a crimson bird perched above bamboo poles wrapped in razor wire.

"Son of a bitch."

The rest of the details were an exact match, almost to a T, with the tattoos inked on my dead Chinese corpses.

"You see, Cass. It's right there in front of you. I don't know how you do it, but you walked right into the lion's den again, my friend."

I exited the web page and placed my phone into its cradle on the dash. Leaning my head back against the headrest, I stroked my mouth with one hand.

"Cass?"

The weight of her findings pressed into my chest, stealing my breath.

"Cass," she snapped.

"So," I said, readjusting myself behind the steering wheel. "The bodies you have on ice, they weren't just bad guys. They were fucking Chinese operatives."

"Exactly. And whatever their mission was, it was worth killing to keep secret."

CHAPTER FIFTY-ONE

THE CR, WEST TEXAS

The roar of a one-and-a-half-ton diesel barreling down the gravel road at eighty-five miles an hour, the scream of sirens hot on its tail, and the thick plume of dust swirling like a jet wash behind the racing two vehicles formed a singular being, an unstoppable juggernaut where nothing could stand in its way. Flint took each curve as if on rails. Boss followed like a bloodhound locked onto a scent. Inside the truck, the phone rang and rang, but no one answered the call.

"Pick up, Raven. Pick up!"

When she did not answer, Flint called Cody's cell. He was out on the property with the rest of the Six M crew, unaware of the situation at the Flying H.

Cody answered after two rings.

"Yeah?"

"Get your asses back to the bunkhouse, pronto."

"Flint? What's—"

"Stop talking and start moving!"

Flint disconnected the call and pressed on until,

edging out of the landscape, the CR emerged in the distance. A mile became a thousand yards in a blink, then five hundred, the entrance fast approaching, but Flint did not slow down. His determination battled his imagination, which toyed with his emotions. At twenty yards, he finally let off the accelerator, coasting like a speeding train along the tracks. At the last possible second, he jammed the brakes and cut hard on the wheel, fishtailing around until the grille guard faced the ranch, its iron teeth pronounced and hungry. With a thunderous growl, the truck flew under the entryway arch and over the cattle guard before sliding to a stop in the center of the yard.

With the engine idling, panting, seething, Flint was out the door and running to the house as Boss's patrol unit skidded to a stop behind him. Hopping out, she yelled after him.

"Cover yourself!"

Flint heard her but was too focused on finding Raven and Charlotte to care. He leaped onto the porch. On a normal day, he would remove his hat and knock before entering the house, but today he all but kicked the door down. The *fwap* of the screen followed by a wooden *thud* of the door swinging open was startling, but Flint did not flinch. He surged into the Callahan's house, head on a swivel, heart racing.

"Raven. Charlotte."

He moved through the living room darting in and out of the kitchen. Empty. Boss met him at the door as he rushed by and down the hall to the bedrooms.

"Miguel. Raven. Anybody?" she asked.

Pounding steps carried him back to the front door, his face blank and unknowing.

"The house is empty," he said.

In that single moment, an image flashed in his mind. The same thought must have crossed Boss's as well, because their expressions hardened as they spoke in unison. "The barn."

Boss whirled around and took off with gun drawn. Flint sprinted past her, headed straight for the barn door.

Ropes, bodies hanging, blood, oh so much blood, and darkness. Those were what stabbed at his thoughts, a replay of what he had uncovered at the Flying H, but superimposed with heightened imagery as if the nightmare bled over to the CR.

He dashed inside, the stale must of the barn wrapping around him like a suffocating blanket.

"Raven? Charlotte?"

The patter of soft feet, like a mouse scurrying along the wall, drew his attention to the stalls. When his eyes fell on Miguel running toward him, all smiles, with arms swinging to his side, Flint bent over, placing his hands on his knees to catch a moment's breath.

"Find 'em? Flint?"

Boss entered the barn, gun at the ready and eyes scanning.

"Flint! Flint! *¡Ven a ver!* Come see."

Miguel grabbed Flint's hand and tugged him toward the stalls. Boss saw and lowered her gun, following two steps behind.

"*¿Qué es, Miguel?*" Flint said, looking down at the smaller wrangler.

Instead of answering, Miguel let go of Flint and scurried ahead, climbing the planks until he see-sawed over the top and into the nearest stall.

"Miguel?" Flint's pounding heart slowed a beat, but he remained on edge.

Boss fell in line with him as they closed the final steps to the point Miguel disappeared. Together, they both looked over the top slat and immediately understood. On the floor, legs and feet nestled into a bed of hay, Miguel sat and gently stroked the nose of the dog Raven had saved. Raven leaned against the far wall with Charlotte in her arms.

Relief washed over Flint. Boss holstered her weapon.

"Ya okay?" Flint said, nudging his chin at her.

"As well as can be, Flint."

"What about…" Flint shifted his gaze to Charlotte.

"Overwhelmed. I don't know how, but she's asleep. Cried her eyes out. Scared. In shock. Just…overwhelmed." Raven glanced at Boss. "Hey, Marie."

Deputy Marie Bostwick, like the rest of the department, had become like family to Raven and Cass. Boss smiled but kept her professional composure iced over her personal feelings.

"Is there something going on besides…" Raven tilted her head toward Charlotte and mouthed, "The Flying H?" Her gaze shifted between Flint and Boss. "The way y'all rushed in here, it seemed like maybe there was."

"No," Boss said, glancing at Flint. "Just wanted to make sure everyone out here was safe. Sorry if we caused any alarm. Got a little nervous when no one answered the door at the house." She walked through the stall door and took a knee next to Miguel near the dog. "But it looks like the CR gang is all together."

"Mostly," Raven replied.

"Cass still over in Houston?"

"Yes, but he said was coming home tonight."

A stampede of hooves reverberated from the yard, drawing Flint's attention. He turned, then spoke over his shoulder.

"Be right back."

Walking to the side door, Flint peered into the yard and saw the Six M crew securing their horses to posts around the corral. Cody and Gilly were the first ones to see Flint and came rushing over.

"Why all the fuss, Flint?" Cody said.

Flint replied, "You notice anythin' strange out there this mornin'?"

"What are you talkin' about, Flint?" Gilly asked. "Ain't nuthin' out there 'cept dust 'n rocks n' cattle."

He shot Gilly a piercing glare, sharper than she deserved, but after all he had been through this morning, a wisp of tension was bound to slip out.

"I know what's out there, Gilly. Floyd Huckabee, Harvey Ogelthorp, and two others over at the Flyin' H were killed last night."

"Killed? How?" Gilly asked.

"There ain't any words I care ta use ta describe it. They're dead, an' that's that."

"Ho-lee shit," Cody said, turning around and waving the rest of his crew over. "Pedro. Jesse. Hustle over."

Flint continued. "I'll ask again. See anythin' out of the ordinary? Activity near the river. Mexicans where they shouldn't be. Tracks ya don't recognize. Missin' cattle. Anythin' ya can think of."

Murmured answers fell and heads shook.

"Nothin' like that, Flint," Cody said.

"There was one thing," Jesse added. "Don't know if'n it means much. Ain't what ya'd call abnormal, but..."

"For Christ's sake, spit it out, Jesse," Flint said impatiently.

"Well. Buzzards."

Flint arched his eyebrows, teetering on losing his temper but a gut feeling held him in check for the moment.

"Buzzards," he echoed.

All eyes were on Jesse now.

"Yep, a whole mess of 'em flyin' around, circlin' over somethin' just southwest of here."

"Ya sure about that? What ya saw. Where ya saw it?"

"Clear as day, Flint," Jesse replied, nodding with certainty.

"Shit." Flint spun, stalked back to the barn, and leaned through the doorway. "Hey, Boss?" He kept his voice low and soft, but the acoustics in the barn carried it like a ripple along the Whispering Wall in Williamstown, Australia.

When Boss emerged from the stall, Flint waved her over. Turning around, Flint looked to the sky, searching the blue expanse, though what he had hoped to see was too far away.

"What is it, Flint?"

Pinching his lips to one side and shaking his head, he turned around.

"I know what's hangin' inside Huckabee's barn. And I know what's missin'."

Boss's face tightened.

"Dammit, Levi! I told you to stay out of there."

Boss looked past Flint, catching wandering eyes from the Six M crew. Shifting her weight to the balls of her feet, she controlled her rising frustration.

"Yeah, ya did. And I didn't. That ain't the point."

"Get to it, then."

Flashes from the barn played in Flint's mind like black-and-white photo clippings scattered across a blood-stained table until one picture stood out, glowing white before fading, dissolving as though it had never existed. He looked over his shoulder, then turned toward the direction of his thought.

"I know where Floyd Huckabee's head is."

CHAPTER FIFTY-TWO

29.71028° N, 95.64308° W

Líng Líng bent over, placing her bag on the floor of the cramped service area inside the maintenance bay of VoltGuard-RTU-3. She rummaged through its contents, fully aware of the view she was offering Jimmy, who stood patiently behind her. Taking her time, she leaned over further, muttering softly to herself as she searched.

"I don't see it. Dang. Maybe in here."

Jimmy leaned to one side, eyes still fixed on her enticing curves, and spoke as if she had addressed him directly.

"Help you find something, Ms. Wu?"

Her face hidden from his view, Líng Líng smiled, flexing her cheeks beneath serpentine eyes. "You can call me Barbara, if you like."

Jimmy gulped. Never in his wildest imaginations did he picture being alone with a woman he considered to be as beautiful and exotic. He touched the end of his tongue to his lips, moistening the skin before speaking.

"Okay. Barbara." His tone dropped, her name spilling from his lips with unkempt desire. "What are you looking for?"

Jimmy stepped closer and leaned over, his hips brushing hers.

Líng Líng felt the rub. She leaned into it, nudging her hips just enough to press the seam of his pant leg against her. A soft breath escaped her lips.

"Ah, there it is," she said.

Jimmy smiled, convinced he was the cause of her delight. She, in turn, was most definitely the reason his stomach fluttered, the tight stretch in the crotch of his jeans revealing his reaction. She turned her head, her face inches from his.

"Guess we ought to get started."

Her scent was intoxicating, the gleam in her eyes hypnotic. Jimmy was already drawn to her, but now his whole being was captured as his mind spun fantasies of what the next few moments might bring. He was hooked, blinded by his delusions that things were about to turn steamy.

"Guess so," he said, heart throbbing.

Líng Líng closed her eyes and exhaled, the soft puff of her breath caressing Jimmy's cheek. When she opened them again, it was as if a predatory creature had awakened inside of her, darkening her eyes and crimping her face. Like a serpent poised to strike, she drew her hand from the bag, the glint of steel flashing in the dim light. In one swift, merciless motion, she plunged the stiletto dagger into Jimmy's left eye, rupturing it with a sickening pop and driving the razor-sharp blade deep into the delicate recesses of his brain.

There was no time for Jimmy to react, no voice with which to squeal. His body jolted as if struck with electricity, then crumpled to the floor, the weight and angle of his fall wrenching the blade from Líng Líng's hand. With a metallic clank, his forehead struck the ground, the hilt of the knife propping his head at an unnatural angle as dark fluid seeped from the wound. Convulsions rippled through his body, his arms and legs twitching erratically in the cramped maintenance bay.

Líng Líng had pivoted, dragging her bag clear of the falling man, and now stood over her victim. Her nostrils flared. Her breath came in sharp bursts. Her fingers tingled with an ecstasy known only to the truly vile in moments like this.

Reaching into the bag, she removed a small laptop, opened the lid, and powered it on. The hum of the machine joined a chorus of electronic *whirs* and *clicks*, finding its place among them as if it had arrived home, once and for all. Next, she retrieved a small canvas pouch containing a DB9 serial cable and plugged it into the RTU, the reassuring click a spotlight in the cacophony of orchestral diagnostic tones.

She focused on the laptop, its OLED screen emitting a glow that bathed her face with brilliant colors. The viciousness in her face softened, but a diabolical glare remained in her eyes. Inserting the free end of the DB9 cable into an open port on her computer, she keyed in a security code, accessing her device and prepared to exploit the RTU.

Her fingers flew over the keyboard, deploying malicious code to infiltrate the RTU's communication protocols, bypass its safeguards, and inject a virus upstream into the SCADA system. Lines of code streamed across the screen, each keystroke bringing her closer to breaching the critical infrastructure defenses. A warning icon flickered. Líng Líng smirked. This was child's play. Systematically, she hacked her way through the security, a mere ghost infiltrating the nerve center of the power grid.

CHAPTER FIFTY-THREE

NEWGULF POWER SUBSTATION, NEWGULF, TEXAS

Scoots surfed through code like a *kaha nalu* on Maui's west shores, his patch clean, his access to data unrestricted. Ray leaned against one of the massive tower stubs, the thick steel column embedded deep in the concrete foundation. He scrolled through apps on his phone, trying to ignore the constant buzzing in his ears. Across the complex, Newgulf Substation supervisor, David Morrell, watched the two through the bent and faded venetian blinds in the operations building. The slats cast jagged lines of shadow across his face, merging with the deep furrows of the scowl he wore.

Scoots hummed R.E.M.'s "It's the End of the World as We Know It" under his breath, his foot tapping to the rhythm in his head. Working in tandem with a favorite tune gave him a deeper sense of focus, stimulating the heightened creativity he only found when fully "in the zone."

Shifting from hums to words, Scoots keystroked further into the system as the song came to an end.

"...and I feel...shit!"

Scoots's voice carried, pulling Ray away from his phone.

"What is it?" Ray asked.

Scoots's eyes stayed glued to the screen, his fingers racing at binary speed. *Hammer. Scan. Process. Repeat.* Too fast to explain. Too advanced to comprehend.

When Scoots did not reply, Ray sauntered over, his feet dragging like a twelve-year-old trudging through the halls between middle school classes.

"You get shocked or something?"

Scoots keyed in the final line of code, tapped Enter, and stepped aside just as Ray stopped behind him.

"Well?" he said, impatience and boredom channeling through his tone.

Scoots whirled around, wide-eyed with tense determination. He ripped his cell phone from his pocket, placed a call, and held it out in front of him.

Ray frowned, but Scoots's agitated intensity had caught his full attention.

The line rang twice on speaker before it was answered.

"This is Callahan."

"Cass," Scoots blurted, his head leaning over the phone, his hand clutching its edges for dear life. "Someone is in the system. They're in right now. And they're close, real close." He spun around to look at his computer screen. "29.71028° N, 95.64308° W. I'll text you the coordinates, but Cass..."

Scoots paused, catching his breath as an airy hush fell over the call. He ran his fingers through his hair, then locked eyes with Ray.

"Cass, that's in Houston. They're in fucking West Houston!"

CHAPTER FIFTY-FOUR

HOUSTON, TEXAS

West Houston!

My mind spun. The northbound lanes of Eldridge Parkway stretched out before me like the halls of the Overlook Hotel, and suddenly, I was Danny peddling my tricycle as fast as my legs could pump. There was no end in sight as the hallway, the roadway grew longer before my eyes, twisting, contorting, changing with each curve, each intersection, each passing car whose horn blared louder and louder.

"Jackass!"

A man in a passing car stopped to lean out his window and yell, then threw a half empty milkshake at my driver's side door. I was halfway out the door when I realized I had come to a complete stop in the middle of the road.

My phone buzzed, announcing an incoming text. I pressed the gas and pulled to the outside lane where I rolled at low speeds and read the message.

10:53 A.M.

ScootsF: 29.71028° N, 95.64308° W

I pressed and held my finger over the coordinates, copied them, then switched to my maps app and pasted the numbers into the search bar. The screen began to load a map of the area around the pin from that location. I zoomed in, but the weak signal on my phone caused the image to vanish.

"Where the hell is a cell tower when you need one!"

I glanced out the window, as if scanning the horizon might magically produce a relay, transmitter, or booster—anything to improve the signal. I shook my hands in frustration, then stared back at the screen, my eyes boring into the tempered glass.

Then, as if my wish had been granted, the map reappeared. The image loaded strong and clear, ready to be manipulated in any direction. I zoomed in, closer to the red dot in the middle of my screen. Roadways sharpened. *Zoom.* Names of surrounding businesses came into view. *Zoom.* Details emerged. *Zoom.*

The red dot seemed to form crosshairs, pinpointing a plain-looking industrial complex. Towers, buildings, a gravel parking lot—each nondescript. It reminded me of military targets I'd seen on the news: laser-painted, distorted grayscale images captured through infrared technology.

And then it hit me.

Zoom.

The coordinates disappeared and the name of the facility, glowing in bold, yellow letters, shown plain as day.

The Barker Substation.

CHAPTER FIFTY-FIVE

THE CR, WEST TEXAS

The sun rose higher, warming the earth and drying the land, a cleansing for a day that needed it more than any other. Flint led the Six M men and Deputy Bostwick on horseback across the CR to the fence line where they had crossed onto the Flying H yesterday, just before the storm. The men were armed with rifles. Flint carried his Colt 1911. Boss stowed a shotgun in a saddle scabbard, her utility belt carrying enough ammunition for both her service pistol and the shotgun. From afar, they looked like a posse straight out of the old-west, riding the range on a manhunt with a show of firepower and grit that no one would stand in their way.

Boss rode Gilly's horse, as Flint had asked her to stay behind with Raven. The deputy was a natural in the saddle, returning to good form after many years of chasing down bad guys with 400 horses under the hood. Now she reverted to one, her experience as a teenage barrel racer paving the way for an easy ride.

As they approached the fence, the group fanned out, eyes scanning the horizon. Jesse hopped off his horse and cut a pass-through section of the fence with a quick snip of the barbwire.

"Ain't far. Ya can see the Flyin' H grove from here," Flint said.

Lost in the backdrop of rising cliffs across the Rio Grande, a small jumble of green stood out like an oasis against the desert's weathered face.

"I see it, Flint," Boss said.

Jesse walked back to his horse, sliding the fencing pliers he used to open the gap in the fence back into his saddlebag. "Look up," he said, lifting his chin to the sky.

Boss covered her brow with a flattened hand and looked. Circling over the patch of green was a kettle of vultures, their black forms like a swarm of tiny gnats against the pale sky. Looking away, Boss lowered her hand.

"Flint, I sure hope you're wrong about this."

Buzzards were nature's garbage men, tasked with cleaning up roadkill, the remains of animals taken down by predators, or the weaker ones felled by disease—or bullets. They were essential, but they did not discriminate, giving each corpse their full attention.

Flint turned in his saddle. "Me too, Boss."

Jesse mounted up and gave a ready nod. Flint whistled, and the others gathered around him.

"Listen up. Keep yer eyes peeled. Ain't sayin' were gonna find trouble, but it may be lookin' out fer us. Hear me?" Grunts and nods of agreement filtered through the bunch. "Once we're off these horses, ya pay attention ta anythin' Deputy Bostwick tells ya."

Flint glanced at Boss, giving her the floor.

"Main thing," she said, her voice firm like a seasoned boss on a cattle drive. "If you see something out of place, leave it alone. Don't approach. Don't touch. Call me over and we'll go on from there."

"You mean like..."

Pedro's voice trailed off before he finished, his eyes bulging as he took a breath to quell his thoughts.

"Exactly, Pedro," Boss said. She pitched back to Flint. "Get us there."

Without another word, Flint leaned forward and nudged his horse's sides, and the posse was off again.

Hooves in sync, heads bobbing, and manes flowing in rhythm of their cross-country trek, they approached the grove. Its green, lush leaves looked like fancy sequins draped on the cottonwood branches, but scattered among the tangles, hungry vultures perched like bruises on the landscape.

More vultures soared overhead, their wings extended and still, gliding on unseen currents. For such ugly birds, they looked graceful, as if floating in the sky, but that was the only quality ever worthy of praise.

Flint slowed their pace and, using hand signals, spread the group out to begin searching the area beneath the blackened swirl.

The Six M crew were expert ranch hands, forged from hardened callouses and burned muscle, searing sun, and frigid cold. They had witnessed most everything that a rancher might see: the miracles of birth, the devastation of death, and the ruin of a man when he chose to give up his spurs, or worse, watch them be hung out to dry. The days were long and demanding, but in their eyes, that was what made it all worthwhile. Ranching was not a job, but a lifestyle, and the Six M crew were masters of their domain.

But even masters have weaknesses.

At the south side of the grove, Cody and Jesse edged closer, steering their horses into the wake of black feathers. Vultures hissed and flapped away, their feathery fog pulling back to reveal a mound formed of drying mud and packed earth, handmade and left in plain view.

"Oh, hell," Cody murmured, his voice cracking, his stomach lurching.

Dismounting, their boots sank into the soft earth as a new, bitter stench clawed at their nostrils.

Carved into the trunk of a tree behind the mound were jagged, angular words. Their meaning was lost on Cody and Jesse, but it did not matter. Neither man dared to look away from what held their focus.

Floyd Huckabee's head sat atop the mound like a forsaken idol, facing the open range. His lifeless eyes stared into nothingness, frozen wide like frosted glass. Beneath him, the mound was scarred black with dried blood, the ground below it crisscrossed by a tapestry of blunt talon tracks.

Jesse pressed his fingers to his lips and gave a sharp whistle. Cody chased two bold vultures waddling closer, their hunched backs bobbing up and down, cursing him with a hiss as they shuffled away from him. Like immature children, the greedy wake stalked around on the periphery waiting for their chance to get back to their desert delight.

Cody turned and began to approach Huckabee's remains.

"Hold up there, Cody," Boss yelled as she and Flint rode up. "Both of you, back away. You can help by getting the buzzards as far from the scene as possible."

Pedro rode in from the opposite side of the grove.

"Pedro," Cody called. "Stay in the saddle. Work the right side. Let's get these scavengers outta here. Me an' Jesse'll work 'em from the ground."

Whooping and hollering, the Six M hands chased groups of vultures away, but the birds were not fooled.

Every time one group flapped off, another took its place. Flint bit his lip, led his horse away from Boss, drew his .45, and fired shots into the air.

BANG! BANG! BANG!

Spooked by the thunderous noise, the vultures scattered, their wings beating furiously as they fled into the sky in a chaotic storm of black feathers and piercing cries. Cody, Jesse, and Pedro spun around, startled for a moment. Cody let out a dry chuckle, sharing a glance with Jesse and muttered, "Guess that's one way to do it."

"All right, Dirty Harry. Put it away." Boss said, shaking her head. While she was an officer of the law, bound by county-wide jurisdiction, out here with these cowboys, she knew she was far out of her element.

Flint holstered his weapon. Boss dismounted and led her horse into the grove. "Y'all tie up in here. Stay wide as you can around the...Mr. Huckabee."

Following her lead, they found their way into the grove without disturbing any more of the ground around the immediate area relative to the remains. Boss posted Jesse, Cody, and Pedro at points along a makeshift perimeter she walked off, scuffing her shoes along the ground to create a crime scene border. Flint followed her, keeping to himself, while also watching the land along both sides of the Rio Grande.

When Boss finished, she crossed into the crime scene, inviting Flint to follow in her footsteps, and approached the gruesome display. Kneeling, she cleared her throat, then turned her head and spat.

"What do you think, Flint?" she asked, wiping her lips with the back of her hand.

"Pretty fucking disgusting."

Boss stood up and shot Flint a glare.

"Really?"

Not waiting for an answer, she turned away, her eyes falling on the inscription carved into the tree trunk.

"*Dios perdona. El cartel no.*" Boss read aloud, repeating the phrase twice before turning to Flint. "Do you understand the message?"

Flint's face hardened. "Yep. Means, '*God forgives. The cartel does not.*' It's one of them narco warnings, right?"

"It's called a *narcomantas*. It's not just a warning," she added. "It's fearmongering, meant to paralyze anyone who steps out of line." Boss looked to the river, her eyes wandering up and down the weedy banks and muddy brambles. "It's retaliatory. A consequence for Curly's actions yesterday, most likely."

Flint pressed his hands to his hips, his jaw tightening as if chewing on the weight of her words. "Son of a bitch didn't know who he was shootin' at, didn't care who got hurt." He shook his head, the futility of the situation gnawing at him.

"Odds are we'll never find justice for the murders," Boss said, her voice trailing with lost hope. "Best we can do for now is care for the remains and keep an eye out."

Flint yanked off his hat and slapped it against his thigh, sending up a puff of dust, his face tight with anger.

"Shit!"

The curse echoed across the flat land, carrying his anger to both sides of the border.

Boss pulled out her radio and reported their findings, her voice steady despite the grim details she relayed.

The sun blazed overhead as a few remaining vultures circled high above, their shadows too distant to touch the ground. The air hung low and dry, carrying a faint, putrid scent of decaying flesh.

After giving their approximate location, Boss turned back toward what remained of Floyd Huckabee. Flint stood beside her. His head hung low.

CHAPTER FIFTY-SIX

HOUSTON, TEXAS

I had no time to lose. GPS calculated a twenty-minute drive to the Barker Substation from my location. So far, I had played my role on TITON close to the belt, acting alone or with only my most trusted allies by my side. But now, navigating the city—a jungle of cars, traffic lights, and pedestrians—between me and the operatives I suspected were highly trained Chinese agents, I felt the need to call in an audible.

"Special Agent in Charge, Dylan Sharp speaking..."

"Sharp." His name spewed from my mouth like the aftereffects of a bad hangover, but I needed his help. "I need you to relay a code 76 to HPD. We have an active *Electric Storm*. Repeat. *Electric Storm*. I am in route to intercept, but I need an open road."

I jammed my foot to the floor, spiking the engine's RPMs as I weaved through two-lane traffic like a NASCAR pro.

"Copy that, Agent Callahan," Sharp replied, his tone clipped, "but TITON protocol dictates your action will not subject civilians to imminent harm. Proceed on your route, but you're on your own."

His response made my head spin.

"Are you fucking kidding me?"

I had no siren, no official identification on my truck marking me as law enforcement, and yet I was being told to go it alone.

"Look, Cass," Sharp continued. "The second I relay the code, HPD will mobilize, which means, while a couple of handlebar heroes jump a few curbs and block a few intersections, the rest of the force will be swarming your target. If what you say is truly happening, we must move with stealth."

"Maybe you're not hearing me Sharp. These are Chinese operatives. PLASSF! Goddamn China's Strategic Support Force!"

"I know the PL...listen. This is what you signed up for, Cass. You are the tip of the sword. The crest of the wave. TITON is the first responder, the one to initiate, protect, no matter the risk. If you can't get to your intercept point without drawing attention to their operation it won't matter if I call the National Guard to back you up. Every government has teams like this with failsafe protocols to follow should their cover be blown or they're captured. Think about it, Cass. Think about what happened yesterday at the detention facility. The guy you wanted to interrogate alone was killed right in front of you."

I slammed my horn at the Volvo in front of me, yanking the wheel hard right to cut off a clunker Toyota sporting an *All Lives Matter* sticker on its rear fender. The Toyota's high-pitched horn chirped in protest, but the sound was swallowed by the roar of four hundred horses under my hood.

"Wait. You know about that?"

"I know about that," he echoed, sounding more like a squawking parrot than my boss.

"Look, Sharp. I am not Tarzan. I can't just swoop across the city, I—"

"Here's what I can do," he interrupted. "I'll get you an escort, but only to a predetermined point. They'll know you're official, but we'll keep it low profile. Something like...pregnant wife in labor. Stay on your current heading and be on the lookout."

My knuckles whitened as I strangled the steering wheel.

"Be on the lookout?" I yelled, but my voice hit the void of a dead line.

"Crrrap!" I growled.

Eldridge Parkway curved left, rising over a bridge before descending into a three-light nightmare at its intersection with Interstate 10. My heart slammed into my chest as I crested the bridge, staring down at a valley of brake lights clogging the road, all waiting for the light to turn green.

My options were limited, and my window for action was closing fast. At the last moment, I swerved left, steering into the oncoming lane of traffic. Since the light had yet to turn, the lanes were mercifully empty, but the intersection ahead was a different story. Cross traffic flowed like a raging river.

Horns blared to my right, and I caught the dubious stare of a young driver behind the wheel of a classic '94 Mazda Miata. He raised a fist in protest as I shot past.

My path ahead was blocked, forcing me to tap my brakes and slow my speed. Less than a hundred feet from the intersection, a burst of flashing strobe lights cut in behind me, two iron horse interceptors closing in with each honk and blare. The lead unit surged up alongside my truck with a deafening roar.

The officer pointed at me with a sharp, commanding gesture, shouting something I could not hear over the noise of the chaos. Slowing even further, I fumbled for my wallet and flashed my TITON badge through the window, fully expecting it would not be worth the price of a two-dollar hotdog at an Astros game.

To my disbelief, the officer gave me a thumbs up, chirped his siren, and tore into the onslaught of cross traffic, clearing a path like Moses parting the Red Sea. The second motor unit slid in behind me, and suddenly, we were off to the races.

CHAPTER FIFTY-SEVEN

29.71028° N, 95.64308° W

Miào Wén-Kē wiped his face with a paper towel from the break area, then used a squirt of sanitizer to scrub away the red-speckled stains from his hands and wrists. He removed his shirt, now a tie-dyed swirl of red over gray, balled it up, and slipped it into a large plastic Ziplock bag from his satchel. He removed a plain black t-shirt and slipped it over his head. The Dri-FIT cloth clung to his skin, outlining the hard curves of his muscles. Removing a small earpiece from his pocket, he fit it in place and tapped the side to power it on. A rising, electronic chime sounded out, followed by noise-canceling silence.

"*Chì Hǔ*, online."

Miào Wén-Kē collected his things, threw away his trash, and returned to a command chair in front of the main terminal monitor. He moved as if he belonged, calm and deliberate, every motion a quiet reminder that his role was vital, but timing was everything. He could not proceed until...

"Read you, Crimson Tiger. *Shèn Yǐng* holds the key."

"You are a mirage indeed," Chì Hǔ replied. "Zhàn Huǒ was right to bring you onboard. Proceed."

With call signs activated, the mission commenced.

Keys clicked over the comms as Shèn Yǐng gave real-time status updates. "Code is embedding. Voltage thresholds primed. Target nodes will cascade in...thirty seconds."

"Copy," Chì Hǔ acknowledged. "Confirm packet trajectory."

"Gulf Corridor locked. Coastal Grid at fifty-five percent. Pushing to San Antonio's subnet."

Chì Hǔ grinned, his crooked smile widening as images of chaos and devastation danced in his mind like a private Imax screening. The Americans would crumble under the weight of their own fragile systems. "Good wo—"

"No...wait." The sharp edge in Shèn Yǐng's voice sliced through his satisfaction. "Something's wrong."

Chì Hǔ leaned forward, his elbows pressing into the desk. The monitor in front of him hummed with steady data flow. The grid map glowed in calm greens and blues. Voltage levels hovered in the mid-range, the numbers unmoving. Arrows pulsed across power lines with rhythmic consistency, while the load distribution chart rotated slowly, every sector within capacity. It was too perfect. Too still.

"Define 'wrong.'"

"The packets aren't landing. There's a block. Looks like a loopback in the transmission chain. I'm trying to redirect..."

Comms fell silent save for the furious clatter of keys. Shèn Yǐng was not just typing, she was hammering commands into the system, each stroke undercut by her mounting frustration.

"Redirect failed," she growled. "The loop's locked. It's cutting me out."

"How the hell does a loop lock us out? That architecture is ours."

"It's not automated," she hissed. "This was patched. Someone's here. Someone inside the system!"

Chì Hŭ's gaze darted across the grid map. The cool greens and blues felt mocking now, a quiet taunt against his rising irritation. His voice dropped to a razor-sharp edge. "Can you isolate them?"

"Tracing now." Her breathing quickened, tension creeping into every syllable. Keys clicked, commands fired, and still, the loop held. "Damn it! It's piggybacking our signal. Whoever they are, they're smart. This wasn't a quick hack. Do we abort?"

"No." Chì Hŭ's response was immediate, defiant. "We are too far in. That trace is now your priority. Find them before they lock us out completely."

"Tracing..." Shèn Yĭng's voice flattened. "Wait. Got a signature. It's routed from another substation south of here. Probably a local tech. I can burn them out, but it'll take time. We're exposed until then."

Chì Hŭ shoved back from the workstation, the command chair spinning slightly from the force. Standing, he clenched his fists at his sides, nails digging into his palms. His cool demeanor fractured, replaced by a searing fire—a hunger to see the blackout sweep across Texas like a storm of vengeance.

"This ends now," he muttered under his breath. "Initiating the final phase will be effortless once the plume of darkness descends on the pitiful Americans, so comforted in their Western arrogance."

His crooked grin returned as he envisioned the devastation about to unfold.

"Chì Hǔ?"

"Do it," he snapped, his tone final. "Disable the intruder's access and finish the cascade."

CHAPTER FIFTY-EIGHT

NEWGULF SUBSTATION, NEWGULF, TEXAS

"So, you think your kung fu is better than mine?" Scoots said, blazing a new script of code across his screen with lightning-fast fingers. "Not on your life."

CHAPTER FIFTY-NINE

My iron horse escort weaved through the crowded streets of Houston, guiding me onto Alief Clodine Road before peeling away just a half mile from the Barker Substation. There was no send-off, no final salute, only the two officers extinguishing their lights and roaring ahead, their motorcycles growling like restless beasts.

Gracias, Ponch and John, I thought as I flashed my headlights.

I drove on, locating the cluster of high-voltage transmission towers, large, boxy transformers with cooling fans, and chain-link fence wrapped around the perimeter of the Barker Substation. Nestled in an open area across the West Park Tollway, it offered a clear view the rest of the way in. From my truck, however, nothing seemed out of the ordinary.

Luck was on my side as I caught a green light at the intersection of Alief Clodine and the Highway 6 access road. I turned right, slowing as I crossed the overpass and approached the entrance to the substation's gravel lot.

Pulling in, the popping sounds beneath my tires made me suddenly think of home. West Texas ranch roads had a way of all sounding the same, its gravely chorus stuck in my head like a favorite tune waiting to play its familiar refrain.

I scanned the lot. Two trucks sat together on the far side, parked near the perimeter fence. A plain white van closer to the gate did not seem out of place—at first glance. But the way it was parked caught my attention. Its perfectly square position in front of the small operations building hinted at a driver with an unusual attentiveness to detail.

The trucks, though, told a different story. Positioned close together, they leaned toward each other at odd angles, like they had been dropped there without a second thought, their drivers more focused on the six-pack waiting at the end of their shift than on how they left their trucks.

The difference sat heavy in my gut. Habit versus control. Two very different approaches, two very different types of people. And if my years as a detective had taught me anything, it was that personality often dictated behavior.

I keyed a security code into the customized gun safe installed in the truck's center console and retrieved my battlefield green Glock 17 along with two extra clips. Opening the door, I stepped outside, slid the gun between my belt and back, and tucked the clips into my rear pocket. Gravel crunched beneath my shoes as I made my way to the security gate. The sun hung high, heating the air and throwing an intense glare off the metal transmission towers.

Stopping at the gate, I trusted my instincts as the

muscles in my gut twitched with the familiar tension of pregame jitters. I knew things were about to get hot and heavy, even though I had yet to meet my opponent. I scanned the complex. No exterior movement. No sound except for the incessant hum from the power lines.

With a firm push, I pressed the button on the call box and waited, the weight of what might come tightening in my chest.

CHAPTER SIXTY

BARKER SUBSTATION, HOUSTON, TEXAS

A harsh buzz sounded out from the security panel in the operations room, signaling that Chì Hǔ and Shèn Yǐng had company at their door. Chì Hǔ glanced at the receiver, then pursed his lips, knowing he could not ignore the call.

He tapped his earpiece. "Someone is here. Have you neutralized the intruder?"

"Working on it. They're good, but I'm better. One minute more." Shèn Yǐng's voice carried the strain of concentration, as if she were locked in an arm-wrestling match, her opponent teetering on the edge of defeat.

"Move quicker. I will handle whoever it is. Boot the intruder out of the system and finish the cascade!"

Clearing his throat, Chì Hǔ answered the call.

"Operations in progress. Entry is restricted unless authorized. Identify yourself."

Silence. Then a man's voice crackled through the speaker.

"Yeah. This is Cass Callahan. I need to speak with the station super."

Chì Hǔ responded quickly. "As I stated, entry is restricted without authorization."

Another pause. Then came the words that sent a cold spike down Chì Hǔ's spine.

"As I stated," the voice repeated, cool and deliberate. "I need to speak with your supervisor. My name is Cass Callahan. FBI."

CHAPTER SIXTY-ONE

BARKER SUBSTATION, HOUSTON, TEXAS

"Cass Callahan. FBI," I said, stepping back to glare into the gate camera. All I saw were frayed A/V wires hanging from an empty mount. Two things crossed my mind: this place was skating on a razor-thin edge of safety regulations, and my Chinese operative buddies were still one step ahead, likely watching me right now.

Silence hung on the line. My hand drifted toward my gun, the nagging sense of something off growing stronger. Was it their words? Their tone? The slight but forced northeastern accent?

I glanced back at the call button, debating my next move. Demanding the gate be unlocked and threatening to involve the DOE seemed like the only card I had left. It was bullshit, of course, but a step up from shooting the lock and charging in alone.

My patience thinned, but a metallic buzz and the click of the lock disengaging held me in check for now.

"The gate should be unlocked, Agent Callahan. Come on in."

The old call box stared at me. Its rusted edges and weathered face seemed to mock me, dredging up an old proverb from my youth: *He who enters the wolf's den must deal with the wolf.*

Holding the gate open with my foot, I pulled my cell from my pocket and sent Ray a quick message. What the call box did not know was that I was a wolf as well.

11:21 A.M.

Callahan: At Barker Substation. I'm going in.

CHAPTER SIXTY-TWO

THE CR, WEST TEXAS

Gilly sat with Raven and Charlotte in the barn while Miguel stroked the dog. The dog was still in bad shape, but with everything that had unfolded this morning, its care had been forced to take a back seat. At least it was alive. That was a blessing. A buzz in Raven's pocket drew her attention. She slid her phone out and read the message. Her expression fell as her gaze shifted from Charlotte to Gilly.

"News?" Gilly asked.

Raven nodded but did not elaborate. Instead, she reached forward and scratched the dog's ears.

"Can you drive us to town, Gilly? Cody won't mind us borrowing his truck, will he?"

"Heck, no," Gilly replied, twisting her mouth as though Raven's question were ludicrous.

"Good. This fella needs more than we can offer. We gave it a fighting chance, but it needs to see a vet."

Gilly stood.

"I'll fetch the keys and pull around. Sit tight, an' I'll come back an' help ya carry the dog."

"I'll do it."

Gilly and Raven both turned to Charlotte. Her voice was meek, and her face still pale except for the redness around her eyes. Straightening her posture, she repeated herself, her voice steadier this time.

"I'll do it. I'll help Raven."

Raven smiled, her heart swelling at the courage this young woman was mustering.

"Okay," she said, her eyes fixed on Charlotte. "Okay."

CHAPTER SIXTY-THREE

BARKER SUBSTATION, HOUSTON TEXAS

hree steps past the gate, I heard the lock engage and saw the operations building door open ahead. A man in a black t-shirt and a white hardhat stepped into view. He paused in the doorway, then turned toward me, raised a hand, and smiled. I nodded and walked over to him.

"Sorry about all that over the intercom," he said, meeting me halfway. "It's been a busy morning."

"Tell me about it," I said, studying the man, my old detective habits taking over: Asian male, five foot six, one hundred forty-five pounds give or take, black shirt, black pants, designer dress shoes. "Cass Callahan," I said, producing my credentials for him to see. I watched his eyes as he glanced at my ID. "Problem with the grid?"

The man looked over his shoulder at the row of towers and electrical equipment.

"'The grid?' That's a common misconception. What you see here is just a small part of a larger web. Something cataclysmic would have to happen for the entire grid, as you say, to experience a problem." He turned back to me. "No, just running tests. I'm Daniel Wu, Barker Substation supervisor. Care to come inside? I'll give you the grand tour."

He pivoted, offering me the lead.

"After you," I said, extending my hand.

The man turned and began walking to the door, when I had a thought. What was it Scoots had said about access points or patches? Something about the RTUs.

"Actually, let's start down there," I said, pointing to the transmission towers and the small buildings like the ones I saw in Newgulf. If the substations were set up the same, the RTUs Scoots had mentioned would be located there, not in the operations building. "That looks more interesting."

I started over to have a look for myself.

"This way, Agent Callahan," the man called out behind me. I took a big risk walking away with my back to him, but I had to play the part of the entitled FBI agent.

"That's okay," I said. "I'd rather start down there."

"I must insist. We are running a series of tests, and..."

I spun around. "Mr. Wu, this isn't my first time paying this station a visit. In fact, DOE and Homeland both take great interest in the safety and security of our nations..." I squinted my eyes and emphasized, "...power grids. Call this a surprise inspection, I don't really give a damn. Let's start with the control stations, the RTUs, and then you can show me whatever you like inside."

My pocket buzzed. I huffed, drumming up my role, and removed my phone to read the message.

"Then you're in luck, sir." Mr. Wu replied. "The RTUs are in the operations building at this location. Better for security and maintenance alike. ERCOT is always looking for ways to improve efficiency, streamline the state's power needs into the future." He swept his hand toward the door. "Please."

I glanced at the screen.

11:26 A.M.

RayT: The kid's still in the thick of it. Watch your back.

It hit me like an electrical surge, sharp and undeniable. Flashes of dialogue, subtle body language, and that look Scoots gave me over breakfast lit up my mind like a live wire. His voice followed, as clearly as if he were right beside me:

A hard patch at the original access point is the only option. They'll tell you otherwise, but they'd be wrong.

"Agent Callahan, regulations state that—"

"You can shove your regulations up your ass," I interrupted, my eyes glued to Mr. Wu, waiting for a reaction.

Of all the roughnecks, juice monkeys, and roustabouts I had met over the years, none of them, not even one, would have let what I said slide, badge or not. But Wu?

"Fine, Agent Callahan. I'll let my man know you're heading his way," he said, surrendering, then marched through the operations building door and disappeared.

I pocketed my phone and made my way toward the small control buildings beneath the transmission towers. The doors to each structure stood side by side like a row of port-a-johns. A flavor in the air, a trace of hot metal, the scorch of burned hairs, scratched at my throat and tickled my nose as I moved closer. The hum of the power lines intensified like swarming bees hovering overhead. I kept watch for Wu's man, but he did not show himself.

I tried the handle on the first control door. It was locked. I moved on to the second, finding it unlocked. I rested one hand on my hip, prepared to pull my weapon as I eased the door open. Looking inside, the overhead fluorescents activated. Blinking amber and green lights flashed on an access panel below a sign: *VoltGuard-RTU-2*. Electrical blips popped like tiny mouse farts, but the small maintenance bay was empty.

I leaned back and closed the door, catching a blur of black from my periphery. Instinct took over, and I ducked as a fist, wielding a long, sharp dagger, missed my head by less than an inch. I slid to my left as my attacker's follow-through clanged into the side of the building. I reached for my gun, pulling and aiming in one fluid motion, but a lightning strike to my wrist by a skilled, precise kick knocked it from my grasp. A second kick struck my chest driving me backward. I stumbled before regaining my balance, then pivoted into a fighting stance in time to deflect the next volley of kicks and swipes of the knife that came at me like a predator clawing and striking at prey.

Long, black hair flowed and high-pitched shrieks followed each attempt to kill me. I kept on the defensive until a small window opened in our action, and I took advantage. Sidestepping to my right, I squatted, then used the power of my thighs and the blunt force of my hand to palm strike my attacker center mass. My hit was perfect, jolting the fighter back like a rag doll. It was at that moment a saw that the snake I was fighting was a woman.

Ordinarily, I would have looked for a more controlled way to end this bout, but the bitch had tried to kill me, so game on.

I bounced on the balls of my feet, my hands on guard, my eyes laser-locked on my target. She could not have been taller than five foot three and had an uncanny resemblance to the actress, Zhang Ziyi minus the killer intent in her eyes. We circled, the heat of the day and the sudden action breaking me into a showering sweat. She lunged forward, the stiletto knife striking at me like a cobra's fangs I rotated, stepped back, then surged ahead after her miss, connecting with a jumping front kick to her knife-wielding shoulder. The woman toppled backward, rolling to the ground. I advanced, muscles tensed and ready to end this once and for all, but she had other plans. She absorbed the roll, rotating backward and kicking her feet over her head. With a spring of her hands on the ground, she flipped onto her feet, rebounding her momentum to jump forward and landed a solid round-house kick to my left ear.

For an instant, the world grew fuzzy. A ringing exploded in my head like the gongs in a Chinese New Year parade. I swung my hands out and felt a sharp sting piercing my forearm. It hurt like hell but cleared my head. Trickling warmth seeped over my skin and along the blade of the knife in my attacker's hand. We locked eyes again. She was a hungry serpent, waiting to spill more blood, and I was, to put it simply, pissed off.

Ignoring my arm, the blood and the throbbing took a back seat to my adrenaline-filled flurry. I had had enough of this shit. I charged, my battle cry loud and vicious. She swung the blade and missed, then jumped backward and kicked at my face. I saw it coming before my yell met my lips. I caught her leg and clamped it under my arm, her thigh pinned tight against my ribs. Using her momentum, I twisted hard, spinning us both until she slammed into the ground beneath me. landing on top of her, I felt the sickening crack of bone giving way under my weight. She let out a blood-curdling shriek, crumpling to the ground. Her leg jutted out at an unnatural angle. I sprang to my feet and for a moment, I stood there, catching my breath, watching the woman writhe on the ground.

She cursed me, though her Chinese insults fell on indifferent ears. The stiletto stuck out of the ground just out of reach of her. Every time she tried to skootch closer, her broken leg reminded her it was better not to move.

Her glare was murderous as I reached down and pulled the knife from the ground. I held it up and gave it its due. The hilt was slimy with a mix of my blood and dust but the blade looked crisp, razor-sharp, not ready to be sheathed away.

"Nice blade."

Locating my gun, I picked it up and held it out next to the knife, inspecting each weapon.

"Lucky kick," I said, sweating and bleeding sarcasm. "Don't you know, never bring a knife to a—"

Bang!

The woman's head snapped backward, her once piercing eyes now popped open in eternal shock. A line of red trickled from the bullet hole in her forehead.

I whirled around, searching for the shooter, and saw Mr. Wu crouching in front of the operations building. Anger seared from his face, his skin taking on a sunburnt sheen, his mouth clenched.

He fired again as I jumped and rolled to my left, finding minimal cover at the base of the first maintenance bay. Shot after shot, bullets zinged by, but none of them seemed remotely close to me.

As the echo of his last shot faded, the swarm of bees sound I had heard overhead now seemed to be trapped inside the building I was using for cover. The buzz turned to crackles and snaps.

Shit! He wasn't shooting at me. He was...

I jumped away from the building just as the door blew from its hinges. Sparks lurched out of the opening followed by a stream of smoke and what looked at first like an electrical snake coiling and recoiling as it prepared to strike.

Caught in the open, I fired at Wu, then ran ahead,

zigzagging as bullets tore into the ground where my feet had been. I fired again, my magazine emptying as I sprinted full tilt. Wu turned and ran for the security gate, his gun in one hand, a brown leather satchel slung over his shoulder. He rammed through the gate and headed for the van when I saw Ponch and John zoom into the gravel lot.

I continued my sprint, witnessing to my horror that Wu had turned his gun on the officers.

BANG!

BANG!

BANG!

The gunfire was deafening, echoing off concrete and steel.

I watched as the first officer jerked back, his bike skidding to the ground in a cloud of gravel. The second returned fire like a cowboy riding down a bank robber, but he too, was shot in the line of duty. He cut the wheel hard left, and flipped from the seat, clear of the bike as it rolled onto its side.

Rage boiled in my chest, mixing with the bitter taste of helplessness. I kicked through the gate, a raw, furious yell tearing from my throat as I sprinted after Wu.

Wu changed direction and ran toward the nearest downed officer. Pulling him away from his motorcycle, Wu yanked it upright and hopped onto the seat. With a roaring twist of the wrist, he gunned the engine, the rear wheel spinning over the loose gravel before regaining traction.

I glanced at the second officer. He lay propped on his side holding the microphone to his PTT shoulder mounted radio. He was injured, but alive, and communicating. I ran over to the first officer. He was unconscious. His nose bled, but that looked like the worst of his injuries. Looking lower, I saw a steaming hole smoked from his uniform just off center of his chest where one of Wu's bullets had dug into the Kevlar vest beneath.

Brave, lucky bastard, I thought.

Wu veered onto the grassy shoulder, blocked from the Highway 6 access road by a slow-moving eighteen-wheel gravel truck. The driver punched his horn as Wu steered away from the near collision, bouncing and buckling into the rough patch of grass on the shoulder. He lost his grip on the handlebars for a moment, and the bike stalled.

"Go!" I heard the other officer yell. "Get that son of a bitch!"

Jumping to my feet, I raced toward my truck, tracking Wu as he struggled to restart the bike.

I slammed into the driver's seat, the door still swinging as I fired the engine. If Wu got away, I might not have another chance to stop him. All 450 horses roared as I tore off in pursuit.

The eighteen-wheeler moved ahead, still blaring its horn and leaving a clear path in its wake. I skidded onto the road, my tires screeching over the asphalt, and jammed the gas again. Another fifty yards, and I would be right on top of Wu.

"Nowhere to go, you son of a bitch." My voice was low, sharing my thoughts with an empty cab as I watched him fight with the bike. I was closing fast when he glanced back at me.

Giving up on the motorcycle, Wu leaped off. He ran out of the grass and darted across the access road in front of me like a wild coyote, then scrambled up the angled abutment slope using his hands to help him climb up to the highway.

I gunned the truck's engine, narrowly missing him, then slammed the brakes, yanking the wheel hard to the left. The treads spun at first in the rising soil before grabbing ahold. They dug in, propelling me and the truck up the embankment behind Wu.

Wu scrambled to the top, his satchel swinging wildly, but the roar of my truck made him stumble. He ran ten more yards, cutting into traffic, then turned back, his face twisted in fury.

And that's when I saw it.

His hand dipped into the satchel, pulling something free, a small metallic cube, its edges catching the light.

What the hell?

Car horns wailed as they swerved to miss him

I gritted my teeth, slamming the accelerator harder, lining him up with the iron teeth of my truck's grille guard. But Wu raised the device, his beady eyes locked on me and tossed it onto the road like throwing dice in a casino.

The cube skidded and spun, until—crap. *Snake eyes.* It stopped tumbling and erupted with a violent *BOOM*. A searing white light followed. Shards of concrete exploded, blasting outward in a fiery burst of heat and shrapnel, hammering my truck's frame, ripping through metal, and cracking the windshield. I slammed the brakes and swerved, grinding to a halt in the middle of the road.

My heart pounded as I scanned the wreckage, but Wu was gone.

No, not gone.

My eyes narrowed, catching the faintest movement darting through the smoky haze.

He wasn't running. He was getting away.

And I had no time to lose.

CHAPTER SIXTY-FOUR

Cars filled the lanes, stopped by the explosion or rubbernecking just out of harm's way, blocking any chance I had of continuing the chase behind the wheel. I jumped out, left my brand new, now in desperate need of bodywork, truck in the middle of Highway 6, and took off running after Wu. Sirens wailed in the distance. Thick, black smoke billowed behind me. And I was weaving through a midday traffic tragedy, Glock in my hand and my face set with that look that said, 'Stay the hell out of my way.'

I had caught a glimpse of Wu through the smoky haze, but now that I was out of the truck and on foot, I lost him in the chaotic shuffle.

But he had not lost me.

A gunshot blasted. The bullet zinged by my ear like a deadly mosquito lusting for blood. I dodged, ducking behind the bed of an old Chevy truck, its driver stuck in the vehicular muck. I caught him out of the corner of my eye reaching behind him and removing a rifle from a gun rack suction cupped to his rear window.

Only in Texas, I thought.

I ripped my wallet out, stepped back to block him from opening the door, and pressed my ID to the window.

"Stay inside and put the fucking gun away."

His eyes met mine, jittering between me and the ID, but stood down. I tapped the window. "And call 9-1-1!"

I returned to the rear of the truck, spotting Wu as he ran down the shoulder before cutting into a shopping center parking lot.

Run, Cass.

I was injured, mad, tired, a swirling chunk of breathing mayhem, but I heard the words as plainly as I had heard them a thousand times. It was Raven's voice, cheering me on, urging me to catch that Chinese bastard and end this thing.

I drew in a deep breath and resumed the chase.

Sirens grew louder and I could now see emergency lights swarming the road. A helicopter appeared overhead. Was it a news chopper? HPD? It did not matter. I was still on my own.

The shopping center was a simple strip of businesses lined up in an L-shaped layout. A coffee shop, a bookstore that sold both books and booze, a fashion boutique, a Vietnamese restaurant, and Happy Hands reflexology—everyday places where the only danger lurking was the high prices forced on the everyday consumer, except maybe the allure of a seedy massage, not the deranged actions of a mad terrorist running rampant along their adjoining sidewalks.

Wu looked back, saw me, but this time he did not fire. He was smart not to draw attention away from the disaster on the road.

I sped up my pace, staying close to the intermittent

stone columns lining the sidewalk, ready to take cover behind one should he change his mind about reengaging. My legs and chest burned, my arm throbbed from the puncture wound, but I did not stop.

A Mexican restaurant dominated the corner of the complex. Red, white, and green banners hung from the ceiling, decorating the entrance. Mariachi music played over exterior speakers, echoing along the concrete walkway, drawing shoppers toward the promise of margaritas and traditional homemade dishes. Large green letters, separated by a bright red pepper, spelled out the name *La Cocina* on a yellow sign.

I watched as Wu rounded the corner, passed the restaurant, then hesitated. He turned around, retraced his steps, and disappeared through the entrance door.

I slowed as I reached the entrance, my heart pounding against my ribs. Why here? Was Wu cornered, setting a trap, or looking to take hostages? Maybe he was just cutting through to the back.

It did not matter.

The vibrant notes of mariachi music spilled from the restaurant, clashing with the distant wail of sirens.

My pulse thundered.

I flexed my grip on the Glock, my injured arm screaming in protest, and glanced through the front windows. Families were inside. Diners. Innocent people, laughing over midday margaritas and chips, oblivious to the danger just yards away.

My gut twisted.

This was bad. Worse than bad. But there was no waiting. No backup. No time to think.

Wu was in there. And I was going in after him.

I drew a sharp breath, squared my shoulders, and pushed through the door.

CHAPTER SIXTY-FIVE

NEWGULF SUBSTATION, NEWGULF, TEXAS

"Come on, come on!" Scoots argued with the screen, his fingers flying across the keyboard, his coding in a battle with the malicious intrusions—a pair of threats as unique as they were destructive: an active packet distribution algorithm and a virus, both wreaking havoc. Scoots was good, a genius's genius, but he was in the fight of his young life.

"What's going on?" Ray asked, hearing the frustration in his voice. He stood back to give Scoots room to work but was as curious as a kid in a candy store after receiving the text from Cass. He read it over and over. *I'm going in.* Cass's words. His last words. Ray hated waiting, hated the helplessness. He wanted to be in the thick of it with Cass in Houston rather than playing babysitter bodyguard in the middle of *Nowhere, Texas.* "Did it work?"

Scoots never took his eyes off the screen.

"Not yet," he growled, his tone sharper than either of them expected.

"Talk to me in English, kid."

"This thing's a polymorphic nightmare! It's self-replicating across the damn subnet and encrypting faster than I can decrypt. It's throwing garbage packets like confetti at a DOS parade and spoofing headers to mask the payload! I've got recursive loops in the main thread, rogue ports opening faster than I can close them, and now it's sandboxing my patches like it's mocking me! Who the hell writes a virus with adaptive cloaking and multi-vector packet injection?!"

"Yeah, kid, I understood...none of that. You winning or losing?"

"Damn it, Ray!" Scoots snapped, his focus glued to the cascading code on his screen.

Ray forced himself to step back, scrolling through his phone to distract himself. Somehow, he always ended up back on his text thread with Cass. He paced like a caged animal, gripping his phone and muttering under his breath.

"Dig in, Callahan," he whispered, his voice barely audible. "Be careful."

CHAPTER SIXTY-SIX

HOUSTON, TEXAS

The first shot rang out before the restaurant door closed behind me. Bits of drywall crumbled to the floor at my feet.

"Agent Callahan," Wu's voice commanded the room, replacing the music that had abruptly cut off. Frightened screams echoed through the room as eyes volleyed between me near the front door and Wu, who stood behind a young waitress. His arm locked around her neck as he held a small pistol, pointed at me, next to her ear. "That was the last warning shot of the day," he said, his tone calm but razor-sharp. "Though it should have preceded your last breath. Please, put your gun on the floor and kick it away."

I scanned the room. Whimpering tears, angry glares, and terrified faces filled the once-joyous space, a vibrant tribute to old Mexico turned into an unforgettable nightmare. The restaurant's charm was gone, sheer terror flooding a place none of the customers would ever dare return.

"Do it now, or I will shoot a customer," Wu said, his gun shifting toward a mother shielding her child at a nearby table.

"No," I said, my voice steady despite my racing heart. I had been in hostage situations before, each one terrifying in its own way, but this felt different. The usual suspects were not foreign operatives; they were frantic, panicked criminals with nothing to lose. Most of the time, these situations ended with brief negotiations and a safe surrender. Sometimes, they turned bloody, another sniper's notch added to the barrel. But I never lost a hostage.

"These people have nothing to do with..."

"*Bì zuǐ, yú chǔn de měi guó rén!*" Wu shouted. "They have everything to do with why I am here. Why *we* are here. For decades, you Americans have paraded around the world, gorging on riches built on the broken backs of those you claim to liberate. Your so-called freedoms have made you weak. Your schools churn out brainwashed idiots, incapable of competing on a global scale, yet you declare yourselves the shining superpower, the model for the world to follow.

"Do not insult me by saying these people are innocent. Look at them! They feast like no one out there is starving. They drink and laugh, obsessing over their petty first-world problems—what overpriced coffee to buy, which designer shoes will make them happy. It is pathetic. It is decadence. In an instant, I can take it all away and it will destroy you."

His lips curled into a snarl as he spat his final words.

I stepped forward, my arms and hands raised by my hips.

Wu gripped the waitress tighter, then leaned over and spoke into her ear.

"The man standing over there is going to get you

killed, girl. Is there anything you would like to tell him before you die?"

Tears overran her cheeks, falling in terrified streams. Mucus clung to her lips as she struggled to form words.

"P-p-pleeease..."

It was all she could say.

"Let me ask you something, girl, before the lights go out. Do you like cake? Every American likes cake. You see, the virus planted at the power station was a means to an end, a way to turn back time so that privileged people such as yourself know what it is like to lose, know what it is like to suffer in darkness, but it was not the entire plan. It was like the frosting of your precious cake. Delicious by itself, but only the top layer of decadent ecstasy."

Wu dipped his head and kissed her ear, his eyes cutting upward at me with a sharp, piercing glare.

"It will not matter if I tell the rest. Things are already in motion, and soon the whole world will see."

Standing up straight, he pointed the barrel of the gun at me, his face losing its bland, yellowed appearance as a rush of fury overcame him.

"When your man, or whoever you thought was clever enough to intervene, initiated his first keystroke, a failsafe process was automatically activated, triggering a series of cyber-intrusions designed to cripple your precious space program. The viruses are flooding the servers at the Johnson Space Center as we speak—overwriting telemetry data, scrambling communication networks, and corrupting the automated flight controls of active missions. Ground control will lose contact with every spacecraft and satellite and there is nothing anyone can do to reverse it.

"And the space station? Its life-support and navigation systems are already under attack. Redundant backups? Gone. The orbital stabilization program is collapsing.

Soon, the station will drift, unstoppable and irreversible, into decaying orbit. Your people up there will burn in reentry or suffocate before it happens. And the world will watch every agonizing second.

"Like your power stations, unprotected, taken for granted, so it is with the security of your skies. It took nothing to fly a simple drone over your precious space center. Using RF signals, we exploited the unsecured communication protocols embedded in your systems. Weak links you didn't even realize existed. With just a signal, we injected malicious code into the network, which then spread like a virus, corrupting critical systems.

"Your power stations, your skies, even the devices in your pocket, they are all gateways. When you turn on your TV, your computer, or your phone, do not think for a second that China isn't watching."

Wu looked pleased.

"Crippling the grid was something I was so looking forward to watching. It would have been...fun. But in the end, it was only the start of the show."

My cell phone buzzed. The room fell silent. Then it buzzed again.

"You've said a lot of things," I said, my voice calm. "I imagine that's President Xi on the line, calling to congratulate you." I motioned to my pocket. "Why don't we find out?"

The cell buzzed a third time.

Wu smirked. "Okay, Agent Callahan. I'll play along."

Using two fingers, I pinched my phone out of my pocket and held it in front of me. I glanced at the screen and smiled.

"Well, would you look at that? Seems like your little virus just got medicated. Would you like me to share this, or would you like to read it yourself?"

Wu's demeanor shifted—a slight tilt of the head, his

eyes narrowing with curiosity, suspicion flickering behind them as he studied me in silence.

"Okay, allow me." I glanced at the message. "It says...Cass, viruses have been neutralized. ERCOT notified and is running system wide diagnostics to verify the clean slate. Also, I was able to trace similar coding signatures across the network and cross-checked key servers statewide. Found a match in Clear Lake and at the JSC. Malicious code eradicated. My kung fu is untouchable."

I looked up, locking eyes with Wu.

"Your plan has failed, Wu. The viruses you planted are being wiped out as we speak. How do you think I found you? Your mistake was underestimating us. My grandparents used to say, 'Don't wake the sleeping giant.' But what you've never heard behind your cold, communist walls is this: Don't fuck with the USA."

"You're bluffing, Agent Callahan."

I raised my cell phone. "Take a look for yourself, asshole," I said, tossing it toward him.

The moment the phone left my hand, a man shielding his family gave me a nod, then lunged at Wu, pulling the waitress away as the phone arced through the air.

In one smooth motion, I reached behind my back and drew the stiletto knife I had tucked into my belt. Without hesitation, I hurled it at Wu. The blade spun through the air—hilt over blade, hilt over blade—like a scene from a slow-motion action movie before burying itself deep in his chest.

Wu's finger jerked on the trigger, but the shot miraculously missed everyone, the bullet shattering a Mexican pot at the restaurant entrance. He staggered back, his face twisted in shock.

I did not wait. Charging past tables, I leaped into the air, slamming my foot against the knife's hilt. The impact drove the blade further into his chest and sent Wu careening backward.

Shrieks filled the air as people rushed for the exit.

Wu toppled backward, crashing into the restaurant's margarita machine, its cold, savory mix spilling over his dead body.

I turned to the man.

"Call 9-1-1!"

"Already been done, boss."

He stepped over to me, and we shared a glance at the dead Chinese terrorist.

"Staff Sergeant Jacob Carter, United States Marine Corps. You looked like you could use a hand."

"Staff Sergeant Carter, appreciate the assist," I said, shaking his hand. "Cass Callahan, Second Battalion, Dragon Company."

"Figured you were more than just an average spook," he said, patting my shoulder before walking away. "Semper Fi."

I picked up my gun and found my cell phone, then walked over to Wu and sat down on the floor next to his body. My arm throbbed, my head pounded, my lungs burned, and beneath it all, my heart ached for Raven and to just be home.

I scrolled through my phone, swiping past contacts as the sounds of sirens approaching echoed outside the restaurant. When I found the number I was searching for, I tapped the call button and leaned my back against the wall, listening to the ring across the line.

A nasally, irritating voice answered the call.

"Special Agent in Charge, Dylan Sharp speaking."

"I bet you just love saying all that shit, don't you, Sharp?"

"Callahan. I'm guessing that you've wrapped up your part of the charade, or you wouldn't be calling."

I looked at Wu, his eyes relaxed and staring ahead.

"Yeah," I said. "But I need a favor."

CHAPTER SIXTY-SEVEN

HOUSTON, TEXAS

Every badge in the city descended on the active scenes scattered across West Houston, with the Barker Substation serving as the epicenter for tactical and investigative operations. Everyone wanted a word with me, HPD, FBI, DHS, and even a specialized ERCOT task force liaison, all clamoring to know my role, demanding answers about my lack of communication, and, above all, asking one question: what the hell was TITON?

It took a call from the lieutenant governor to the chief of police, the Houston DA, and the special agent in charge of the FBI Houston Field Office to clarify the jurisdictional authority granted to me within the *Texas Intelligence and Tactical Operations Network*, though a full explanation of my duties remained classified. Skepticism spread like wildfire through the ranks, but word from the top had to be treated as a directive. There was a job to do, a cleanup to manage, a deep investigation in which to dive, and a country to protect.

A different ripple swept through the local force, painting me in a new light. This shift was spurred by two Iron Horse officers whose endorsements of me, along with their gratitude for my actions, helped clear the slate with Houston's true heroes and my former employer, HPD. Ponch and John, two brave men I did not have the chance to meet before they were whisked away by ambulance, bought me the time I needed to stay in the hunt for the Texas terror, Daniel Wu, if that really was his name. I was relieved to learn that both had survived, and I deflected any words of thanks or praise directed at me back onto them. *I got your six* rang deep blue today, and I will never forget that.

It had been a hell of a day, and now that the anthill was in full repair mode, time seemed to return to normal. It was approaching three o'clock before I escaped the onslaught of bureaucracy that wanted me to answer the same revolving questions. Spotting an EMT loading supplies into a side compartment on his ambulance, I seized the chance to remove myself from the chaos and seek both treatment and a moment to breathe.

The events of the day brought me clarity. I thought about what had been in motion, what might have happened if it had not been uncovered in time. The consequences of action and inaction, the online chatter and political fallout—this was not just Houston's problem. This was an international incident. Yet, through the chaos, I realized something simple: there will always be dangers, enemies, and threats. I served my country. I served Houston. Now, I am a guardian for the state. But deeper down, I knew there was an even greater responsibility to uphold, and I knew what I had to do.

As he bandaged my arm and checked for further injuries, I sat on the rear bumper of the West Houston

EMS rig and looked across a sea of officials, people, Americans, and thanked my lucky stars that I was one of them.

"Make sure to give this chump a rectal before you're through with him," a crass, grumbling voice called out, cutting through the noise. I could not help but grin, surprised and quite relieved to hear it.

"Yeah, he's in need of an immediate systems upgrade," a second voice chimed.

The EMT had just finished and stepped aside.

"Look at you two," I said. "Batman and Robin in the flesh."

"More like Bruce Wayne and Alfred," Scoots said, ribbing Ray's limited but critical role in the events at the Newgulf substation.

Ray huffed. "You look like shit, Callahan. As usual. Think just once you can catch the bad guy without blowing up the place?" Leaning in, he wrapped his arms around my head and squeezed before turning to look at Scoots like a proud father might his son. "This kid is by far..." He paused, cracking a rare smile. "The scariest son-of-a-bitch I've ever met. If you think he's fast with numbers and thinking and all that nonsense, try riding in that rocket coffin he calls a car."

"Oh, man. You know you loved it, detective."

"Ray, kid. Call me Ray. Now, bring it in."

Ray extended an arm, pulling Scoots into our tight embrace.

"The hair," Scoots cried jokingly. "Watch the hair."

The moment Ray let go, the world around me seemed different. It felt different, but I had one more very important thing to do before the end of the day.

"You get me outta here, Scoots?" I asked.

"01111001 01110101 01110000."

"You see, there he goes again," Ray playfully complained. "Scary as hell."

I stood up, understanding Scoots's code, and turned to Ray. "You cover for me here?"

"Always have, always will, Private. I'll catch a ride with a uniform. Where you off to?"

I nodded at Ray, conveying an unspoken gratitude for our friendship and years of service together in one simple glance. "I have a promise to keep."

I slipped my hand into my pocket. "No need to catch a ride though," I said, pulling out the key fob for my truck. "I'll pick it up from you next time I'm in town, just take good care of it, okay?"

Ray held out his palm, and I handed it to him.

"Don't worry, brother," Ray said. "Not a scratch."

I laughed to myself as Scoots and I walked away. When we got to his car, he opened my door and asked what was so funny. I molded myself into the passenger seat as he carefully closed it behind me.

"Oh, nothing, kid. Just...Damn it, Cass."

EPILOGUE ONE

My head rocked against the window, the steady vibrations lulling me, while the crackle in my headset faded into the background as the plane soared over Central Texas at ten thousand feet. The plush seats, the cool airflow, and the sensation of near weightlessness all worked to soothe my battered body and ease my mind. The flight out of Sugar Land, Texas, was smooth. SAIC Dylan Sharp came through with the favor for me, flying down to pick me up before bringing me back across the state toward the CR. Toward Raven. It was not the first time he had swooped in for the save, and I was sure he would not let me forget it. I had just drifted into sleep when chatter in my headset startled me awake.

"Cessna Eight-Six-Niner Foxtrot Sierra, radar contact. Maintain ten thousand feet. Traffic, two o'clock, five miles, westbound at thirteen thousand."

"Copy that." Sharp's voice came through steady. "Maintain ten thousand. Looking for traffic, Eight-Six-Niner Foxtrot Sierra."

"Eight-Six-Niner Foxtrot Sierra, contact Fort Worth Center on one-three-five-point-three."

"One-three-five-point-three, Eight-Six-Niner Foxtrot Sierra. Thanks for the help."

Sharp glanced at me, his eyes hidden behind Ray-Bans. For someone in a position of authority, he did not dress the part, at least not on this flight. He wore an El Paso Chihuahuas Minor League Baseball team hat worn backward, a black Grateful Dead t-shirt, and jeans. If I did not know any better, he had taken a page right out of my playbook.

"Sorry about that," he said. "San Antonio air traffic control runs a tight ship. Shouldn't have too many more interruptions. West Texas is a lonely bitch."

I nodded, shifting in my seat. "What's our ETA?"

"Couple hours. Just enough time for us to discuss your next assignment."

That jolted me awake. Wide awake.

Sharp reached over his shoulder and pulled a manila folder out from behind my seat, handing it to me.

"Joint task force out of SoCal. They've..."

"I don't want to know," I said, pushing the folder away.

Sharp smacked his lip like he was chewing gum with his mouth open.

"You think you don't, but you do. Trust me, Callahan. You do."

His cockiness was next level, and I could see there was no winning this fight, so I diverted to one simple truth I had planned on sharing with him once we landed.

"I'm out."

"I get you. Take a few days. Bang the wife." My eyes broke him in half, my mind punched his face over and over. "But I know you better than you know yourself."

"Doubtful," I said, my mental fist burning and blood soaked.

"Don't believe me? Fine. It'll be tough losing a guy like you. But..."

There was always a 'but,' however, in Sharp's case, make it an ass.

"...for old time's sake." He backhanded my arm with his knuckles like we were old chums. "As a thank you for flying across Texas just to bring you home *today*, take a peek at what's inside."

He held the folder out, his hand as steady as the one on the yoke.

There was no way in hell I was going to budge on my decision to leave the bureau, but I swiped it from him and broke the seal holding the flaps together. Annoyed, I flipped it open. With one glance, my gut twisted as if the plane had plunged a thousand feet and was barreling toward the ground. My heart thumped. My fingers tingled as if the tips had fallen asleep.

"Bullshit!" I said, slamming the file closed. "Total bullshit."

"It's not, Cass. The picture came across my desk just this morning. The Southern California Task Force on Organized Crime and Illegal Activity, fucking terrible name if you ask me. Anyway, they put out a bulletin with photographs from recent catch and release illegals as well as other persons of interest. I knew once I saw that," he said, reaching over and opening the folder bringing the cover photo into plain view. "You were the first one I was going to call. That's our guy. *Your* guy."

I looked at the photo. The dark hair. The suave mannerisms. The familiar complexion. A face that had haunted my nightmares long after I had watched him burn. It all stirred a fire within me I thought had been snuffed out.

"If I'm wrong," Sharp added, "you can kick me in the

balls until my face turns blue. But that right there, that goddamn picture you're holding, is none other than Carlos Ruiz-Mata. Camargo's very own cartel sicario, the one we thought we'd blown straight to hell. Fucking *El Despiadado*."

EPILOGUE TWO

I walked across the tarmac at Lely International Airport in Presidio, and never looked back. Not even when Sharp called after me. His voice was swallowed by the churn of the engine, the whirl of the prop, and the weight of the last two hours spent in silence. Reflective silence. All I wanted was a ride home. He might as well have pushed me out at ten thousand feet without a parachute. Whatever the Special Agent in Charge had to say, it was not worth hearing.

Yet, clenched in my fist, rolled tight like a weapon in waiting, was the folder, the dossier with everything Sharp had on my old enemy.

There was no one to meet me, no one to read my face and ask why I looked so frustrated. So defeated. The small, rural airport did not support commercial travel, catering mainly to private and government planes, but it did have a rental car service just outside the terminal. I took the first car I was offered, paid the fee, and hiked across the dim parking lot. Spotting the car, a 2020 Chevy Malibu, I hopped in and noted the time.

9:45 p.m.

Glancing in the rearview mirror, the dome light cast a shadow across my face, giving my reflection an eerie appearance. For a moment, I felt as if I were not alone. The image in the mirror was dark. I blinked, and before my eyes, in a flash of fatalism, I saw *El Despiadado* staring back at me. Taunting me.

I killed your friends, the deputies you worked with, the innocents in your hometown, and had it not been for an extreme case of luck, your son as well, my friend.

I could hear his voice rising, deepening, slithering in my head.

I crammed my eyes shut and yanked the door handle closed. The hard *thwump* of the car door slamming, the interior pressure of the vehicle shifting, then silence. As if I were caught in a vacuum, the quiet consumed me, yet inside my head, I screamed. I screamed aloud for all to hear, releasing my frustrations, my anguish, and my impenitent rage until, finally, I could scream no more. When I opened my eyes, the world came into focus. The darkness settled in, hiding the grim reflection, concealing my outer turmoil.

"Get it together, Cass," I said, urging myself to let go of all the anguish I had allowed back into my thoughts. "Little Bird is only forty-five minutes away."

I took a deep breath, slid the key into the ignition, and with a twist of my wrist, was rewarded with the gentle grumble that settled into a slow, easy idle. The radio sprang to life, and I heard an old, familiar voice singing.

"Almost heaven. West Virginia..."

I turned the volume up, letting the melody fill the car, letting it wrap around my frayed nerves. Forcing myself to sing along, I followed the homespun words, letting John Denver guide me as my own country roads, winding and shadowed, took me home.

EPILOGUE THREE

Gravel popped under the car, spitting into the undercarriage with sharp metallic *clinks*. The grind of tires turning from one patch of underdeveloped back road to another sent butterflies bouncing through my stomach. Ahead, the warm glow of the porch light came into view as my body shook from the vibrations of the old iron cattle guard rattling beneath the car. Light from the barn stretched outward, illuminating the dusty yard where pickups parked side by side seemed ready to share a beer after a long day's work. I caught the orange glow of a cigarette and its ghostly smoke trail rising over a trusted, hardened friend, his boots perched on the handrail of his tiny house. Faint country western music drifted from the bunkhouse next door, and the butterflies danced again.

Coming to a stop in front of the house, I noticed empty chairs on the porch and a side table where a single brown Shiner bottle stood watch, left behind but not forgotten. Not at my house. Not on the CR.

I cut the engine and stepped out, closing the door with a gentle push. The night air was warmer than usual and carried a scent only West Texas natives would call comforting—a hint of manure, a waft of fresh hay, a subtle mix of fresh earth and dust, and fragrance of creosote and mesquite. Together, the aromas confirmed what I already knew: I was where I was meant to be.

Hinges in dire need of WD-40 creaked and squeaked as the screen door slowly opened. Light spilled from inside, wrapping around the figure appearing in the door-way, painting a golden fringe around the most beautiful person on earth.

My feet felt heavy, as if sunken into the ground. My legs tightened and my arms fell to my sides, limp as rope. The door closed with a slap, the house light softening through the gray sheen of the screen, its golden hue fading as sweet footsteps carried over the wooden planks of the porch.

One sound. One peep. One affirmation of everything I held dear was all it took to feel...saved.

"It's ten forty-five."

My feet lightened, and I took a step. No angel had ever sounded sweeter. No bird had ever glided softer on the backs of the wind. No one ever felt what I felt in that very moment—the moment I heard Raven say, "You kept your promise."

ACKNOWLEDGMENTS

Every book has its challenges, some forecasted, others unseen until they are staring me in the face, and I want to take a moment to thank some very important people who helped Texas Terror become a realistic glimpse into fictional life.

First, my family, whose support on this writing journey has been legend...wait for it...dary! Thanks, Barney! While I am upstairs—yes, that's a feat in itself, but a story for another time—I can hear my wife, Joellan, hard at work in her office down the hall. Each click of her keyboard, online chat, or the "shuffle-squeeze" she's forced into when passing by the attic stairs because they block the hall while I'm in my lerkim, challenges me to do better, write more, and harness my creativity. It's because of her I have the freedom and time to bring stories to life. I only hope I make her proud with each new plot twist, descriptive phrase, or crazy character. And to Ryan and Jackson, my college-aged sons, you give me life and keep me younger than you can ever know. Thank you for always listening when I say, "Hey...check this out."

I've thanked my parents and sister in past acknowledgments, and I will again. Family circles may be biased but meet this small team of readers and I guarantee they rival any Big Five editor out there. It's not all French toast and syrup when discussing pages with them. Sometimes it's the shot of a Cactus Killer (ask me about that drink later!) or the raw rub of a frayed rope slipping across the palm of your hand. Other times, it feels like sitting down to a family-style breakfast. Truth can hurt, especially when creativity and vulnerability go hand in hand, but every writer needs to hear it. How else will we improve?

I've also had countless conversations with friends, experts in various fields, random deputy sheriffs at my favorite morning writing spots, clergy, and talented authors but one person stands out for keeping my technical terminology, computer-savvy realism, and edgy (yet public knowledge) information not just believable, but accurate. Scott W. Howard, or should I say Scoots!—thank you for all the chats, driveway drinks, and for burning rubber down 359 in one kick-ass classic ride. The Miata Kid would be proud.

Lastly, but never least, thanks to the team at Wolfpack Publishing. Your support, and especially Patience, continues to make this writer's dream come true.

ABOUT THE AUTHOR

Chris Mullen is an accomplished and award-winning author, recognized for his captivating storytelling and literary talent. Hailing from Richmond, Texas, he is a proud graduate of Texas A&M University.

With a career spanning twenty-three years in education, Chris has been a dedicated teacher in both Kindergarten and PreK, cultivating his passion for storytelling and nurturing young minds. In 2019, he received the prestigious Connie Wootton Excellence in Teaching Award—a testament to his commitment to education and his profound impact on students' lives, bestowed upon him by the Southwest Association of Episcopal Schools (SAES). It was during this time that the idea for his young adult western adventure series, Rowdy, was born.

When he's not weaving stories, you can find Chris honing his craft in local coffee shops, pizza places, or even the neighborhood grocery store.

www.chrismullenwrites.com